Author's Note

Christopher Doveton spent his early life in South Africa and completed his education at Sutton Valence School, Kent.

Having completed a spell in the Royal Navy as Communications Officer aboard HMS Ark Royal he then qualified as a Company Secretary and eventually started his own business.

Following the death of his wife in 2002, and tempted by the dream of owning a place in the sun, he chose the Moorish Town of Mijas, in the Costa del Sol only to experience the traumas and disasters of buying a villa during the Spanish property boom.

The Spanish Dream is the thriller he was compelled to write.

Acknowledgement

To Jen, with many thanks,
and to Derek Fox for his encouragement and help

THE SPANISH DREAM

Christopher Doveton

Published 2011 by arima publishing

www.arimapublishing.com

ISBN 978 1 84549 516 9

© Christopher Doveton 2011

Printed and bound in the United Kingdom

Typeset in Garamond 12

Swirl is an imprint of arima publishing.

arima publishing

ASK House, Northgate Avenue

Bury St Edmunds, Suffolk IP32 6BB

t: (+44) 01284 700321

www.arimapublishing.com

CHAPTER 1

The coastline of Africa was just visible on the horizon, the evening sun setting over Torremolinos, twinkling lights gradually emerging to illuminate the town of Fuengirola. The air was still, the deep blue Mediterranean, calm.

Peter Grant relaxed on the balcony of his hillside villa, absorbing the peaceful scene below as he sipped an extremely palatable glass of red Crianza wine.

Drifting night noises and scents of the warm continental evening should have made him feel alive, yet he didn't. Peter Grant faced a number of major crises in his life.

His dream of owning his own villa in such an idyllic setting had resulted in the failure of his marriage, the near collapse of his thriving, profitable business and two wasted years trying desperately to finalise his purchase of the property.

Draining his glass he decided to take immediate action against the perpetrators who had made his life hell, nearly bankrupted him and turned his "Spanish Dream" into a nightmare.

Stupid then to have been so naïve in trusting the plausible and conniving group of developers who together had promised to sell him a new and different future.

In hindsight maybe he should curse that beautiful late spring day in the Georgian city of Bath when he walked up Milsom Street lured by the seductive invitation to a place in the sun.

*   *   *

Peter Grant looked immaculate as usual. He wore a light grey suit, blue checked shirt and flamboyant matching tie. There was not a strand of his brown, slightly greying, hair out of place. Fastidious to a fault was Peter to whom appearance meant a lot.

A keep fit fanatic and keen golfer, his slim, athletic figure, together with his rugged and tanned good looks lulled his many admirers into accepting he was ten years younger than his forty-seven years.

Today he stepped into the warm, comforting May sunshine into Lower Borough Walls on his way to meet with his accountant, Alan Parker, to discuss the expansion of his printing company, St Helena Press, founded ten years earlier. He paused taken by the magnificent Bath Abbey, framed by the entrance to the Abbey courtyard, its mellowed stone glowing like old gold in the sunlight. Beautiful! And that was something Peter appreciated in all its forms!

Reaching the top of Milsom Street his attention was drawn to a window filled with breathtaking images of marble villas, rising majestically from a deep blue Mediterranean. Mesmerised, Peter took in the significance of the large sign:

THE SPANISH DREAM

Appended to it a phrase: "Professionals in finding your Spanish Dream Home".

He crossed the road into Edgar Buildings. And there was beauty with its attractive figure looking, he thought, directly at him from the large floor to ceiling Georgian window.

Golden hair hung loosely on bare shoulders. Dressed in a low cut blouse and knee length skirt, accentuating tanned legs, was sufficient incentive for Peter to make his next move through the open door of Bull Ring Properties.

He gazed into her emerald green, sparkling eyes and resisting the temptation to run his fingers through her natural waved hair.

'Good morning,' he greeted, 'a lovely day.'

'Good morning. I'm Julie. How may I help?' She smiled wickedly, her look consuming him in a way that made him feel wanted.

'Spanish Dream sounds very inviting,' he said nodding towards the mural depicting the picturesque harbour of Puerto Banús, crammed with luxury yachts, its parking bays filled with Ferraris, Porsches, Bentleys. Nothing less.

He noticed how Julie's eyes sparkled with the anticipation of another lucrative sales contract.

Her seductive voice and body language made Peter feel he was the only person important to her, as she began to set the scene, first by laying a glossy brochure on the table that depicted luxury properties, landscaped gardens and swimming pools.

'This is the area of the Costa del Sol coastline where we are building affordable luxury town houses and apartments extending from Fuengirola to the magnificent harbour of the Sotto Grande. You will be able to purchase a stunning three bedroom apartment for as little as £175,000 and … wait for it, a four bedroom town house for only £250,000. How does that sound?' Julie revelled in her opening lines.

'Well,' said Peter, 'I am not familiar with prices of property in Spain, but they seem reasonable to me.'

'The other good news is that we offer you guaranteed rental income and a 50% mortgage when you purchase the property.' Julie deliberately didn't explain that the terms of the rental scheme required the purchase of an expensive furniture package from the company.

They exchanged glances. Peter's body language displayed certain excitement, almost as if he'd already committed to a rewarding and exciting time in sunny Spain.

Would his wife, Angela, think the same?

'Are there any reasons why you would not wish to proceed with a purchase contract?' Julie asked. Peter said nothing.

'Good,' she said. 'The next stage is to take you and your partner, all expenses paid, to visit our locations on the Costa del Sol. We will fly you to Malaga, your accommodation for the three days in a luxury five hotel near Marbella. I will be your guide. Once there you will meet our resident staff including our Operations Director, Conrad Hemmings.'

' Right,' said Peter grinning broadly, 'When do we leave?'

CHAPTER 2

Bill Young was no academic. In his youth he was more interested in watching Birmingham City play in the first division and re-building cars rather than pass 'O' levels.

He had an insatiable passion for cars. Acquiring Austin 7s destined for the scrap heap, re-building them and selling to collectors for a healthy profit.

He followed his father's footsteps and joined Midland Motors as an apprentice.

However, engineering talents, a quick brain, articulate and with his inbuilt greed for success, assured his meteoric rise to Managing Director, at the age of thirty five, sound like a fairy tale.

The Agenda for the Board Meeting had reached the item of "any other business".

There was no requirement for Directors to give prior notice of any special subjects to be discussed at a Board Meeting.

The Chairman and major shareholder of Bull Ring Properties, Bill Young, leapt up from his seat at the magnificent boardroom table whose shine reflected his immaculate charcoal grey suit and ultra white shirt, his animated features alive with excitement as fifteen expectant pairs of eyes made contact with his. Bodies leaned forward nervously, in anticipation. Bill's thunderous baritone shattered the silence giving vent to the energy contained in the meeting so far.

'I am informing you that the subject I am about to present will not be minuted. The content of my proposals is strictly confidential and is not to be discussed outside this room with any employees, secretaries, wives, partners and, or lovers, or with any shareholder of this company. You will not, repeat not, make any notes.

'If I find there is a mole amongst us then you will be removed from office for gross misconduct'. He surveyed them all adding: 'Is that quite clear? Good. Then let's proceed.'

Now a multi-millionaire, having sold his share options on the acquisition of Midland Motors by the Chinese, he resigned from the company.

He purchased Bull Ring Properties, a successful property developer, until the collapse of the housing market in 2003, when they had filed for administration.

Bill Young continued: 'Since my acquisition of Bull Ring Properties, our company, gentlemen, is one of the most profitable and successful "buy to let" developers in the UK.

'Our annual sales are in excess of £200 million and with profits reaching £30 million we are ready to consider a flotation on the London Stock Market. I am sure that some would welcome this news, as the move would make a few millionaires.

'However, I do not believe this is the right time to consider going public for a number of reasons. Agreed, we could generate more capital to finance the proposed expansion about to be discussed.

'We would achieve growth and an increase in market share. This is not a priority at present. The business plan we are about to unveil will give us the financial strength and stability to complete a successful flotation in five years time.

'The only directors I have briefed on the new business plan, on a "need to know basis", are Conrad Hemmings and our new financial director Simon Peters.'

The Chairman thought about the Board. Could he trust all of them to agree his new business plan? He had taken a gamble on his new finance director – Simon was a senior partner in Symonds Reed, the company's auditors, with responsibility for the European market. Matthew Larking, senior partner had been concerned about accounting anomalies following the takeover of Bull Ring Properties, and had persuaded Bill Young to employ Simon Peters on an annual contract as Financial Director, with Matthew to continue as a partner in the firm with a dual reporting responsibility.

Conrad Hemmings posed a different threat. Bill Young had bought his company.

A typical wheeler dealer salesman, Hemmings's ruthlessness and bargaining skills would be ideal as Operations Director. Bill would like to think he could trust him; after all he had saved him from bankruptcy and financial ruin. However, unanswered questions about his past still lingered.

'Conrad,' said Bill Young. 'Would you please elaborate on the business plan we have discussed.'

'Good Morning gentlemen,' said Conrad.

His muscular tall, athletic figure dominated the room. His thick blond hair almost reached his shoulders; a style which should have been almost feminine on most men, merely added certain dignity, along with his "who gives a shit anyway" attitude. Steely brown eyes offered a hint of aggression, hinting at his manipulative nature. Yet, Conrad's charming, debonair, charismatic and persuasive qualities, always attractive to the opposite sex, were in direct contrast to his ruthless, arrogant and uncaring attitude to those who dared cross his path.

Directly contrasting his 'rough diamond' character, Conrad, unknown to Bill Young and fellow directors had, dare one say, hidden qualities.

He'd graduated with honours in accountancy from Bristol University; employed by one of the leading practices in the UK, Peat, Young & Haskins, specialising in Corporate Finance and Off Shore Tax Havens. Five years of confrontation with HMRC was the deciding factor that forced him to duck from beneath the umbrella of a large corporation for the excitement and rewards of building his own international empire.

'As Bill has said, our success in the property market is due to the rapid expansion of the "buy to let market". However, the market is becoming more and more competitive with the availability of second mortgages, low interest rates and increased money supply. We must look for new markets,' Conrad thundered, both arms aggressively raised to make his point.

'I have looked at the property market in Europe and consider Spain will provide the platform for our future investments in capital and people.'

The new European Operations Director had prepared a Power Point presentation.

'The rental market in the Costa del Sol is expanding rapidly and demand is exceeding supply for town houses and apartments. There are over 700,000 ex pats who have bought properties in Spain, the majority live along the coastal belt of the Costa del Sol.

'The value of properties purchased by UK residents reached £3 billion in 2002. By 2007 the potential market value will have risen to a staggering £6 billion.'

Adrenalin coursed from Conrad's heaving body as fifteen pairs of expectant eyes absorbed the map images on screen of the Costa del Sol, highlighting areas for development.

Conrad sensed his attentive and mesmerised audience were beginning to accept his proposal with the hidden agenda that would turn fantasy into reality, making him very rich. His fellow directors, including the Chairman, were oblivious that his own Spanish property portfolio already existed: a lucrative joint venture with his lawyer in Marbella, Franco Pérez.

'Now I will pass you over to Simon who will elaborate on our business plan.'

'Thank you Conrad, I have chosen the right time to join this progressive company.'

Greying hair swept back from his high forehead, long and graceful fingers drumming the boardroom table nervously, sparkling, soft blue eyes found those of Judy Archer, the HR director. Simon relaxed, Judy already smitten by this charming, attractive, talented and obviously very successful person. Yes, she thought, we could be very good friends.

Simon continued, 'The Marketing programme will involve our twenty franchise agents who will take potential clients to our "off plan sites", covering the development areas you have seen. Clients will be flown to

Malaga and hotel accommodation will be provided in the four star hotel, the Kon Tiki Beach, near Marbella. All costs will be paid by the company. The Kon Tiki is a luxury hotel with a private beach, three swimming pools, beauty salons, saunas, fitness suite and three restaurants.

'There will be a team of sales personnel employed by the company, living in Spain and working from our offices in Puerto Banús. They will be responsible for presentations to clients, working with our franchise agents who will close the sales and secure a non refundable reservation fee of £5,000 on every property.

'Specialist lawyers are being appointed in Birmingham and Marbella. It will be conditional in the contract that clients use the services of these lawyers for exchange and completion of purchase contracts.

'The company will provide owners with an opportunity to rent out their properties through our Spanish company. We will be responsible for rental contracts and in return receive 50% of the letting fees. Interior design and furniture packages will be mandatory for owners entering into rental contracts.

'Finally, there is one announcement Bill has asked me to make. The next company meeting will be in Puerto Banús and you are all invited.'

Chairman and Directors leapt to their feet, a number of fists banging the table, all adding to a riot of applause.

CHAPTER 3

Conrad Hemmings found the offices of Fernandez Sanches in the Avenue Ricardo Soriano, and strolled beneath palm trees heavy with yellow/orange fruit, mimosa's in full blossom of golden yellow, sweet perfume filling the warm air.

In the foyer he was greeted by the pretty receptionist, large gold earrings catching the light adding to her stunning appearance. Her bright red sleeveless dress, revealing tanned shoulders, her golden hair tied back with a matching ribbon.

With his imagination in overdrive, Conrad watched this golden goddess walk towards him, emerald eyes sparkling, almost seductive, he thought, as they never wavered from his.

'Hola, buenos días, I have a meeting with Signor Gomez,' Conrad spluttered, oblivious to the fact that 'Gomez' is pronounced 'Gometh'.

'Bueno, you are expected, please take the lift to the first floor, Signor Hemmings, Signor Gomez will be there to meet you,' she said in perfect English.

Manuel Gomez fixed Conrad with steely blue eyes from behind gold rimmed bifocals as Conrad stepped out of the lift. He greeted him with a warm, well flossed smile, as always looking immaculate in pin-striped suit and white shirt. For a man who had achieved so much for justice in Spain he looked relaxed, indeed a man who had nothing to prove, such was his position. Gold cuff links caught the light as an exquisitely manicured hand stretched out to welcome Conrad.

'Good morning Mr Hemmings, good to meet you,' he said in well modulated tones. Shorter than Conrad he appeared overwhelmed by the towering figure.

A senior partner in the firm, he had qualified at Madrid University, gaining a law degree specialising in criminal law. Working closely with the prosecutor's office in Marbella, he was now being tipped for the appointment of Chief Prosecutor. Normally he would refuse to act for a property developer, especially from England, his talents more productive in helping police prosecutors convict drug barons and corrupt mayors.

It appeared Bull Ring Properties intrigued him.

'Thank you,' Conrad said. 'Good to be here Manuel. Property Conveyancing, our solicitors in England, highly recommended your firm.'

'Where do we begin?' asked Gomez taking Conrad's arm and directing him to an opulent office that reeked of power, achievement and position.

'Firstly, would you like a cool drink on this warm day? I suggest our typical Spanish drink, a portion of Crianza red wine, lemonade, slice of lemon and lots of ice, in a large glass.'

'Sounds very tempting,' said Conrad, directed to a leather chair placed off centre before a huge teak desk – less intimidating than face to face – Conrad explained the expansion of Bull Ring Properties covering the purchase of land and aggressive building programme on the Costa del Sol.

'We need to incorporate a company in Spain and register the company as Bull Ring Properties (Spain). The directors will be myself and Bill Young, who as you know is Chairman of the holding company in England.'

Gomez nodded in all the right places, obviously understanding the intentions Conrad put forward.

'I understand,' he said, 'that following registration of the new company ten million Euros will be transferred to Banco España.'

'That is so,' Conrad confirmed. 'The acquisition of land, completion of purchase contracts, obtaining NIE numbers for our clients, liaising with Property Conveyancing on reservation fees, sales contracts, will all be handled by your firm.'

' Owners will make stage payments covering fifty per cent of their property value, the remaining fifty per cent, a guaranteed mortgage through Banco España over a period no more than twenty five years.'

Gomez steepled his fingers and nodded. 'So, tell me, how many properties to start with?'

'We plan to sell five hundred properties over the next two years.'

'Have you any plans that will benefit owners financially?' enquired Manuel.

Conrad paused to sip his drink, smiled and nodded. ' Excellent choice, cooling.'

'And yes Manuel, we have plans to exploit the lucrative rental market. Owners will be offered a special package giving them a twenty per cent return on their capital investment. Your firm will be involved with legal issues resulting in extra fees linked to the rental contracts.

'The new company will include a department negotiating the contacts on behalf of the owners. Bull Ring Properties will be guaranteed fifty percent on all letting fees generated through participants in the rental scheme. Interior design and furniture packages will be mandatory for owners signing contracts.'

He paused again to allow what he'd said to sink in.

'In return our company will market properties through travel companies such as Thomsons, First Choice and Sovereign. Hopefully, they will agree to include our rental properties in their glossy brochures and web sites.'

Gomez clapped his hands. 'Well, what exciting times we have ahead of us. I have always wanted to become involved in the lucrative property market and now it is about to happen. Thank you for instructing my firm to handle such a large portfolio,'

he added trying to sound the part.

'We will meet again when the new company is registered.'

' Looking forward to the launch,' Conrad boomed, vigorously shaking the outstretched hand. 'If we've concluded the business for now then I'll leave. Plenty to do.' He finished his drink. 'Thanks very much for the refreshments.'

Gomez accompanied him to the lift.

Signor Gomez remembered reading an article in the Times and London Gazette. Mr William Young, now Chairman, had purchased Bull Ring Developments saving the company from insolvency. Apparently there'd been something concerning the deficiency of current assets in the company's Balance Sheet, exposed by the auditors. He recalled one of the directors was involved, no name given.

Gomez's intuitive brain took charge. Conrad was hiding something. Why had he really come to Spain?

He grabbed his unique and treasured Salvador Dali lobster phone and dialled David Wiltshire, head of the Serious Fraud Office in London. David would know everything.

* * *

Conrad left the offices of Fernandez Sanches and walked through Villandrado, surrounded by cooling fountains, palm trees, bougainvillea, hibiscus and oleander, close to where the Plaza del Toros towered over the square.

Uncertain about the directions to Huerta de los Castales where he was meeting his lawyer, Franco Pérez, Conrad looked for someone who might be able to help with directions. His potential target an attractive young woman seated on the edge of a water feature, feet dangling and splashing in the bubbling water. A cool way to pass

her lunch break.

Maria Carmen looked up, and to Conrad she smiled as if they knew each other already.

'Perdón,' Conrad said. 'Hablas ingles?' (Do you speak English?)

'Perhaps,' came the reply in perfect English.

'Good,' he said, 'But surely we have already met; how could I forget such a gorgeous lady?'

'Don't think so,' replied Maria, feigning puzzlement.

'Oh well,' Conrad was not convinced. 'Could you please direct me to Huerta de los Castales?'

'With pleasure. I know the area well, if you tell me the address I maybe able to assist.' Working with astute lawyers had trained Maria to offer help in exchange for valuable information.

'Thank you, I need to find No 56, the offices of my lawyer Franco Pérez.'

'I know them. You go past the Plaza del Toros, turn right and you will come to Serenata; this leads to los Costales. Number 56 is at the end overlooking the marina.'

'Muchas gracias!' said Conrad.

'De nada,' (don't mention it) replied Maria with an engaging smile.

Maria, secretary to Signor Gomez had seen Conrad in the office, but why she wondered would Signor Hemmings engage another lawyer? Might it be that Signor Gomez had clashed with Signor Pérez in the courts when acting as defence lawyer for corrupt town hall officials? It was, she supposed, a good enough reason.

Maria had overheard a conversation between Signor Gomez and the prosecutor's office implicating Franco Pérez for allegedly paying bribes to officials in return for illegal building licenses.

Once Conrad was out of sight, Maria stood, brushed water from gorgeous tanned legs, realising something was wrong, Of course, she must inform Signor Gomez of her suspicions immediately.

CHAPTER 4

Wouldn't mind meeting her again, mused Conrad, setting out to find his lawyer.

Conrad, debonair, good looking, charming, and with a suave and persuasive manner, always turned the heads of the opposite sex, much to his amusement and often gratification!

Ann, his wife of twenty five years, unaccepting of his blatant affairs – and who could blame her? – instigated a painful divorce, affecting the future of his two sons.

With such a lavish lifestyle, notwithstanding his wife's divorce settlement, it meant Conrad saying goodbye, eventually, to their period Jacobean six bedroom mansion, nestling in idyllic Staffordshire countryside. Investigation by the serious fraud squad into the sale of company assets, prior to acquisition of his company, was ongoing. A well kept secret from Ann and Bill Young.

For certain Bill would rue the day he had saved Conrad Hemmings from extinction.

Definitely Conrad's decision that his new position as Operations Director justified the purchase of a villa, and to this end Puerto Banũs would be ideal. The harbour filled with luxury yachts, chic shops, gourmet restaurants, night clubs and bars, he could integrate into the glamorous lifestyle, why he might even afford and a Rolls Bentley coupé. Money was no concern now the divorce settlement had been agreed. Director's fees in Bull Ring would be in excess of £100,000 per annum plus a performance bonus. He smiled broadly. The Spanish property venture with his lawyer friend Franco Pérez, would make him rich.

Walking through cosmopolitan upmarket Marbella, Conrad located the offices of Franco Pérez, to be confronted and dwarfed by a large solid oak portal, fronting a structure resembling an entrance to a castle, a perpendicular shaped door set into the stonework.

'Signor Franco Pérez'... **'El Abogado'** were engraved on a gold plaque in large very professional Copperplate script.

Conrad tugged the thick heavy bell rope.

'Hola Conrad, come in,' shouted Franco from an opening above him, again the window, like the doorway, in keeping with the style of a medieval castle. The inner door swung back with a thud. Stepping over the raised threshold, he walked into a large mosaic tiled courtyard where a central fountain spouted large columns of blue water, and where magnificent palm trees strained to reach the open dome some twenty feet above.

Franco, arms outstretched, and standing at the top of a magnificent shining gold spiral staircase, waved and shouted at Conrad to join him.

Strange, thought Conrad that their first meeting, two years ago, had been as guests of the Spanish Ambassador, Signor Antonio Gonzales at the Spanish Embassy in London. A magnificent evening, one he remembered well, spent in the lively company of Spain's leading flamenco dancers from Andalusia. Conrad and Franco had remained in contact ever since.

Ernesto Carlos, lawyer friend of Franco, graduating together from Barcelona University, had been kind enough to arrange the introduction to Conrad.

In addition to being an astute lawyer, Ernesto Carlos enjoyed the position of Chairman of an international property investment company *Carlos Investments* with offices in London and Barcelona.

He had contracted Symonds & Reed to act as accountants and auditors for his company. At the time Conrad was a junior partner in the international firm of Chartered Accountants and as luck would have it he'd been assigned to oversee the account of Carlos Investments, his flair for tax evasion and international finance having greatly impressed Signor Carlos. In return Carlos would play a major role in saving Conrad from total ruin – a small price to pay for all the years of profitable growth and success attributed solely to the accountancy expertise and financial skills of Conrad.

Ernesto Carlos had purchased a large block of luxury apartments from Conrad near New Street station in Birmingham for two million pounds whose 'cash' proceeds- equivalent to two million four hundred thousand Euros – were transferred by him from investment accounts held in Spain directly into the joint accounts held by Conrad and Franco.

Money laundering regulations had been successfully breached, or it seemed so at the time by the three perpetrators.

Conrad's accountancy qualifications and the invaluable experience of working with a large reputable accountancy practice, had given him specialist knowledge in the legal manipulation of company accounts, tax avoidance and money laundering regulations.

With insolvency looming for him and Bull Ring Properties, the buy to let market was becoming competitive; profit margins were tight, not helped with recession taking hold on the economy. Liquidity, negative cash flow and now banks, reigning in loans, resulting in major financial and operation problems. Conrad knew that the ratio of Fixed Assets, represented by the fifty million pounds valuation of his property portfolio in his Balance Sheet, were not in line with Current Assets. The liquidity ratio could not improve unless ten million pounds worth of property was liquidated immediately, Conrad realising only too well that Bull Ring Properties was in serious trouble.

This inevitably, meant he'd need to extract funds before the company was sold to Bill Young.

Extracting five million pounds was hardly practical, two million a more sensible amount and sufficient for the proposed Spanish property venture with his friend Franco Pérez.

Conrad, in desperation, paid Radley Williams, estate valuers in Birmingham, twenty thousand pounds in cash, to revalue his property assets for two million pounds less than the current balance sheet figure, the said revised valuation supported by an Inland Revenue Certification document.

The 2007 Companies Act and the Articles of Association would require him to hold an extraordinary general meeting to discuss special business, he also knew that the directors would normally be required to pass a unanimous resolution agreeing the write down of Company assets. Such a special resolution would of course be minuted for inspection by the company's auditors and shareholders. Then again, Conrad had no intention of calling a board meeting to pass any resolution or minute anything.

With on line access into the company accounts, from his workstation in the plush study of his Jacobean mansion – taken advantage of whilst time permitted – Conrad opened the 'Suspense' account and entered two million pounds in the debit column, with a note: "Depreciation of fixed assets, property revaluation". Next he accessed the Fixed Assets property register, that indicated fifty million pounds and entered the revised figure of forty eight million pounds thus deleting all reference to the sale of the New Street property to Ernesto Carlos for two million pounds, all outstanding debts and loans on the apartments settled prior to the sale.

His creative accounting skills told him that the entry in the Suspense account would not be linked to the two million pounds paid by Ernesto Carlos for the apartments. No entry would be made in the company's cash account showing the sudden disappearance of the money. Smiling, he had the satisfaction of knowing that the double entry would be fraudulently completed once the €1.4 million transfer reached Conrad's and Franco's joint bank account in Marbella.

Yes, Conrad's property fund would be safe.

The fraudulent write down in assets would take sufficient time to be discovered, hence the transfer of money by Ernesto Carlos from his investment company in Spain would avoid money laundering regulations and Capital Gains Tax for Conrad. Only Signor Carlos could be held responsible for contravening regulations.

'No sweat,' said Conrad quietly, 'he's been given a very good deal on purchasing the apartments.'

And the other thing to come from all of this, the fact that Bill Young would be unaware of Conrad's deceit in selling Bull Ring Properties short;

well at least until the new auditors had produced annual accounts eighteen month's down the line.

A good deal, it seemed, for the perpetrators of justice at the time.

Conrad looked to be in no hurry to reach Franco and took his time climbing the long spiral staircase. Hand resting lightly on the magnificent gold hand rail, he paused to admire the features of the water garden below. Exotic species of water lilies, their brilliant colours appearing to change as droplets of water, caught in the sunlight from the open dome, nestled on their stamens. Mesmerised, he eventually reached Franco at the top of the staircase.

'Buenas tardes, Franco. Cómo estás?' (How are you?) Conrad offered a broad grin, and embraced Franco like a long lost brother.

'Well, thank you, good to see you again.'

'What a wonderful entrance hall you have for your office, we could be in the Alhambra.'

'You have obviously visited the Royal Palace. Actually I did get the idea from the Moorish court in the Palace. If you look past the water garden,' Franco pointed, ' you will see a water canal taking the water from the garden and running underneath the glass wall into a swimming pool, just like the one at Alhambra.'

'This must have cost you a fortune.'

'That's another story. Come on we have many things to discuss.'

He took Conrad's arm and led him into his office. Conrad transfixed by the high fan vaulted ceiling supporting an enormous sparkling crystal chandelier, and beautiful teak panelling which lined the walls, their matching furniture adding to the air of opulence and wealth. Large shuttered windows stood open revealing a large balcony filled with exotic plants, and allowed a magnificent view of Marbella's billionaires paradise harbour.

Franco, dressed in a silk white suit, looked relaxed behind the red leather teak desk.

'Would you like a drink?'

'Thank you for asking, Manuel Gomez at Fernandez Sanches has just had me share your Spanish drink, Crianza, lemonade and ice. Very cooling.'

'Ah, you know Signor Gomez?' Conrad said with an inquiring smile.

'Oh yes indeed,' Franco spluttered trying hard not to choke. 'We have clashed many times in Marbella's criminal courts when I have been acting as defence lawyer.'

Franco waved his finger. 'Some advice my friend, don't trust him he is very manipulative and ambitious, and has set his sights on becoming Chief Prosecutor.'

'That said,' replied Conrad, 'you should know Signor Gomez has been appointed to oversee all transactions for Bull Ring Properties in Spain.'

'Fine, I wish you well but you have been warned.' Franco cocked an eyebrow.

Conrad had already made a mental note to investigate his dislike and distrust for Gomez, despite his being a lawyer held in high esteem for his ceaseless efforts in bringing ruthless criminals to justice.

'Now to our business.' Franco slapped the desk top, anxious it seemed to continue. 'You, my friend, will be pleased to know that contracts have been signed on all twenty apartments at Elvira and deposits paid. Our agent, San Salvador, is confident the habitation license will be issued by Marbella's town hall in two weeks.'

Conrad gawked for a second time at the, to him, surprising revelation.

'How on earth have you managed to obtain the release of the first license so quickly? I mean corruption and prosecution of Town Hall officials, including Mayors, as you well know, has resulted in serious back log of licenses being issued, sometimes taking over a year to be granted.'

'I assure you, my friend that it has not been at all easy, all the ground rules have changed and are getting worse.'

Conrad wandered to the balcony and back, perhaps returning with a small dream of owning a yacht, since they all looked majestic in the bay.

'I have already saved some Town Hall officials and mayors from prosecution and lengthy jail sentences, through lack of evidence,' Franco explained. 'Whilst remaining in office, for the time being at least, it is surprising how much these officials are extremely willing to reciprocate by waiving building regulations and granting licenses in my favour.'

'And, more importantly…' Franco winked, 'I have not acted illegally.' 'And', he added laughing and again thumping the desk, 'we have not paid any bribes to these greedy people. What about that my friend?'

Conrad hesitated before deciding he'd play it lightly replying, 'You have done well Franco.'

Totally unaware of Franco's involvement as defence lawyer for corrupt officials who had caused so much suffering to investors and people who had sold their homes in the UK to settle in Spain, Conrad did wonder if Franco's duties as "defence lawyer" were more far reaching and encompassed "Costa Criminals" generally.

'Before we go to lunch, I have something to show you.' Taking Conrad's arm Franco steered him back to the balcony overlooking the harbour.

'I noticed your envious look a moment ago.' He gestured. 'Do you see the large white cruiser, moored below us?' Conrad nodded. 'It belongs to Mohammed V, the King of Morocco. Interesting, his title changed from "King" in 1957 when it ceased to be a French Protectorate. The King has employed me to oversee two large housing developments in Rabat and Tangiers. The contract includes the use of just one of his many luxury yachts, MS Hercules, for business and private use. The crew and all running costs are included.

'It has ten double berths on board, an outdoor swimming pool that becomes an indoor pool at the touch of a button, a conference room and cinema. Hopefully you will be among a party of guests I will be organising to visit Morocco very shortly.

Not a bad deal eh?' He slapped Conrad's back.

Using a pair of high powered binoculars lent to him by Franco, Conrad inspected the boat.

Built into to the stern of the cruiser was a bathing platform housing a twin screw motor boat. Twin turrets fore and aft concealed a rocket launcher and a Bofors 40mm Oerlikon gun, it's quarter deck enclosed by bulkheads, lending it the look of a Type 23 Royal Navy Frigate. An officer of the watch stood on the deck wearing the white uniform of a Moroccan naval lieutenant.

His education at Pangbourne College guaranteed Conrad entry into Dartmouth Naval College, where he passed out as a Sub Lieutenant. The frigate HMS Magpie was his first commission, based in Hong Kong on surveillance duties for illegal gun running and drug trafficking.

It meant he could recognise the so-called luxury cruiser being similar in design and construction to a vessel he had boarded to arrest drug dealers. Perhaps the boat was registered under a new country of origin, with a name change. There were likely to be sealed bulkheads below deck, hiding the contraband of drugs and cigarettes. He had also read that the Spanish Costas are home to more than 20,000 foreign criminals of 70 nationalities; that gangs operated with little fear of detection by police or coastguard patrol boats. Yes, he would be very interested to accompany Franco on his trip to Morocco almost certain he could be involved in something more sinister than just property development for the King of Morocco.

From the office they made their way at Franco's invitation, to the man's favourite restaurant on Marbella's golden mile beach.

Seated at a table at El Merlo Blanco (The White Bird) they ordered the speciality of the house, the menu sporting every variety of fish you could find locally – lobster, crayfish, longestine, crab, octopus and squid. A bottle of local dry white wine *Esmeralda* complemented the different flavours of their fish platters.

'Franco,' Conrad said, wiping his mouth and taking a sip of wine, 'I would welcome your professional views on proposals covering the expansion of Bull Ring Properties.'

'Go ahead, I will do my best to help.'

'Well, the Ramos Group, as you know are the largest developer on the Costa del Sol. They have purchased land enabling us to build five hundred town houses and apartments on twenty sites, over the next two years.'

He shovelled in another fork full. 'Excellent fish,' he said expecting what he anticipated being a guarded reply from Franco.

'How on earth will you persuade the Town Halls to agree planning applications, building regulations and habitation licenses for so many properties in such a short time frame?' Again the arched eyebrows from Franco.

'I have stated earlier, Town Hall officials are severely hampered by the clampdown in granting licenses, many have lost their jobs due to their own corrupt ways.' Franco sipped his wine, savouring the taste; he glanced through the window purposely, choosing his next words carefully.

'Oh yes,' he eventually said, 'let us not forget that your Signor Gomez is leading the attack against your future allies, and attempting to put them all in jail. I regret to say that you do not have a chance of achieving your ambitious targets. And you can tell that to your Signor Bill Young from me.' Franco's blood pressure was up, seen in his colour. Or maybe it was just the wine.

Conrad was surprised at the outburst: all he'd asked for was some advice on the best way to overcome the problems of licensing. But he decided in the circumstances, it would be inappropriate to elaborate on the cunning rescue plan Bill Young was negotiating with the Spanish Government and developers Luis Ramos, overcoming the problems involving building licenses. More especially since Franco might think to use the highly sensitive information to his own advantage.

'Would you like a dessert?' offered Franco deliberately changing the subject.

'I can recommend the mouth watering fruit sorbets,'

'I really couldn't, thanks. A most enjoyable lunch.'

The sunshine beckoned. The two men sauntered along the promenade, attention drawn well and truly to the gorgeously tanned nubile females wearing revealing thongs and nothing else.

Who the hell wanted to talk about leases?

CHAPTER 5

Deep ravines and tortuous hairpin bends added to the excitement as the luxury coach, filled with Bull Ring clients, raced up the mountainside above Estepona.

The mysterious coastline of Morocco, overshadowed by a curving tower of black stone – Gibraltar – rising like some extraordinary behemoth out of the deep blue Mediterranean, could be glimpsed in the distance.

Julie Nash, blonde hair falling gracefully on her bare shoulders, faced her guests, and switched on the microphone.

'Shortly we will arrive at the Duquesa development. You will be able to view the town houses and apartments nearing completion, also the fully furnished show house. Conrad Hemmings, our director…'

An unexpected lurch of the coach forced the interruption. The microphone leapt from her hand, Julie flying backwards attempting to prevent a fall; she grabbed the back of the driver's seat the momentum throwing her from side to side. Her head hit the windscreen with a resounding thud; she slid to the floor.

Conscious but shocked, Julie saw a white Bentley coupé overtaking the coach on the bend. She couldn't believe her eyes. Conrad Hemmings, blonde hair flying, sat nonchalantly behind the wheel arm raised in a defiant clenched fist salute. She was convinced he would pull over to see if any of the passengers had sustained any injuries. Wrong! He continued speeding up the mountain oblivious that the coach was full of potential clients.

Within the space of seconds what could be described as an idyllic coach ride had transformed into something far worse: once attentive passengers were now screaming in terror as the coach carved an erratic course towards the deep ravine below, its driver Manuel desperately trying to control the beast and steer it away from the edge.

Brakes squealed, locked up. The nearside front tyre hit a boulder which served to throw it sideways. Out of control it slid backwards towards certain disaster. Screams and shouts echoed back and forth; sheer terror gripped all there. Manuel crossed himself, his prayer eventually answered as rear tyres struck a line of large boulders at the edge of the precipice, bringing the coach to an abrupt halt.

Angela, Peter Grant's wife, and trained nurse, leapt to her feet. Manuel handed her the first aid box.

Julie, two hands now locked over a seat back refused to let go until Angela persuaded her to sit down, 'It's OK, we've stopped.'

'You are very fortunate,' Angela told her after inspecting the wound. 'It's superficial, won't require stitches.' She raised a smile adding: 'Your looks are intact.' It helped.

Peter clawed his way to the front of the coach shouting and waving his arms. Never one to stay cool, Peter. 'That bloody madman in the Bentley damned near murdered us. Only thanks to Manuel's driving skills we're still alive.'

'Did anyone see the driver or the registration number?' Angela asked. 'What about you Manuel, did you see anything?'

'No signora, *lo siento mucho*, I try stop, I see nothink.'

The traumatised passengers remained silent. Julie, thankful to Angela, whose comment had done her good, let instinct take charge.

Exposing Conrad would result in serious misgivings by her clients, her credibility would be in tatters, and the company would never be trusted again. As for Conrad he would be ruined. Serve him right for being such an idiot.

Conrad was furious the coach hadn't pulled over to let him pass, bend or no bend.

He had an important meeting with clients who were about to purchase his properties.

He was late. Looking into his wing mirror, he saw the driver had managed to stop the coach from going over the side and that it was now stationary. No need to investigate, there would be no injuries. He raced on up the mountain.

The coach limped slowly to the summit of the Duquesa development. Conrad, looking relaxed dressed in whites, greeted his shaken guests. No white Bentley coupé in sight.

He looked puzzled, not having the sense to realise just who the coach had conveyed here.

'Why so long Julie and what about the injury to your head?' Conrad asked trying to sound sympathetic.

If a look could be called a sneer, Conrad received one from Julie who pointedly stated: 'Some maniac in a white car overtook our coach on a bend and tried to push us off the road into a ravine! Thankfully Manuel's driving skills and his knowledge of the mountain saved us from certain death. Unfortunately he was unable to save me from hitting my head on the windscreen.'

Julie continued to glower at Conrad in disgust.

As blasé as ever he came back with, 'Hope you managed to get the number.'

She wanted to slap the smile from his condescending face; instead she retaliated with, 'You do realise that you came very close to killing and maiming fifty potential customers who will probably spend over two million pounds with us over the next three days? Not to mention the adverse publicity you would have generated had there been a disaster; the client base demolished in one stupid move, Bull Ring project exterminated. Not very clever!'

'Well, well, you do have some strong views on something that *didn't* happen. Anyway, you are the only person who is able to identify me and I strongly suggest you keep it that way.' His flint-hard gaze made a point.

'Now shall we join our "valuable and alive" clients for my introduction and details of the programme over the next few days.' Sarcasm was one of his failings.

They headed for the site office where the visitors were being compensated and regaled with refreshments.

'Good morning everyone, it's really good to see you all.' Conrad oozed sickly charm.

Peter, in complete innocence, interrupted. 'You nearly didn't see us at all. We are extremely fortunate to be alive, some madman overtook our coach on a sharp bend and we nearly ended up dead.'

'I have to say that I am very sorry you've had such a distressing experience. Unfortunately I am unable to help you with any details of the er, madman.'

'Anyway let's forget it. Since you are all in one piece,' Conrad was really enjoying this, 'we will make certain you enjoy your few days with us. It will help you forget the incident.'

Peter was not convinced by the glib and uncaring reply from Conrad, and determined to find out the identity of the vehicle and driver.

'For those I haven't had the privilege to meet, my name is Conrad Hemmings, Director in charge of operations in Spain for Bull Ring Properties.

'We have an action packed programme starting with a tour of the various sites that are nearing completion, and sites where construction has recently commenced. We break for lunch at *El Salvador,* a superb Spanish restaurant above Marbella. After lunch we go to the Mijas development and then return to the Kon Tiki for a relaxing few hours where you can spend time in the pools or on the hotel's private beach.

'The evening will start with a cocktail reception at 6.30 p.m. where you will meet Bill Young, our Chairman, and the main board directors. There will be full displays of developments you will visit to-day, together with pricing details, investment potential and current availability. At 8 p.m we leave for Puerto Banús for a fantastic evening at the La Manga.. At the end of the evening I hope you will be proud owners of your Spanish Dream home.'

The smile that would charm the Devil lit his face.

'I will now hand you over to John Gates, head of our resident team who, with Julie's help, will show you the development here at Duquesa. I have a meeting with the developers so I will see you all this evening.

Hope you have a productive and enjoyable day." He clapped his hands once. 'Are there any questions?'

Julie led her party to the show house. They entered the complex through a stone archway, leading into a magnificent courtyard decorated with nature's finest – palm trees, bougainvillea, hibiscus, mimosa and olive trees. Beyond this garden of paradise stood what had been named the *Infinity Pool*, surrounded by wattle shelters and recliners.

Julie went into her well-rehearsed sales pitch

'The town houses and apartments you will be given the opportunity to purchase are all finished to the same high specification you see here. Marble floors throughout, air conditioning, wood burners, granite work top surfaces, integrated kitchen units, communal pool, all are included in the prices for town houses and apartments. It is advisable you install security bars on all windows and doors. We call them "wreckers" in Spain.

'A new innovation is to transform the open patio area upstairs into a conservatory. This is simply achieved by installing glass curtains, the effect of which can be seen when I show you the patio areas.

'Any opinions so far?'

Ecstatic, excited voices, smiling guests, now freed from the ordeal of their journey, burst forth almost as one.

'Absolutely fantastic. When can we have one, and how much?'

'We thought you would be impressed,' replied Julie. 'I suggest we discuss pricing details, availability, completion dates and rental potential, at our reception to-night.' She paused, waiting for them to quieten more before saying, 'Now, I will let you into my little secret. Hopefully this will give you a certain amount of confidence concerning the market and buying your property off plan in the Costa del Sol.

'I have obviously had time to look at the investment potential, capital appreciation and rental returns. Prices are likely to increase by at least 20% in the next few months, due to demand exceeding supply and the strength of the pound against the Euro and other currencies.

'I've reserved three properties. An apartment, here on the Duquesa development for my parents who are moving to Spain, a town house in Estrella and another on the Mijas site.' She smiled as she scanned eager faces.

'W ell,' said Angela, 'that sounds fine for you but there are still many uncertainties for all of us. We are buying in a foreign country, town hall officials are being prosecuted for granting illegal building licenses, meaning we could easily be taken for a ride. Properties will need furnishing; there is a 7% Spanish Income Tax (IVA) to pay, on top of the purchase price, plus solicitors fees, local taxes and other hidden costs. We don't know anything about Bull Ring Properties except they have moved rapidly into the Spanish property market. This is totally different from the "buy to let" market in the UK. Can we see copies of your annual accounts?'

Angela was on a roll. In fact she'd elected herself spokesperson for all.

'Tell me Julie, how do we know that our properties won't be bulldozed into the ground as a result of the land being purchased illegally by the parties involved in the developments? Will Bull Ring provide guarantees protecting our money should you or the developer go bust?'

Julie attentive and nodding in all the right places, came back with:

'You have raised some very important issues, Angela, and hopefully these will be answered by our management team. I can assure you that there is no way Bull Ring Properties will go under, otherwise I would not have invested nearly €1 million in my properties if there were any doubts concerning the company's viability.'

Julie shared some of Angela's concerns, albeit she refrained from voicing them. Agreed, perhaps there were gaps in the company's grandiose plans that did require investigation.

With an added promise that all queries of this nature would be answered, she ushered the now extremely thoughtful guests into the coach departing for Sotto Grande, Estepona and Estrella.

They finally arrived at El Salvador restaurant, exhausted and yet exhilarated by their morning's work.

'Julie, you speak Spanish, would you please translate?' asked Peter pointing to the large tapas menu.

'Delighted. The seafood selection includes *gambas al pil pil.* That is prawns sizzled with garlic; *remojón*, an exotic combination of oranges, onions, cod with octopus and fresh anchovies. This can be followed by meatballs, rabbit in almond sauce, pork cutlets, kidneys in sherry sauce, lamb stew or tortilla, a thick potato omelette.'

Julia warmed to this, aware everyone listened, and were almost salivating at the appetising dishes mentioned. She went on, 'The full flavour of the gourmet Andalusían food will be complemented by an agreeable light dry wine called *Rueda.'*

She laughed. 'Once replete and after staggering to the coach you are allowed a siesta!'

Everyone applauded, and thanked her.

Much happier following the meal, they'd reached the fresher air of Mijas with its fine views down to the coast. The clean white Moorish houses and green shutters depicted good examples of the Spanish genius for giving even tourist traps a certain enchantment.

The new complex had been built into the hillside with far reaching sea views, its luxury millionaire villas, owned mainly by Germans, providing the affluent backdrop to the new town houses.

'Fantastic!' exploded Peter, stepping down from the coach. 'That's the one we are going to buy.' He indicated the villa at the far end of the complex, with uninterrupted views from the sun terraces and a view of the Infinity Pool.

Julie, happier at their change of attitude from that of maudlin doubt to one of exciting anticipation, found she had difficulty in keeping pace with them.

'This is it, darling,' Peter told Angela, ' our Spanish dream home at last, no further development, unique location, quiet, excellent rental potential, fantastic views. It ticks all the boxes for me.'

He turned towards her. 'What do you think? We have visited four locations and found nothing to our liking.'

'Before you answer him,' interrupted Julie, 'you see the large hilltop just beyond the apartment block?' They followed her eye line. 'I can tell you that will be demolished thus extending your views to Gibraltar and Africa.'

'That will be amazing, getting better every minute.' Peter was ecstatic.

Angela demurred. 'I think this is the best property we have seen, however, I do have some reservations.' She looked at Peter.

He arced an eyebrow. 'And they are?'

'I just cannot believe that the planners or the owners of the fantastic villas behind us would allow this superb development to include apartment blocks that would effectively remove all their views.' Angela turned towards Julie for answers.

'I mean how can we be assured that Mijas Town Hall will give their final approval to this development and grant the habitation license?'

'That is something you need to ask Conrad,' Julie's phone rang. Turning away from Peter and Angela, she looked slightly relieved.

Back with them Julie said, 'I'm afraid your concerns are irrelevant. Head Office have just informed me that all properties on this site have been reserved. I am very sorry for you both.'

Peter almost uttered an expletive; needless to say he wasn't well pleased. 'Why does it always happen to us. We haven't actually gone in raptures over anything else we've seen and we certainly do not want an apartment.'

Julie's mobile rang again. She answered it and grinned at them.

'This must be your lucky day, the moment I put my phone down the current owner called the office to say she was unable to proceed. Your dream home, is for sale again.'

'This must be a miracle. I can't believe . . . Call it fate but we are meant to have this villa.' He embraced Angela.

'Peter,' Julie interrupted, 'I do not wish to sound over-enthusiastic or push you into a hasty decision but you need to make a decision now. There are a number of clients on our coach who have shown serious interest in the site. The property will be relaunched on our web site immediately and will be snapped up very quickly.'

'Right, we need to know the price,' replied Peter.

'Let's see Plot 10.' Turning over pages in her schedule she said, 'Ha, yes, three bedroom town house, priced at €360,000, equivalent to £250,000 based on the current exchange rate of 1.42 or 68 Euros to the pound. IVA tax of 7% and legal costs of £10,000 need to be added. A reservation fee of £5000 is payable on signing the contract. You are also guaranteed a 50% repayment mortgage with Casa Espana over twenty five years.' She didn't lose the smile. 'We have thought about everything to give you a trouble free property package.

'Would you like to make a reservation now? It is very unlikely you will get a second chance,' Julie emphasised wearing her sales hat.

'We will take that chance and give you an answer this evening when I have spoken with my financial advisers,' replied Peter.

CHAPTER 6

Gomez, watering can in hand, was tending to his rare species of exotic plants on the balcony leading from his office when the phone rang.

Maria's voice echoed from the phone's speaker, 'Manuel, David Wiltshire from SFO is on the line.'

'Thank you,' he shouted. 'Please put him through, and Maria, could you organise a coffee for me? Thanks.'

'Hello David, good to hear from you and so soon, must be important!'

'Where are you Manuel? From the bird song it sounds as if you are in a garden of paradise with peacocks calling.'

'Nice one, I am on my balcony garden, watering the plants. Only seagulls I'm afraid!'

Maria came in, left the coffee, and laughed loudly when she heard about the peacocks.

'All right for some. Hey, that's better, can't hear the peacocks now you've turned off that darned loud speaker,' David chuckled then got serious.

'There have been major developments since our last conversation, Manuel. You were correct in voicing your concerns following the meeting with Hemmings.

The serious fraud office have opened the case brought to them by Symonds & Reed, Bull Ring's accountants and auditors. Following the takeover of the company by Bill Young, they did indeed discover a deficiency in the Company's assets.

'Their interim report states that someone with accountancy experience entered a debit entry in the property account, depreciating the value of the fixed assets by a staggering two million pounds. There is no record in the company's ledgers of any property being sold, nor any credit entry in the bank accounts. You already know someone leaked information to the Times and London Gazette on a deficiency of fixed assets following the acquisition. We could not confirm our suspicions until now.' Serious, yes but David had kept his tone even without losing his temper. To say he was annoyed was an understatement.

Manuel took a little time to sip his coffee before countering with: 'Well, well, Conrad Hemmings will have to find answers to a growing number of questions, assuming he had the acumen to alter the accounts—'

'Sorry to interrupt you, Manuel,' David said, 'but did you know that Hemmings is a qualified accountant? He was employed by an international firm, Symonds & Reed where he specialised in corporate tax avoidance and international finance. A very clever and ruthless person.'

Gomez was becoming even more intrigued and engrossed by the speed at which the story was unfolding.

'I'm having trouble believing what you have just told me. I specifically asked Conrad about his professional background when we met. I remember him being evasive about wanting to discuss anything his business or personal life, except for property developments in Spain.

'This is staggering news to me. I have to say I felt extremely uncomfortable being unable to discover the make up of this suave, personable and persuasive stranger who suddenly came into my life.'

Gomez sipped his coffee. He noticed his hands trembled a little and blamed a heavy watering can! Birdsong had ceased, and quite rightly given the shocking circumstances of what he'd heard.

'David, I am accustomed to dealing with international fraudsters. However, I do understand Hemmings could be even more dangerous and manipulating with his professional status. Indeed a deceitful and ruthless character.

'By the way I didn't tell you. Shortly after leaving my office, Hemmings found himself in a big square by the Bull Ring in Marbella. Maria, my secretary, was enjoying her lunch break by the fountain, dangling her lovely legs in its cooling waters…!

At the other end of the line David had a momentary vision of beautiful, tanned legs.

Conrad, apparently approached her asking directions to the offices of a Signor Pérez, a lawyer renowned for defending corrupt town hall officials and criminals convicted for drug trafficking offences. Our paths have crossed in the courts. I should add he doesn't like me.

'He is also involved in property deals. My suspicious nature tells me that Conrad could be involved in Pérez's shady activities.'

'Mm very interesting Manuel. Confirmation of your findings could be a significant development in tracing the link to the disappearance of the money, and possibly implicating Signor Pérez, and "the third man", I am about to mention.

The pun is intended by the way.

'Matthew Larking, senior partner of the auditors is convinced the fraud of the disappearing assets would not have been discovered had it not been for Simon Peters. As you know he is the newly appointed Financial Director for Bull Ring. Apart from the Chairman, neither Directors nor employees are aware that he's also a partner in Symonds & Reed. Simon is also a qualified director, and shareholder, but is employed under a special contract by Bull Ring. His insider knowledge and access into the accounts allowed him to expedite a special audit on the company's property portfolio. Instead of accepting properties listed in the property asset register he paid a visit to The Land Registry, where details of all owners of property in the UK are listed. He discovered that a large apartment block in Birmingham, originally owned by Bull Ring, appeared in the register owned by a finance organisation called Carlos Investments. This, my friend, is owned by Signor Ernesto Carlos, another Spanish lawyer. Apparently there is no entry in the Land Registry ledgers to confirm the property had changed hands.'

Manuel drained his cup, and pulled a face at cold coffee, right now bewildered and numbed by more unsettling news.

Matthew, on a deep breath, said: 'Finally, Manuel, following this lengthy conversation I have a favour to ask of you. Matthew Larking, always aware of Simon's movements, contacted me to say that Main Board directors and Bill Young are in Marbella. As the company's ɩnish lawyer, would you please arrange to meet the Chairman and make him aware of ongoing investigations. Naturally, you will appreciate there are very serious financial implications affecting the future of his company. Apart from the auditors and ourselves no one is privy to this confidential information.'

David heard a loud snort from Manuel.

'Thank you very much indeed, for giving me the dirty work.!' Manuel chuckled despite his feelings. 'To be honest it is a coincidence. I have been invited to the company reception at the Kon Tiki by none other than Conrad Hemmings. I'll keep you posted.'

'Many thanks for your invaluable help Manuel, and I am extremely sorry your new client has so many problems. We'll speak again soon and thanks again.' Matthew replaced his phone.

Gomez flipped the off switch on his phone, closed his eyes and mused about the recent conversation. He was beginning to rue the day his path had crossed with that of Conrad Hemmings.

CHAPTER 7

'Hola', the attractive girl smiled.

'Hola, Buenos dias, dos café con leche, por favor,' Simon Peters stuttered trying to emulate the "teach yourself" Spanish tapes he had been studying since he joined the company.

'Algo más?'

'What does she mean?' whispered Bill Young.

'She asked if we wanted anything else.'

'No gracias,' Simon smiled broadly, confidence in the command of the Spanish language growing by the minute. His mobile rang to the tune of Beethoven's Fifth.

'Hello, Simon here.'

He cupped a hand over his new Blackberry phone.

'It's the office, Bill. The reception is very bad, I'll go over to the fountain and hopefully it will improve.' The signal was actually excellent, but the caller, Matthew Larking, aware that Bill Young and Simon were together, was emphatic that Bill should not overhear their conversation.

'Simon, David Wiltshire from the SFO has just phoned me saying he has briefed Manuel Gomez, Bull Ring's lawyer in Marbella, about the disappearing assets.

Gomez will meet Bill Young at the reception and explain everything. When Bill Young hears the news from Gomez his reaction will not be positive to say the least. Gomez will ensure Bill understands but for your timely intervention, the financial situation of his company could be extremely tenuous. Would you make certain that you are "in the wings" so to speak and fully prepared to pick up the pieces?'

'Finally, it is imperative that the suspicions of Bill Young, Conrad Hemmings and the developers you are about to meet are not aroused. If there is any leak at all it could be the end of the Spanish operation. Do you understand Simon?'

'Yes, OK David,' Simon snapped, feeling irked that David had taken this tone. It made him feel like a bloody imbecile. 'I'd better get back, Bill will be getting suspicious. Will be in touch.'

He strolled around the fountain, confused by the conversation with his boss.

Why would Signor Gomez need to explain the outcome of his lengthy and inspired investigation, resulting in the discovery of the fraud? After all, Simon was more conversant with UK accountancy procedures than a Spanish lawyer. Matthew had asked him to "wait in the wings". Would he be standing back stage, waiting for a cue from Gomez to draw back the curtains and reveal himself, entering the arena to "pick up the pieces"? He couldn't help his strong feelings of sarcasm and resentment. 'Perhaps I am being over reactive,' he mumbled. Though he doubted it.

Bill Young happily sipped his coffee, seated in the open air café, which was one of several in the main square of Puerto Banús; absorbing the sound of gushing fountains, floral designs, tented shops, look alike Picasso sculptures, all blending into the notorious cosmopolitan shopping area. Puerto Banús was certainly affluent, he mused, home base for many fashionable names including Gucci, Zara, Louis Vuitton and recently James Hewitt's dining establishment, "Polo House".

Pleased to be alone for a moment, relaxing in the sunshine, he understood for the first time in his many visits the overwhelming desire which prompted clients to own their dream homes in this land of sun, sea, cheap living, gourmet food and classic wine. Even the Spanish are nice people. Yes, he would definitely consider purchasing one of the larger properties reserved for directors. Perhaps Conrad would follow suit? Bill was blissfully unaware that Conrad was already purchasing a penthouse overlooking the billionaire's paradise of Puerto Banús harbour, and with *his* money!

His thoughts were interrupted by Peter's return.

'Sorry for the intrusion, the accounts department had a problem agreeing the trial balance for the month end accounts,' Simon lied.

Simon finished his tepid coffee in one gulp and settled the bill. They started to walk across the beautiful square.

'You see the offices on the corner, the low level building with a blue glass frontage,' Bill pointed.

Simon pulled Bill's shirt sleeve. 'Do you mean that enormous neon flashing sign?' They stopped to stare at the illuminated sign.

"BULL RING PROPERTIES (SPAIN)"

"DREAM HOMES IN THE SUN"

'How could you miss that message, whatever the time of day?' Simon muttered in disbelief. He had second thoughts about adding "a bit over the top" just in case Bill Young had designed and approved the Blackpool illumination.

Conrad, his usual immaculate self, dressed in cream slacks and white shirt, viewing them from across the square, stood poised to open the massive glass door.

'Good to see you again and welcome to our prestigious offices,' he enthused shaking their hands vigorously.

Simon couldn't look this man in the face, knowing his scheming and ruthless nature. Thank God, it wouldn't be long now before his dishonest life would be exposed.

'Very impressive sign Conrad, makes a statement, reminds me of Southsea or is it Clacton?' Bill laughed thumping Conrad on the back and nearly knocking him off balance.

'Our guests have arrived,' Conrad said leading Bill and Simon into his plush oval office, beautifully carved oak panels were covered with life size pictures of Bull Ring developments. At the highly polished board room table sat two Spaniards.

'Let me introduce Bill Young our Chairman, and Simon Peters the Financial Director,' Conrad smiled.

A tall slim handsome figure with dark complexion, rose from the table, jet black hair swept back and tied in a bun, steely blue penetrating eyes matching the topaz and diamond ear studs. The Adonis offered his beautifully manicured hand to Bill and Simon.

'Luis Ramos, President of the Ramos Group. Very good to meet you Signor Young and Signor Peters.' He handed Bill and Simon a gold lined business card, with a portrait of "Luis Ramos" engraved on the front.

How ostentatious is that? Simon reflected looking at the reproduction on the card.

Signor Ramos placed his gold ringed hand on the bare shoulder of the signora seated next to him. 'I would like to introduce my Business Director, Carla Flores.'

Simon leant forward expecting to be offered the hand of this Spanish beauty, whose low cut black dress clung like a wet suit to her sensuous voluptuous figure. He was very disappointed when she failed to take his outstretched hand. Perhaps Spanish protocol is different, Simon decided.

'Please help yourselves to the iced water in front of you and Luis, could you please give an update on the developments and completion dates?'

Ramos had done his homework. He passed around bulky information packs.

'You will find all the information you require covering the seven sites in your folders. The main issue will be achieving completion dates, which as you are aware, are linked to habitation licenses being granted by Town Halls in good time for your clients to set up mortgage arrangements enabling Banco España to release funds. This is the only way my company will receive final payments.'

Luis gulped back his refreshing cold water and asked Carla to continue.

'Estepona, Duquesa, Mijas, Estrella will be ready for occupation in three weeks time. It is now July 15th and we need to receive final payments by the end of August enabling the builders to be paid. Conrad, how does the time-scale fit in with the sales contracts you have in place?'

'Carla, before Conrad answers your question,' Bill interrupted, 'we must address the most important issue, occupation licenses. There is no way owners can complete the purchase of their properties if local authorities cannot grant these licenses. No money can change hands and nobody can be paid.

'Times have changed in Spain. I understand the current dilemma is that Town Halls are being forced to restrict the issuing of licenses as a result of the widespread corruption. The seventeen autonomous Regional communities in Spain, in our case Andalusia, are ultimately responsible for the issue of building licenses in their regions. It is the powerful Andalusían government who ultimately control the property market in the Costa del Sol and *not* as everyone thinks, the local councils. The regional offices are vested with powers for issuing demolition notices where local authorities have issued illegal building licenses in the past. Properties built ten years ago along the coastal region are being flattened as a result of illegal building permits.

'Luis, am I correct in my appraisal of the new initiatives currently being adopted by the authorities?' Bill frowned. He looked worried.

Ramos jumped to his feet at the same time waving a large bundle of papers towards Bill Young.

'Signor Bill,' his anxious demeanour making him forget to say "Signor Young".

'You may think you have completed la investigación, I think it is "research" in English. However, the recent actions of regional communities will not, I repeat, will not destroy the completion and handing over of properties.'

'I think you mean "jeopardise" not "destroy", Simon interrupted.

Ramos sat down. A man who didn't take criticism easily.

'I feel sure you would like to know,' Simon continued with a hint of sarcasm, 'with the help of a Spanish lawyer, also an elected member of the European Parliament, we investigated the new initiatives of the regional communities. Our findings concluded that there is "a wind of change" affecting the building programmes of many local regions. The Costa del Sol being the hardest hit.

There is no need, Signor Ramos, to push this dramatic change of fortunes "under the table", as we say in English. Bill Young is absolutely correct in voicing his concerns.' Simon glowered at Ramos.

'Gentlemen, please, there is no need to have this, how do you say in your country, "confrontation", when we have the perfect solution,' Ramos shouted.

'Who is the Spanish lawyer representing you in Spain, Conrad?'

'Manuel Gomez, senior partner in Fernandez Sanchez.' Conrad smiled.

'Signor Gomez is a very competent lawyer and a good choice. However, he is not flexible and "sticks to the rules", Ramos laughed, his self confidence growing in his command of English idioms.

'Carla, isn't Gomez involved with the prosecutors office in Marbella?'

Carla nodded. 'Si Luis, he is in line to become Chief Prosecutor next year.'

'Does anyone, apart from Carla, know Signor Franco Pérez, he is a lawyer and business friend of mine?' Ramos smiled.

Conrad Hemmings, a budding artist in his youth, bored by the continuous dialogue, was drawing the beautiful Spanish lady sitting opposite him, when suddenly he heard the name "Franco Pérez". He sat bolt upright, his multi coloured pencil hit the floor.

Desperate to regain composure without giving anything away, he anticipated Ramos's next move and blurted out, 'Why do we need to employ another lawyer? Everyone agrees Gomez is a good choice. He might prove to be very useful in the future, if the Andalusían regional authorities attempt to reverse decisions on licenses already granted.' Conrad was stalling for time and playing Devil's Advocate.

Luis rose to his feet yet again, this time without waving his papers.

'Must be a control freak,' Simon whispered to Bill.

'Franco Pérez will assist us to overcome the problem of obtaining licenses.

Ramos Developments have completed on over fifty sites in Andalusia over the past two years accounting for over 2,000 properties,' Luis's voice reached another octave, his speech staccato.

'Our success is entirely due to Franco Pérez's skills in negotiating planning licenses, building licenses, occupation licenses, any licenses you would like to name, with the officials and his friends in the Town Halls.' Luis was back in control, so he thought, until Bill Young interrupted.

'Yes, Luis I understand completely the relaxed approach you are adopting to solve the problem, but at what cost to my company? We are possibly talking about a figure in excess of 500,000 Euros for the arrangement fees to your friend Franco Perez and bribes to mayors and officials in Marbella's town hall.' Bill thumped the table, unhappy at the thought of corruption and the cost to Bull Ring.

Carla noticed Luis's hand shaking as he lifted the glass of water to his mouth. He knew Bill Young had a point and would be against any corruption.

'Listen my friends, this is Spain not England. Our culture, our way of life is totally different from your country. Here in the Costas, crime, corruption, drug trafficking, smuggling, tax evasion are all part of our lives. We sit in this plush office and two hundred yards away in the streets and bars of Puerto Banús, there are gun battles, murders, rapes, every day. Mostly drug related and carried out by organised gangs from all over the world, including England. Do you think I like all this?

'Please believe me, it is quite normal to offer bribes to Town Hall mayors, this is part of our survival. You should not worry about the regional governments issuing demolition notices, believe me, by the time this happens your money will be safe and there will be no legal actions against Bull Ring Properties or Luis Ramos Developments.'

Beads of perspiration ran down his face.

' If you are unable to involve my good friend Franco, licenses will not be granted and your investments, Conrad, of over 100 million Euros will be lost for ever.' Luis sat down.

There was an awkward silence.

The silence was shattered by a knock on the door.

'Come in,' shouted Conrad.

Jasmine, Conrad's beautiful blonde secretary entered the room.

'Excuse me, so sorry to interrupt, I have an urgent message for Mr Hemmings.'

'Yes, what is it Jasmine?' Conrad said abruptly.

'Could you have a word with a gentleman calling himself Signor Pérez? He muttered something about being a business acquaintance of yours. He seemed very anxious and insisted he spoke with you immediately,' Jasmine tried to whisper.

'Please say I can't talk now I'll call back after my meeting.' Conrad sounded important.

'He is not on the telephone Mr Hemmings, he is in reception waiting to see you.'

CHAPTER 8

Peter and Angela froze as they saw the waterfalls, stalagmites and stalactites at the far end of the Kon Tiki's ballroom. Cascading chandeliers completed this magnificent setting.

'Amazing,' whispered Peter. 'Angela, did you know you are looking at the replica of the Theodore Roosevelt Hotel's dining room constructed in New Orleans, in about 1925, in honour of the new President's inauguration? Pity I can't remember his name.'

'I suppose,' Angela smiled, 'you are about to wind me up further by saying there was an assassination attempt on the President's life during the Mardi Gras evening in the ballroom of this fictitious Theodore Roosevelt Hotel.'

'Actually, I—' Peter was distracted by Julie, waving her Pina Collada excitedly whilst trying to negotiate a path across the crowded ballroom. He noted the sense of urgency in her hurried strides, as if her life depended upon reaching Angela and Peter for fear a sale would be lost.

'Buenos noches,' Julie laughed, embracing Peter and making certain he could experience the feel of her beautiful body. Angela was content to offer a hand.

'I hope you have enjoyed a relaxing afternoon. Have you thought about the property at Mijas?' Julie had wasted little time homing in for the kill.

'Indeed,' replied Peter, 'I have just spoken with Alan Parker my accountant. He likes the investment potential. Angela and I like the idea of the attractive rental income, and owning a fantastic retirement home in sunny Spain. What else could we want?'

'Wait a minute Peter,' a scowling Angela interrupted, 'that is not all your accountant said to you. Mr Parker is concerned about the viability of Bull Ring Properties and the working capital available for the company's expansion into Spain.'

'Excuse me Angela,' Julie interrupted. 'I fully understand your accountant's concerns. As I said to you earlier to-day I will be investing nearly one million Euros in three properties, not for pleasure but as a viable capital investment yielding a minimum return of 10% per year. I am sure Bill Young will put all our minds at rest this evening when he emphasises the financial stability of the company and the cash reserves available for the expansion into Spain.'

'Sounds fine to me.' Peter smiled and rubbed his hands. 'Let's proceed with the reservation, we have nothing to lose, have we my darling?' Angela looked up at the ceiling in disgust.

'I am so pleased you have made the decision to proceed, and only just in time.' Julie smiled in a knowing way. 'I was being harassed by another client who wanted to purchase your villa. I couldn't get away from her and resorted to the old sales tactic of saying: "sold I'm afraid". Luckily for me this is now true.'

'Thank you so much for the order,' said Julie squeezing Peter's hand in delight.

Peter turned to answer a tap on his shoulder. His friend and guest Jim Connolly, internationally renowned neuro surgeon, based at the Royal Hospital in Bath, extended his hand.

'Evening Jim.' Peter shook his hand and gripped his arm.

As Doctor of Medicine at the Royal who handled most of Connolly's patients, Angela pecked him on both cheeks.

'Jim, have you met Julie?' Peter enquired.

'Oh yes indeed, I'm getting to know her very well thank you. Jim chuckled and winked at Julie.

'How are you enjoying sitting on the touchline enjoying the ambience and witnessing fellow guests spending their savings?' a smiling Peter asked Jim.

'Actually I am having a splendid time; as Julie knows only too well, and to her credit,' Jim Connolly enthused again acknowledging the beautiful Julie.

Julie responded. 'Mr Connolly is purchasing, wait for it, two town houses, one in the Sotto Grande, the other in Duquesa Park.' She laughed loudly.

'Jim, I can't believe what Julie has said.' Peter's jaw had dropped.

'You come over as my guest, adamant that you did not have the slightest intention of buying anything in Spain and parting with your money. Now you fall for Julie's sales patter, and not content with buying one villa, you buy two, both in upmarket exclusive areas. It's no surprise Julie is laughing all the way to Banco España as her cash register goes into free fall.'

'Julie, the sales you have closed today must be worth over one million Euros.' Peter remained in shock.

'And the rest,' blurted the jubilant Julie.

A sudden hush descended over the exuberant guests. The lights dimmed as the deep red velvet stage curtains, embroidered in gold with life size images of Thor Heyerdahl's famous Kon Tiki boat, drew back to the sound of classical guitar music.

'Perhaps Craig Ogden is going to give a recital,' Angela whispered to Peter.

A tall man appeared from the wings, his face in shadow, the impact on the audience something as he paused centre stage attired in white tuxedo, trousers and shoes, even a flashing white bow tie, the whole ensemble crowned with white hair. This ghost-like figure tapped the microphone.

'Buenas noches, mis amigos, bienvenido a Espana y Plaza de Toros Propiedads,' the mysterious bass voice boomed in a broad "Brummie" accent.

Spotlights flooded the stage, the white figure removing a white wig to reveal a shining bald head. He beamed at his speechless guests.

'Evening all, Bill Young Chairman of "Plaza de Toros Propiedads". I hope you appreciated my excellent Spanish translation of Bull Ring Properties.' The microphone hummed with feedback as he bowed and boomed, his laugh over loud. A few cringed.

A low groan came from the dance floor, followed by a loud, "Evening Bill."

'Thanks for that.' Bill was still smiling. 'Didn't want you to forget my first public appearance.'

'Good to see so many happy and smiling faces in front of me.' Bill rubbed his hands with glee.

'Obviously from the reservation figures I have been given by the sales team you are having an enjoyable visit to the Costa del Sol. There are two hundred guests on this trip and to-day, an incredible fifty per cent of you have signed sales contracts.

'Amongst us tonight,' he pointed to his guests, 'are accountants, solicitors, lawyers, doctors, surgeons, footballers, entrepreneurs . . . Sorry if I've missed anyone, just don't wish to bore your socks off! All, *are* searching for a Spanish Dream.' Bill didn't include high ranking police officers amongst his list, equally unaware that one eminent guest about to make a purchase, was Philip Varley, a Commander in the MI5 division of the Metropolitan Police.

'Thank you all,' Bill continued, 'for placing your faith in our company. I look forward to meeting you personally during the exciting evening ahead.

'Before I hand over to Conrad Hemmings, are there any questions?' Bill grabbed a glass of water handed to him by Conrad.

Angela, not prepared to miss a trick, had positioned herself in front of the stage.

She raised her empty glass towards the chairman.

'Mr Young,' Angela shouted. 'My name is Angela Grant and I am a Doctor of Medicine. I have some questions.'

Without waiting for an invitation she went on: 'Firstly, we need confirmation of Bull Ring's financial viability in supporting their rapid expansion into Spain, preferably in the form of a balance sheet for the year end accounting period. I must stress that we are not interested in historical information from Companies House, but current, up to date figures.' Angela responded strong and assertive. Deliberately.

'Secondly, we are concerned…' She turned to face her audience as if she had been nominated to act as their chief negotiator, '. . .about the latest crackdown by town halls on the Costa del Sol granting building and occupation licenses. I understand this new initiative has been introduced by the Andalusían Regional Government.

'Finally, Mr Young, can you confirm it is the aforesaid autonomous Regional Communities, and not the local authorities, who are issuing demolition notices on properties already built and occupied mainly by British investors?'

Dr Angela Grant was flying.

'Can you guarantee our newly built town houses and apartments will not be bulldozed into rubble this year, next year or in ten years time?'

A pause, albeit brief, held the recognised emphasis before Angela added with extra gusto: 'Well, Mr Chairman? How do you intend to answer that one?'

The guests started applauding, the majority calling 'Well done, Angela.'

Bill, on the other hand produced a false smile to hide obvious unease, thinking: How on earth would a medical consultant know about balance sheets and the powers of Regional Government communities in Spain?

One thing in his favour, his position as European Director for Midland Motors had trained him to think quickly on his feet.

'Thank you Dr Grant for your most interesting and searching questions. Perhaps you would like my job.' Bill made it a joke.

'I presume you have been elected as chief shop steward by your fellow guests.'

He guffawed, the audience by then in hysterics. Angela failed to see the funny side and scowled at him.

'Typical delaying tactics,' she whispered to Peter.

'You asked about the company accounts,' Bill continued. 'I can assure you that the company is solvent with cash reserves in excess of £30 million.

'Might I suggest,' waving his discarded white wig in Angela's direction, 'that you have a word with Simon Peters, our financial director, who will be delighted to give you copies of the accounts. Alternatively, if you prefer, you can search the Companies Registrar on line for the information.'

'Simon,' Bill shouted into the microphone, 'are you with us?'

There was no reply, Simon waiting in the wings with Franco Gomez.

Bill continued, taken aback by Simon's apparent absence. 'Julie please ask Simon to discuss the finance issues with Dr Grant and anyone else who is interested.'

To the room he said, 'I believe the next question Angela Grant raised was the concern over licenses.' The Chairman tried hard to sound vague hoping the issue would disappear.

'I have just arrived from a lengthy meeting with Luis Ramos, president of our developers, Ramos SL.' Direct to Angela, he said, 'Dr Grant, I asked Luis exactly the same question you have raised and was given assurances there would be no problems arranging the first habitation licenses. I am convinced there will be no delays in completion dates.

'No doubt you will all be interested to know, Signor Ramos uses the services of a lawyer, can't remember his name though,' Bill lied, scratching his perspiration sheathed pate. 'This legal friend liaises with all the local authorities in the Costa del Sol that cover the issuing of licenses.'

Angela intervened. 'Excuse me interrupting again.' Angela was trying with difficulty to be polite. 'What about the hefty bribes this lawyer friend of Signor Ramos must be paying to the corrupt mayors who have so far escaped prosecution for issuing dodgy licenses?'

A shocked muttering enlivened the proceedings, and as quickly died as most were eager to learn more from Angela, and her prompting of concise and truthful answers.

'Are we all,' she said, arms outstretched and facing her supporters, 'paying for the cost of these bribes?' Angela smirked knowingly before completing a well executed about turn to face Bill Young.

Conrad, eyes suffused with hatred, entered stage right in an attempt to defuse the onslaught on his boss by Angela Grant, thus saving him from further embarrassment.

Conrad had already concluded that this so-called doctor of medicine appeared oblivious to the fact that property deals in Spain involved some aspects of corruption.

Dr Grant's investigative abilities and leadership qualities acting as spokesperson for Bull Ring clients, more than hinted at danger to the success of the company.

'Perhaps Mr Chairman,' Conrad stared ahead, 'I could answer the question put so eloquently by Mrs Goode…'

Angela rose to her full height. 'My correct name and title is Dr Angela Grant, Mr "Conman" Hemmings, *not* 'MRS' Goode.'

'My sincere apologies for the name change, Dr "Angel" Grant. And touché.'

Conrad laughed. Quite a novelty to be called a "conman". Action for slander? Or something more sinister for the "Angel"?

Bill Young, relieved by Conrad's unrehearsed entrance, replaced the microphone and exited discreetly back stage.

'Believe me my friends,' Conrad bellowed, 'building licenses, occupation licenses, all the bloody licenses you can conjure up will be legal. Bribes do not exist since the local town halls have been purged and officials removed from their offices right here in Marbella.

'There is nothing to worry about.' Conrad thumped the microphone.

'Now all your questions have been answered it is time to put negative feelings aside and leave for our evening's entertainment in Marbella, where I will be your host.' How smug he sounded, what charm he oozed.

Angela raised her voice to Peter. 'Shall we jump ship now!'

CHAPTER 9

Bill Young staggered from the stage, reeling after Angela's unexpected onslaught, and damned pleased Conrad's appearance had rescued him from further belittling.

Seated in the wings on a rickety old stool, Bill mopped his brow; hidden by shadows he started to pray, baulking when he felt a gentle tap on his shoulder.

'Evening Bill,' Simon smiled, 'good thing Conrad made his dramatic entrance.

For once in his life, he's done something right.'

Bill was confused by the remark, totally unaware Conrad had done anything "wrong" in his life. Blame my naivety, Bill concluded.

'Bill, there's someone to meet you.'

'Oh yes pull the other one,' Bill shot back. 'I thought we were leaving for the Norwegian Restaurant? I haven't any meetings arranged.'

'It's a long and complicated story.' Simon sighed. 'Signor Gomez, as you are aware is acting as Bull Ring's lawyer in Spain. He has not yet had the opportunity to meet with you and needs to update you on various developments.'

'Simon, after that drubbing, whatever, I am not in the mood to meet anyone at the moment, least of all another crooked lawyer.' He paused, and then added, albeit reluctantly, 'I could give him ten minutes, I suppose.'

Simon took Bill's arm and led him through a side entrance into an open courtyard, screened by an avenue of pergolas covered in white and pink wisteria. A chuckling stream ran though this sea of colour to end in a fountain decorated by a replica of the infamous "Boy and Dolphin" bronze sculptor by Rodin.

Manuel Gomez rose from the bench to greet his clients. Simon introduced them.

'I'll leave you together and see you in the foyer after the meeting.'

'Fine. And Simon would you please organise a couple of beers? Thanks.' Bill

then addressed Gomez. 'Now Signor, to what do I owe this unexpected pleasure?'

'It is very much a "pleasure" to meet with you, Mr Young,' Gomez said, apparently failing to understand Bill's idiomatic meaning. 'I am very sorry to take you away from your guests and at such short notice.

'To get to the point, earlier to-day I received a call from Matthew Larking. As you know Matthew is the senior partner at Symonds & Reed, your accountants.'

The drinks arrived. Time then for Bill and Gomez to clink glasses, utter a "salud".

'Matthew was insistent,' Gomez sipped his beer, 'that I meet with you to discuss a delicate and highly confidential crisis that has developed.'

'Go on,' Bill muttered, throwing Gomez a suspicious look and thinking *what now?*

'It appears—' Gomez hesitated trying to find the right words, 'that your Simon Young discovered a large discrepancy in Bull Ring's, how do you say, "property portfolio?"'

Bill alarmed, interrupted. 'How large a discrepancy?'

Gomez ran his fingers down the condensation on his glass. 'Well . . . I am very sorry to inform you the figure is in excess of two million pounds,' He sounded nervous. And looked it.

'Good God Manuel!' Bill lurched to his feet, shouting, 'How the hell could that happen?'

'It's . . . it's OK Bill, the Serious Fraud Office are—'

'What about the Fraud Office, are they involved?' Bill fumed.

'Indeed just that,' Gomez muttered.

'Then this *discrepancy*, as you call it, must be serious. They would not be interested unless they considered fraudulent dealings were involved, and in excess of one million pounds. No doubt HMRC will be included in the investigations.' Bill gulped his drink.

Gomez lifted a placating hand, 'Bill, without raising your blood pressure even higher, let me explain the background to this unfortunate situation.

'It seems Simon Peters expedited a special audit on the Company's assets, following his appointment as Financial Director, and after your acquisition of Bull Ring. Mr Peter's discovered, on the heels of a visit to the Land Registry, that a large apartment block owned by Bull Ring was registered in the name of a Signor Ernesto Carlos, a Spanish lawyer, turned entrepreneur, who has his own investment company in London.

'Your Mr Hemmings decided he needed a large sum of money for a property investment. I may be wrong but I think a Spanish lawyer, Signor Franco Pérez is somehow involved with Hemmings in property deals.'

'Excuse me Manuel, you did say Franco Pérez?' Gomez nodded. 'This is the second time to-day Pérez has been mentioned. Quite bizarre. Your fairytale improves by the minute. I wonder, what else do you have in store for me?'

Bill laughed nervously.

'Conrad Hemmings as you know is a qualified accountant. At one time he was a senior partner in the international firm of Peat, Haskins &Young.'

'Good God Manuel, I had no idea Hemmings was an accountant least of all employed by such a reputable firm. He led me to believe that his background was in the computer industry, European marketing manager, I think, with Apple Computers.'

Bill was rattled. Gomez was concerned for his new client there being more bad news to follow.

'It appears Mr Hemmings sold the block of flats to Ernesto Carlos for over two million pounds, "cash".' He paused to let it sink in. Then, 'Before the sale, Hemmings falsified the asset register and devalued the fixed assets.

'Wait for it, mi amigo,' Gomez again silenced Bill who by now had gone puce. 'He carried out this creative accounting before you purchased his company, Bull Ring Properties. You were sold a company for a valuation figure over two million pounds more than it's actual value!

'What is more, Matthew Larking is convinced the Fraud Office will issue an extradition order for the deportation of Mr Hemmings to stand trial in your country.' Gomez finished his beer.

A deeply shocked Bill Young stared into somewhere he really didn't want to be, shame and anger seated in equal portions.

'Manuel.' he muttered quietly, 'to think I rescued Mr Bloody Hemmings from bankruptcy, starvation, the gutter and then paid £20 million for his ailing company.

No wonder Hemmings said nothing to me about being an expert in financial accounting. His actions were pre-meditated and criminal. I just cannot believe he had the balls to swindle me out of another two million after all I'd done for him. Now he's building his property empire with my money, not the bank's money. *My freaking money, Manuel.'* Bill was close to breaking down.

'I should listen to my instincts, they told me he might be dangerous. How could I be so foolish and naïve enough to ignore my gut feeling?'

'Manuel, I need to present Conrad with the facts and get rid of him.'

'No Bill!' Manuel said vehemently, 'I know how you feel but that is not the right action to take at present. You may not know I am involved with the prosecutor's office in Marbella. My job, in addition to my legal practice, is bringing drug traffickers, corrupt Town Hall officials, bent property developers and builders to justice.

'I have my suspicions that Hemmings is somehow involved with Franco Pérez, possibly in property developments. Pérez protects and defends all the criminals in the Costa del Sol whilst I am attempting to prosecute them.'

Bill listened without interrupting, certain the more he could get would further help his predicament.

'The police in Marbella,' Gomez said, 'think Pérez has a connection with Morocco. They have seen him aboard a luxury cruiser in Marbella. The MS Hercules is registered to the King of Morocco and flies the

Moroccan flag. Drugs such as hashish and marijuana are shipped from Morocco into Gibraltar. The Spanish government believes that over a billion pounds worth of drugs a year are imported via the Rock for onward transmission to Europe.

'Oh yes,' Gomez smiled, 'Conrad's business dealings and friendship with Pérez could provide the breakthrough in tracking down these wealthy and crooked drug barons.'

He leaned forward. 'Did you know Bill, that these barons own most of the estate agents in the Costas? They have controlling interests in the developers and building companies. I wouldn't be surprised if they were building Bull Ring's properties as we speak, and with money illegally earned from drug trafficking.' Gomez indeed sounded passionate about his mission to end corruption.

'Manuel, why should I worry about cracking "Crime on the Costas" when my company could be in serious financial trouble in the UK and Spain?

'I can't wave a magic wand and conjure up an insurance policy to cover the two million pounds I have just lost..'

'Bill, I understand and sympathise with your dilemma. If you are able to *co-operate* with us and allow Hemmings to "run with the hounds" – I think that is the English saying – I will guarantee there will be no problems from the town halls in obtaining the various licenses needed for the completion of your developments. Your business will not suffer. What is more the Spanish Foreign Office will liaise with London in delaying any extradition order until our respective Foreign Ministers agree a transfer date. We will keep everything hush, hush.'

What Gomez needed to accomplish was to convince various people in high places that his plan to use Conrad Hemmings as a pawn in the game would lead to widespread prosecution of criminals who were ruining economies and the lives of millions of innocent people. Not to mention the daily killings taking place here in the Costa del Sol, all as a result of drugs.

Such a master plan would place him in a strong position to be appointed Chief Prosecutor in Marbella, and may eventually lead to his becoming Chief Prosecutor for the Regional Government of Andalusía. Oh yes, Signor Young held the key to his future. A good move then for Gomez to act for Bull Ring Properties after all.

At least, this was his game plan to prevent anyone suspecting ulterior motives for his devious schemes. The arrival of Conrad Hemmings on the scene could prove to be a blessing in disguise.

'Mm,' mused Bill, 'I suppose from an ethical and humanitarian point of view it would be churlish of me if I didn't accede to your requests. To be totally honest, helping to bring these heartless, deceitful murderers to justice will give me enormous pleasure.'

Manuel grasped Bill's arm. 'Thank you, one day you will be rewarded by my country for the enormous sacrifices you are making.'

Simon was about to send out a search party for Bill and Manuel when they stepped into the hotel's foyer, joking and laughing loudly.

'Come on Simon, what are you waiting for? We're going to be late for the cabaret,' Bill shouted. Manuel agreed.

CHAPTER 10

Standing in the entrance to La Manga Restaurant, looking the epitome of a millionaire content and happy with life, Conrad Hemmings waited to welcome his guests.

Why suffer shame for his incapacity of showing any remorse or feelings for swindling his very own "Good Samaritan" and friend out of two million pounds? His new life in Spain surrounded by like minded shady individuals was good. His expanding property portfolio had led to an opportunity to join forces with his friend Franco Pérez in exploiting the property market in Morocco; plus he owned an exclusive town house in Puerto Banús, and let's not forget his classic Bentley coupé.

'I have everything I need for the rest of my life and soon the gorgeous Spanish women will come flocking after me.' He chuckled with glee.

Conrad, filled with "joie de vivre", greeted Bill Young and Manuel Gomez at the entrance to La Manga, oblivious that both men had been de-briefed about the disappearing assets in Bull Ring's balance sheet.

'Evening Bill, evening Manuel,' Conrad gushed, preening himself.

'You're a bit late, all our guests have arrived. Did something keep you that I should know about?'

'Well,' replied Bill, 'if we reveal the reason for our delay, you wouldn't believe us.' Bill waived it. 'Anyway it would take far too long to explain.'

He turned to Gomez. 'Isn't that right Manuel?'

'Si, correcto,' Gomez replied with a wink.

'Perhaps we can get together another time,' Bill sounded emphatic and pushed his large frame past the enemy.

Gomez sensed Conrad's anxiety; noticed how ill at ease he seemed at Bill's response. A man who loathed being excluded, if Conrad persisted in his attempt to extract an acceptable explanation at being kept out of the picture, any negative response could spell danger to their plans. Gomez took the initiative.

'Don't worry Conrad, Bill's worried about obtaining the various licenses, and ensuring Bull Ring are paid on time to avoid cash flow problems. I have re-assured him there will be no delays with license issues.'

'Bill's worried! What about me? This is my bloody show and I'm more than just worried I'm absolutely delirious! If you are both intent on hiding something from me affecting the Spanish operation, I need to know about it now, not sometime in the future. Do you hear me? Now!'

He was spitting fire, muttering obscenities; his sense of well-being bottomed out. He tugged Gomez's lapels lifting the man's diminutive frame off the ground.

Gomez, broke free from his clutches, smoothed down his ruffled suit and shouted, 'I'll remember your outburst. No one, I mean no one, manhandles me as you have done *Mister* Hemmings. I could have you charged with assault but I'll wait until I see you in court when the charges will be more serious!'

Gomez shrugged his shoulders, stroked his hair and followed Bill Young, unable to prevent himself wondering what Hemmings would resort to if he were to discover that he, Manuel Gomez, would become Bill Young's saviour, and not Franco Pérez.

Conrad, arms outstretched, and trying to forget his tantrum, faced his starving guests, placed his hands together and looked towards the heavens.

'"*Benedictus, Benedicat*"', he intoned in perfect Latin, followed by an attempt to chant "his" version of "The Grace".

'*Good Bread*'

'*Good Meat*'

'*Good Wine*'

'*Why Wait*'

'*Let's Eat*'

'Shouldn't we say "Amen"?' a basso profundo voice shouted from one of the tables.

The somewhat inebriated guests clapped and cheered.

'Simon,' Julie slurped enjoying her deliciously cold Carpaccio de Boeuf, 'can Bull Ring afford three days of extravaganza for over a hundred guests: the air fares, hotel costs, transportation and now this sumptuous feast?'

'Good question.' Simon sipped his 25 year old Krug champagne. 'Unfortunately the budget was agreed prior to my joining the company. I tried very hard to persuade Conrad to reduce the costs to a realistic figure of £50,000, thus showing a 50% saving.'

Julie was incredulous; she spluttered and ejected soup narrowly missing Peter Grant sitting opposite.

She mopped her mouth with a table napkin, smiled an apology at Peter Grant, and gawked at Simon. 'Wait a minute Simon, if my maths is right, that means the cost to the company for this little jaunt, is in excess of £100,000. I mean, we'd need to sell a minimum of *ten* town houses to cover that sort of expenditure.'

'Yes Julie, quite correct. Conrad wasn't prepared to budge an inch saying entertainment costs would be clawed back in property sales. I have found no evidence of this in my profit analysis to date and it worries me . . . together with other things.

But let's not talk "shop" it's boring, let's enjoy the evening! Don't you agree?'

'I am not convinced. This excessive expenditure could ruin us. If you and Conrad don't control the budget Bull Ring will go bust, we'll be out of a job and there will be a glut of empty properties.' Julie sounded perturbed and angry, unlike the placid and accepting person she normally portrayed.

Maria Carmen, Gomez's beautiful secretary, sat strategically opposite Simon. She looked radiant, attired in a revealing red dress, long golden hair draping tanned shoulders.

Everything about Maria was perfect. Simon's eyes riveted on this ravishing beauty with piercing blue eyes; even Pamela Anderson would be proud of her figure. Not wishing to waste the opportunity, he immediately engaged in conversation with this sensuous Spanish female.

'Buenas noches. ¿Cómo te llamas?' Off he went trying to impress again.

'Me llamo Maria Carmen,' she blushed. 'And you are Signor Simon Peters.'

'How on earth do you know my name, we have never met.'

'Ah ah, I was told to look out for you. I have heard many good things about you.'

Maria avoided a direct answer, not inclined to involve Signor Gomez as her informant.

She surprised herself by the attraction she felt for this debonair, articulate and astute accountant from England, forced to smile as he tried desperately to speak her language *and* with the correct Andalusían accent. 'Very commendable,' she wanted to say.

The arrival of the Filet Mignon aux Oignons avec Gratin dauphinois, served with a vintage Margaux 1982 to complement the Pork Filet, saved Maria from further searching questions.

Conrad mingled with his guests – the polite approach – before descending upon his main target. With large hands on Peter's shoulders, he leaned over to whisper: 'Don't turn round, it's Conrad. Can we have a chat? Not here though, shall we say at the bar?' He was aware of Angela's fixed gaze, sitting opposite, trying to read his lips; without success, he hoped.

'Let me finish my delicious chocolate soufflé and I'll be with you,' Peter responded, intrigued by the approach, at the same time puzzling over Conrad's scheming motive to see him alone.

'What did that rude man want?' Angela hissed at Peter, her eyes blazing hate and suspicion.

'Nothing darling, he wants to discuss the possibility of St Helena Press printing Bull Ring's colour brochures,' Peter lied. Not bad for a spontaneous idea when under pressure from the wife. Certainly worth selling the idea to Conrad and in return making money from Bull Ring. He began to feel more positive about the tête-à-tête with Conrad.

'That's a good one, my dear, quick thinking on your part.' Angela knew Peter's habits to a T. 'I can't imagine Conrad having the slightest intention of giving you any business with me in the background.

'You be careful, you already know he's a dangerous wheeler dealing SOB.' Angela added loudly and deliberately, making certain everyone within earshot could hear exactly what she thought of *Conman* Hemmings.

'Excuse me,' Peter said like a true gentleman, and smiling at Angela, 'see you shortly my dear.'

He headed to the small bar at the far end of the restaurant where Conrad waited, a pint of beer in his hand.

'Thanks for joining me, would you like a drink?' he asked Peter, his tone somewhat subdued, and uncharacteristic. To say he was worried about his outburst with Gomez and possible repercussions would be understatement. Why would Gomez say he'd see him in court . . . the charges will be more serious? Might it be conceivable that his contacts with the police had unearthed evidence against him? Perhaps he should apologise and make a note to be more careful in the future.

'Thanks, a glass of the palatable Margaux we drank earlier would be fine,' Peter replied trying hard to relax in the present company.

'By the way,' he continued. I'll let you into a little secret, but not a word to Angela. Promise?'

'How can I promise if I haven't been told this "secret"? Anyway I don't make promises,' Conrad added quickly taking a sip of his beer. 'Go on, I'm sure I will agree.' He laughed, the laugh replaced by a supercilious grin.

'I lied to the wife about our clandestine rendezvous, saying you wanted to discuss the idea of my company supplying Bull Ring with printing material. My quick thinking was an escape route to overcome her objections about having any contact with you.'

Conrad waved his hand impatiently. 'Yes, I know my friend, and that is exactly what I want to discuss.'

'Wait a minute please, I haven't finished.' Peter sipped his Margaux '82, swilling the wine in order to catch the unique bouquet before swallowing.

'I would like to agree reciprocal business in return for the purchase of our villa in Mijas by giving St Helena Press the opportunity to print your four colour glossy brochures. What do you think?' Peter sounded pleased to take the initiative from Conrad. For all his surprising cordiality towards the man he was determined to make him pay for the atrocious way Angela had been treated.

'Very plausible,' he replied. 'I admire the way you have turned our get together into a sales platform for your company. A man after my own heart,' he said, followed by a patronizing smile.

'I will e-mail Steve Wright, Head of Media Services at head office and give your details. This will open the way for you to arrange an appointment.'

'Thanks Conrad, sounds great.' Peter too grinned and raised his glass in mock toast to the offer. 'Now it's your turn,' he said smugly, delighted that he hadn't lost his negotiating skills.

'Peter, I am deeply concerned and sorry that the relationship between your wife and I has deteriorated so rapidly since we first met.' Conrad was trying hard to be diplomatic and sincere for once in his life.

His desperate efforts at sounding contrite, almost apologetic, nearly lulled Peter into a sense of false security, though not for long.

How could this monster forget the incident in the mountains where his complete disregard for human lives, damned nearly pushed the coach into the ravine and killed everyone?

'I would like to re-build our relationship and start again.' He downed his beer in one, thoroughly enjoying playing the dual role of Jekyll and Hyde. 'I desperately need to have you in *my* party especially since you have many good contacts. It goes without saying that it will be useful to Bull Ring.

'As a goodwill gesture to mend broken fences I would like you and Angela to be our guests on a visit to Morocco. We leave Marbella at the weekend in a luxurious cruiser; we berth at Tangiers. Visits to the wonderful medieval city of Medina, Tetouan, the Rif mountains, Rabat and perhaps Marrakech are included in the itinerary, always assuming we are successful in commandeering the King of Morroco's private jet, which incidentally is all included in our whistle-stop visit. I'm sure all will be a breathtaking, exciting experience visiting kasbahs, riding camels, seeing an oasis. It's a chance in a lifetime to see the real Morocco and enjoy the belly dancing.

'That said, I particularly like the idea of Angela being approached by the dancers to perform a belly dance. Now that would be fun to see.' He slapped Peter on the shoulder laughing loudly.

Peter failed to see the funny side. 'Yes, I'm sure you would like Angela making a fool of herself. Somehow Conrad, I don't think that will happen.' He sounded stern.

Ignoring the rebuff Conrad continued: 'I have invited your medical friends from Bath, Mr and Mrs Connolly. Of course there will be other guests.' He considered it unwise to mention that Franco Pérez was arranging this little trip as an excuse for a legitimate sightseeing excursion, with the intention of avoiding scrutiny from customs officials.

'Sounds very exciting, we've never been to Morocco, it could be quite an experience.' Inquisitiveness entered the conversation. 'Er, you mentioned something about the *King*. Do you have connections with him?'

'Not personally.' Conrad had been remiss, wishing he'd never mentioned the word *King*. 'The cruiser is owned by the King and is on loan to a friend of mine. It seems they have business interests.' Conrad hoped his woolly explanation would silence Peter for the moment.

'One problem Conrad, I anticipate Angela's reaction will be a firm 'Not on your life, even if you gave me a million pounds'. He would need a master plan to persuade his wife to take part in Conrad's escapade, and concluded that nothing is impossible.

'Peter, you've asked me to keep a secret, would you please do the same for me?' He didn't wait for an answer. 'Don't on any account mention this trip to Angela, make it a complete surprise. You never know, if she understands the Connolly's are on the guest list and have accepted the invitation she will feel more comfortable.'

'Yes, that's true, but I foresee difficulties in convincing her.'

Peter's attention was diverted to the far end of the restaurant. Angela, standing on a chair, napkins in both hands, waving madly in his direction.

'My wife is sending me semaphore signals ordering my return. I'd better join the party. Thanks for the drink. You'll have a decision later this evening.'

As Conrad returned to a refill surreptitiously placed by the barman, he looked up and could not believe his luck. Mesmerised by the sight of a gorgeous Spanish female making her way towards him he deduced quietly, 'Probably on her way to powder her nose.' Ego took over. 'Then again she's maybe searching for me.' He chuckled at that.

As she drew nearer he could hardly let this golden opportunity pass by without introducing himself, after all they had met briefly by the Plaza del Toros in Marbella, although Conrad was totally unaware that this beauty was Maria Carmen, personal assistant to Manuel Gomez.

If I play my cards right I could get lucky to-night, he decided before attracting Maria's attention.

Leaving the bar to intercept Maria, he discovered the Gods were not on his side. Without warning incandescent flashes of fork lightning filled the restaurant windows, a brief intro' to deafening peals of thunder. The lights failed.

'Oh my God!' shouted a terrified voice, 'we've been struck.' Thick reddish black smoke glowed in the semi-darkness, and as suddenly began to swirl towards and amongst the guests.

The building was on fire.

'Just my bloody luck,' Conrad thought as he joined the panicked throng making their way to several exits.

CHAPTER 11

Bill Young, clutching an enormous white tablecloth in both hands, waved to his stricken, frightened and drenched guests.

The torrential rain was falling with such velocity and strength that the flood waters had nowhere to go; drain covers were lifted and dragged across the road, such was the force of the fast flowing torrent; large colonies of giant rats were lifted into the air by the upward force of the water and carried downstream.

In a night crammed with deafening noises, not least the rain, sirens blared as the emergency services chased in from all districts of the Costa del Sol; a police helicopter hovered above the stricken building engulfed with flames, sparks shooting into the sky as if thousands of Roman Candles had been fired at once in a maddening climax.

'THIS WAY.' Bill waved the soaked and wine stained tablecloth as if he were commanding a platoon on the verge of ambushing an enemy hideout. 'We must leave the area around the building immediately before it collapses.'

An anxious voice from behind quipped: 'That's all very well but there are no air raid shelters around this area.' Some guests laughed nervously.

'Don't worry everyone,' Bill countered, trying to keep them all level-headed, 'we will head for the underground car park. It's not far from here.'

'CONRAD. SIMON,' Bill cried, 'you two cover the rear of our party; just make certain there are no stragglers.'

He threw a wary glance at the building, wincing at the crackling, searching flames. And he was scared; what man wouldn't be? Bloody storm!

'Julie.' He'd spotted her and now faced her. 'You speak Spanish, right?'

'Yes,' she called back above the din and moved closer to Bill.

'I assume you have your mobile, if not borrow one, and phone the hotel; tell them the situation and organise the coaches to meet us in the central square near the Bull Ring.

'The Plaza del Toros,' Gomez interrupted.

'Thanks Manuel. And Julie, ask the hotel to set up the ballroom for a free bar and refreshments, whatever the guests will need to relax and calm frayed nerves. Ask the manager if he can find us a Spanish group to liven up the evening. Oh, and Julie, ask for at least fifty towels to be loaded into each coach.'

'OK Bill I'll see what I can achieve,' she responded, Julie too in deep shock by the sudden and dramatic turn of events.

Bill turned to face the crowd, voice still raised: 'We need to cross the road, this leads us into the main square and the underground car park.'

There appeared no sense of urgency to carry out his orders. The water's depth was lapping the pavement's edge; shortly there would be no pavement or road to cross.

The crowd's dilemma increased at the sound of rapid gun fire erupting from a bistro opposite Bill's intended landing.

Five hooded figures, carrying Glock automatic revolvers and AK-47's, weapons blazing, appeared from the open door of the bistro, and dragging a struggling female with blonde hair.

Bill felt a tug on his shoulder; he turned to find a massive bull like figure before him.

'Mr Young, I am one of your guests, Philip Varley, Commander of the Murder Squad division, M15. Will you please leave this incident to me and do exactly as I say. Get the guests away from this area and head for the square, without further delay,

I'll see you later.'

Varley rushed across the road, as the gang were trying to drag the hysterical girl into a waiting car. He spread eagled his massive frame behind the Mercedes, crawled round the side, and withdrew an automatic weapon from his jacket. This he carefully aimed at his target, in this case a pair of feet dangling from the vehicle's running board, and fired.

A livid scream joined the rest of the noise. 'BASTARD', the victim shouted as Varley's bullet splintered his ankle.

'Policia, bajas tus las pistolas,' (police, drop your guns) Varley shouted in perfect Spanish.

'We don't bloody-well care who the hell you are, so sod off or we'll shoot,' said a broad Glaswegian accent.

An automatic weapon strafed the rear of the Mercedes narrowly missing Varley's legs. Perhaps the swirling waters had prevented the gunman finding his target. But why had the gunfire come from behind him? Wasting little time he whirled to see a black BMW X5, four men wearing bullet proof vests and holding AK-47's, jump out and fire their weapons at the Mercedes' tyres and windows. They advanced towards the Merc. 'POLICE. This time throw your weapons out of the windows and stay where you are,' Inspector Nacho Valdez demanded in perfect English since hearing one gang member replying in a Scottish accent to Varley's challenge.

The Merc's occupants heeded the warning; weapons clattered on the wet road as men stepped into its murky waters. The Spanish blonde, shaken and bruised, was lifted out of the car. Inspector Valdez and his team removed the gangs masks without any courtesy whatsoever.

'Many thanks for your help Commander Varley,' Valdez acknowledged. 'I am pleased we don't need to interrogate you for being in possession of a hand gun.' Valdez smiled, extended his hand, 'Nacho Valdez from CEISD, Secret Service at your service.' He almost clicked his heels.

'How on earth did you recognise me and know my name?' Varley wanted to know. 'CEISD eh, must be serious criminals you're after.' He sounded bemused.

'We know all about you Commander, M15 informed us you were with a party from England. We've kept surveillance on your movements since you arrived in Spain; we even know your seating position in La Manga.' Valdez offered a dark frown, and an even darker smirk, implying he was a man who did his job. 'You are a major security risk. Criminals you have convicted in England, like Hitman Luis and Artful John are now in Marbella. We are aware there are contracts being handed out to exterminate your colleagues in M15, already in Spain attempting to negotiate extradition orders for British criminals.'

'I never thought there would be such a high price on my head.' For perhaps the first time in his police life the Varley of MI5 sounded worried.

'This is Spain my friend; we are in the Costa del Crime. Nobody is safe. Intense gang wars have been raging between British and foreign criminals over the last ten years along our sunny coastal regions.

'Anyway, Commander thank you for helping us to arrest this mob.' He waved his automatic towards the handcuffed criminals. 'We've been tracking them for months; their leader recently escaped from Spain's top security jail in Alhaurín, for murdering a retired British couple in their villa at Estepona, just down the road.

'I trust the rest of your visit will be a more peaceful one.' Valdez chuckled and helped to bundle the gang into the X5 and a waiting ambulance.

Flood waters receding, Varley made his way towards the main square to find the stranded party. Naturally concerned by the Inspector's remarks and the high level of crime in the Costas, he reasoned that fellow guests should be made aware of the probable disruption to their 'Spanish Dreams' by gang warfare raging along the coast.

Directors of Bull Ring Properties would certainly not be interested in publicising the scale of violent crimes raging in their development areas around Marbella, Puerto Banús, Estepona, Fuengirola and Benalmadena. And that was a fact!

By the time he arrived to find the guests boarding their coaches Varley decided he must think more carefully about investing in property over here.

* * *

A lively group of Spanish vocalists and guitarists greeted the depleted party of drab and sombre guests to the Kon Tiki's ballroom, their renderings at least fetching a few smiles, drinks encouraging the rest of the crowd.

Bill Young climbed the three steps onto the stage, tuxedo replaced by beach wear comprising white shorts, bright yellow and red striped tee shirt and, wait for it, a sombrero.

'How do you like the outfit?' Bill shouted executing a pirouette; his attempt to break the ice and plant yet more smiles on disgruntled faces.

The scantily attired guests looked up at Bill in mute silence.

'Oh well, can't win 'em all,' he chuntered and continued with his solo act.

'We have all been through a frightening ordeal this evening and to think we should be enjoying the cabaret at LaManga is a welcome bonus.

'I am very grateful to Julie for organising this unscripted event and somehow attracting such talented musicians at such short notice. I look forward to seeing you all dancing the Paso Doble.' Bill laughed nervously.

Also, I want to thank Commander Varley, from M15, for his prompt and courageous action in attempting to apprehend the dangerous gang of criminals outside the bistro.'

There was loud applause from the floor. Varley nodded in appreciation.

'Please do not think,' Bill continued, 'that the unfortunate strike by a tornado, yes, it was a tornado, is a common occurrence in southern Spain.

'Equally rare is the appalling shoot out you witnessed in the centre of Marbella.

It appears Spain and America are similar where crime is concerned. There is plenty of discussion about the high level of crimes in both countries but very few people witness the murders, the rapes, the gang violence and break ins. You need not feel intimidated or threatened by what you have seen to-day.'

He was trying desperately to defuse the evening's dramatic events. His main concerns were his buyers worried they might re-consider their purchase options as a result of the dramatic events.

'Mr Young, excuse me,' the deep voice came from Philip Varley.

'I'm afraid to say that you are much mistaken. Crime on the Costas is happening under our very noses; Bull Ring's development locations are in the midst of daily organised crime being carried out by the British, Russians, Polish, Romanians, Slovaks… I could go on.

'Why do you think "wreckers", alarm systems connected to police stations and CCTV surveillance cameras are recommended as standard fittings in all properties by the police?'

Varley was not enjoying his outburst, but felt it was necessary.

'Even these measures are insufficient to deter some criminals, desperate for money to fuel their drug related lives. Do you know, last week a gang raided a villa above Estepona, just above the road where our coach nearly disappeared into the ravine.

Imagine, a gated community containing thirty properties, and all the latest security equipment installed! The gang, with sophisticated wire cutters, literally chopped the main gate into pieces before driving to the villa aware it was occupied by a wealthy retired couple from England. They proceeded to cut the electricity, phone and CCTV cables. Unable to unlock the front door they used oxy-acetylene torches to melt the steel; they then donned gas masks, opened highly toxic gas canisters and placed them under the gap in the front door.

'They jimmied the steel main door to gain entry and found the couple lying on the floor in the hall, killed by the poisonous gas. The rest I leave to your imagination. Needless to say the British gang were caught and are now serving life sentences in Alhaurín, Spain's top security prison.'

A huge gasp filled the room, shocked faces apparent.

'Oh my God, how terrible,' someone said loud enough to be heard.

Varley lifted his beer and drank thirstily.

'Let me be more specific, Mr Young. The number of crimes in the Costas is on a par with South Africa and in that country it is not just bad, its bloody horrendous. I know it from first hand experience.' He surveyed the crowd. 'Sorry to dampen your enthusiasm,' Varley went on taking in fellow investors, 'but when you are about to embark on an exciting mission to buy your dream homes, make your final decision with your eyes wide open and you won't have any regrets.'

Varley sat down to loud applause.

'Well said Commander,' shouted Angela, clapping loudly.

'Mr Young,' she said, 'would you care to give us an answer to the disturbing issues Commander Varley has raised?'

Angela turned to face the stage only to find Bill Young had already made a second hasty exit back stage.

Conrad had applauded the suggestion by Bill Young to stage an impromptu party in an attempt to calm frayed nerves and bring a sense of enjoyment to clients purchasing Bull Ring's properties. And, helping to end the day on a high note.

His enthusiasm was shattered when Bill Young had decided to perform Act 2 Scene 3 of Macbeth, committing commercial suicide in the process.

He whispered to Simon Peters, 'Bill has shown his true colours. What a bloody fool; he's been planting doubts amongst our clients!' Conrad's fists were clenched in anger.

'There is a good chance his scene from Macbeth could destroy the outstanding sales efforts by my team in securing reservations for over fifty town houses and apartments in one day, an incredible achievement. Cancellations could be on the cards after this little fiasco!

'What do you think Simon, am I being unreasonable in my criticism?'

Simon hesitated, aware of Conrad's intrigue and persuasive character, and realising he was being targeted as a conversion, an effort to change him into a "Conrad ally".

'Well,' Simon said, 'Bill certainly opened the way for the Commander to introduce some home truths.

'Personally, I think Varley gave us a constructive and truthful picture of the criminal activity over here and offered something all purchasers of property in Spain would never consider as a deterrent. I just hope you and Bill Young can come up with plans to prioritise security on all the sites and convince clients you have taken notice of the warning by the Commander.'

Simon considered he had given a diplomatic, intuitive and constructive reply.

Conrad was nodding. 'Good thinking, Simon, I'll discuss "security" with Bill to-night and inform our clients of our new proposals. I will need to obtain quotations from Luis Ramos covering the security systems for you to cost into the Trading Accounts.'

Conrad, deep in thought, made for the bar, weaving past a few inebriated guests, as they attempted following Bill's suggestion to perform the Passé Doble whilst staying on their feet.

At the bar Conrad sipped another Miguel mulling the fact that there would be no business left to run if all the negative vibes and criticisms from various members of their distinguished guests continued. Now was the time, he concluded, to act and silence the opposition to the business plan.

Such evil thoughts were distracted for a second time in the evening by the sight of Maria Carmen entering the ballroom; she wore borrowed white shorts and tight fitting red top that did its utmost to reveal her ravishing figure. Conrad made a hasty dash across the dance floor to greet her.

'Good evening,' Conrad drooled. 'I'm afraid I don't know your name but you will probably remember meeting me at the fountains of Plaza del Toros, last week.'

'Oh,' she replied, appearing stunned by it. 'I don't remember the occasion or meeting such an attractive stranger at any of the fountains in Marbella,' Maria lied. She was enjoying every minute of her second unexpected encounter with Signor Hemmings and wondered what the outcome would be this time.

'Perhaps you are mistaken and met another Spanish lady cooling her feet in the water, I think you meet many attractive ladies. She added a coquettish wink.

Conrad was careful he didn't rise to the bait.

'I remember how well you spoke English,' he said. 'When I asked you directions to find the way to Huerta de los Castales, near the harbour in Marbella. Don't you remember now?' He sounded confused.

'Ah, lo siento, mi acuerdo.' (Sorry, I remember) 'You were going to see your lawyer friend Signor Franco Pérez, correcto?' Maria loved having fun.

'Yes that's right, Franco Pérez. But you don't know who I am do you?' He took Maria's hand as an excuse to get closer.

'Conrad Hemmings, Director of Bull Ring Properties in Spain. How about you? What can I call you, apart from Pamela Anderson,' he laughed.

'Very amusing, Signor Hemmings. You can call me Maria'. She knew how important it could be for Signor Gomez's ongoing investigations into Signor Pérez's business dealings if she revealed as little as possible about her connections. Her investigative skills might prove very useful in assisting Gomez to bring the drug barons to justice, and at the same time advance her career in the prosecution service.

'Maria, I'm so glad we met this evening especially after the tornado and the dreadful gangland incident.' He tried hard to sound convincing.

' I know this might sound presumptuous, but I am arranging an excursion to Morocco in a couple of days time. We board a luxury motor cruiser, HM Hercules in Marbella, travel to Tangiers and visit places such as Medina, Tetouan and even go riding camels in the Rift Mountains.

'The guests will include some of Bull Ring's clients, all of whom are extremely accomplished and nice people. We would really like to have you on board and hopefully you will help me to entertain our important guests.' Conrad was the epitome of charm as he attempted to woo this Spanish beauty.

'How about it Maria, will you join us?'

'Sounds an exciting invitation, thank you. I have visited Morocco. Historically, the country has many close links with southern Spain and I find this very interesting. I learned Arabic at school, so I can appreciate the customs and varied backgrounds of the country, and Moroccans much better.'

She genuinely warmed to the fact of visiting Morocco again and broadening her knowledge of the country's history. However, it was the much broader picture that interested her; finding out first hand about Signor Pérez and his operations and keeping a close eye on Signor Hemmings, a man she agreed she could never trust.

Yes, she thought, Manuel Gomez will be very supportive of my involvement in contributing to the capture of the drug barons and criminals. But then Maria also realised that Gomez might consider the mission too dangerous.

'Well, Mr Hemmings I have thought about your suggestion and will give you an answer when I have spoken with my company about having a few days leave.

'Just one thing, who owns the luxury yacht?' she asked smiling broadly. Conrad merely smiled.

The unexpected encounter with Conrad Hemmings had taken Maria by surprise. Her immediate reaction to this deceitful man approaching her with such a tempting offer regarding some kind of liaison, was one of aversion and distrust. That she, Maria Carmen, a pillar of the faith, should have anything to do with such a rogue, revolted her. 'Why,' she muttered to herself, 'didn't I have the courage of my convictions and turn down his invitation to a blind date in Morocco? Perhaps one day I will know the answer,' she concluded.

Behind her smokescreen of disinterest there dwelt an unexplained desire and fascination for this debonair, charming, attractive, articulate and intelligent suitor – a chemistry she'd sensed between them on their first meeting in Plaza del Toros.

The prospect of helping Signor Gomez to expose the vast network of gangsters operating throughout Europe appealed both to her conscience and the strong belief that justice was of paramount importance in this shady, evil world.

And what of the other side to her impeccable character? Only close friends had witnessed what could easily be termed "split personality". Behind one façade, this charming, sophisticated, highly intelligent Spanish beauty was ruthless and demanding, and would stop at nothing to achieve her aims. Her appointment as legal secretary to Gomez, she would see as a masterful step in her career to follow him the moment his appointment was confirmed as Chief Prosecutor in the Andalusían Regional Government.

Alone with her thoughts, indeed pleased by it, she understood Signor Hemmings's motives completely and although not trusting or condone his "modus operandi", guessed he had an exciting lifestyle. Perhaps she could become part of it, enjoy the thrills and dangers of life again by playing hide and seek with the enemies. What fun, she concluded

I will not mention anything to Signor Gomez about my invitation to Morocco; simply send him an e-mail explaining a need to visit my frail parents in Granada. Yes a good thought.

After all, I have only deduced that Conrad Hemmings was involved in some kind of property scandal in England. His links with Franco Pérez could make him a multi- millionaire. Her smile broadened. Nothing wrong with that at all, Maria convinced herself.

She headed for the revolving doors at the entrance to the Kon Tiki not reckoning on seeing her boss, busy talking to Bill Young. One highly polished reverse turn accomplished to avoid any confrontation with Gomez, she found her change of direction led her into the outstretched arms of Conrad, poised for an unexpected embrace.

'Maria, are you trying to avoid something? From the speed you executed that turn, I would say you were,' said Conrad reluctant to release Maria's hand.

'Anyway, the most important question is, will you be joining the ship's crew?' He smiled in anticipation of his new conquest.

'I have spoken with my boss and he has given me three days leave,' she lied.

'Fantastic news Maria.' Conrad was genuinely elated. 'If you send me your e-mail address, I will forward joining instructions; we leave early Monday morning.'

Maria's mobile rang.

'Perdón. *Hola, Maria aquí.*' she said.

'Signor Hemmings, I'll be in touch.' She moved away from Hemmings and found a corner to take the call.

'Maria, it's Simon Peters, you remember we met at La Manga. I was wondering if you would like a trip to Cadiz to-morrow, Sunday, there is a flower festival? You would make a perfect guide and interpreter.'

She remembered the tall dashing accountant from Bull Ring who had taken more than a keen interest in her well-being during the evening's dramatic events.

'Sounds good Simon,' she replied, thinking she might extract information on Conrad Hemmings, in addition of course to enjoying the company of a considerate and attractive male.

'*Excelente,*' came the joyous cry.

'I'll see you in the foyer at 9.30. *Buenas noches* and sleep well!'

*   *   *

'Angela,' Peter shouted to his wife as she turned a lovely shade of tan on the hotel terrace overlooking massive palm trees and an amoeboid looking pool complex.

'Guess what? I've just received a text message from your favourite person.' He laughed loudly.

'Oh yes, and what does Mr Conman Hemmings want this time?' she replied with added scorn.

'Nothing much,' he said dismissively, except an invitation to be his guests on a voyage to Morocco with the Connolly's.

'Nothing much!' Angela jumped off her sun bed dislodging her bikini top in the process and exposing her ample breasts, much to the delight and amusement of fellow sun worshippers.

Angela didn't give a shit how much of an eyeful they got; Angela was incensed by the blatant— She bellowed, again uncaring who heard her this time, 'The invitation is an insult. Not on your life, even if you gave me a million pounds, would I go anywhere with such a . . . a . . . tyrant.' Rage mounting, she gulped water from her bottle of Evian and nearly choked. Cold water spattered those ample breasts, and only then did she heave up her bikini top.

'How very interesting my dear, you have just managed to quote the exact response I said Conrad could expect to his suggestion.' Peter sounded flippant, Angela ready to splash the asinine grin from his face with her water.

'Beg your pardon Peter, do you mean you have already discussed this absurd proposition with the enemy? Ah yes, I remember, you had a tête-à-tête with our friend in La Manga restaurant before the inferno took charge.'

They had moved away from the balcony realising their heated discussion was beginning to disrupt the peace and tranquillity.

'Angela dearest, there is really no need to put yourself through such purgatory and get so upset about such a triviality. Conrad would like to re-build his relationship with you and start again. His words not mine.'

Peter tried to take Angela's hand without success.

'We have never been to Morocco. The idea of cruising to Tangier and flying to Marrakesh in the Sultan's private jet, sounds exciting, don't you think?' At least he was trying hard to broker the peace deal.

' Well I'm not coming. I couldn't be so a hypocritical and accept anything from that man. You do what you think best and I'll take a trip to Granada, much more rewarding.'

Angela stalked away in disgust, leaving Peter beneath a palm tree totally dejected by the uncompromising and yet understandable attitude of his wife.

CHAPTER 12

A strengthening breeze blew as the gleaming white cruiser, HM Hercules, rounded the breakwater entering the harbour of Puerto Banús. All guests had assembled on the waterfront as instructed.

'Good morning everyone,' Conrad shouted from his Bentley coupé as he parked in one of the most exclusive bays on the notorious quayside.

'Are we all here?' He smiled at Peter.

'I think so.' Peter was disappointed at Angela's absence.

'We look a bit depleted,' Conrad said shaking Jim and Jane Connolly's hands.

'Angela and Maria don't appear to be with us, perhaps they are powdering their noses. They should get a move on, we'll be boarding in a few minutes.'

Three long blasts sounded from the boat's horn as she went astern narrowly missing a bevy of millionaire luxury yachts.

Maria, golden hair streaming in the breeze, rushed from a boutique towards the waiting group.

'Hola Maria, glad you made it.' Conrad, introduced her to Peter and the Connolly's. He scanned other faces. 'No Angela. What have you done with her Peter?'

'I think she's on her way to Granada,' Peter replied quietly not wishing to provoke comment from others.

A loud shout sounded from the quarter deck. 'Come on Conrad, the gangway is secure, come and join us.' Franco Pérez, dapper in white suit, and wearing a naval hat denoting the rank of a Naval Captain, stood to attention at the top of the gangway. Three ratings piped the party aboard in true naval fashion.

'Just like being a bloody snottie again.' Conrad smiled as he returned Franco's salute, and stepped smartly onto the quarterdeck.

'Cast off forw'd, cast off aft, slow ahead both engines,' came the order from the bridge.

Peter, dejected his wife hadn't condescended to join him, stood alone looking towards the quayside as the Hercules glided from its moorings.

There! A figure dressed in bright pink, hand on head holding a large, equally pink hat, hastening along the cobbled jetty, waving a holdall and shouting loudly, 'STOP THE BOAT . . .I'M COMING WITH YOU.'

Peter knew that voice. Angela, who else?

'Conrad, Captain, someone stop this ship now,' Peter shouted. 'We've left behind one of the guests.'

The Captain heard the plea. 'Wheel amidships, stop engines, half astern port engine, half ahead starboard engine,' he ordered. The stern came round as the starboard engine manoeuvred the bows into the quayside thus bringing the large vessel under control.

'Stop both engines.'

Good seamanship from the crew managed to secure a rope around the last bollard on the quay before the breakwater; a gangplank was secured between stanchions on the starboard side.

Conrad, puffing an enormous Havana cigar, both arms on the railings observed the spectacle below him, cupped his hands and called out:

'Good to see you again Angela. Making such a dramatic and timely arrival too; couldn't have done it better myself. Why didn't you put us all out of our misery and go to Granada?' Conrad was far from happy; he fumed, every shade of sarcasm evident. He stomped away from the *rescue* operation.

Angela, breath and breasts heaving, was hoisted by two burly seamen across the makeshift crossing between the boat's lower deck and the jetty. Once aboard she found Peter's arms engulfing her.

'So very sorry,' Angela said.

'You were extremely fortunate to make it aboard, another minute and we would be rounding the breakwater into the main channel. You owe the Captain a big apology, his boat was under way and there was no obligation to make him turn back and put his ship in danger.

'On the brighter side, good to see you changed your mind. And don't worry about Conrad's outburst; just him showing his true colours. What exactly made you have second thoughts about the visit to Granada?' He wiped her tear stained, distraught face with his handkerchief.

Angela took it from him, disengaged herself from his embrace, on the face of it unable to appreciate or respond to genuine affection and concern from anyone, least of all her husband.

'I was boarding the coach for Granada and suddenly realised my inconsiderate actions were impulsive. It was not right I should leave the "action" here, allowing Hemmings to dictate the outcome of our futures.' She dabbed her eyes.

'Angela, for one wonderful and memorable moment I really thought you had changed your mind because you loved me and couldn't imagine being without me.'

Did he sound sarcastic? Did he care? He added with passion, 'I was quite unprepared for your half baked excuse about Hemmings trying to control our lives. Actually, love, you are the control freak, not sodding Hemmings, don't you think?' Like Hemmings, Peter fumed.

Feeling like a bloody castaway, Peter looked out over the ship's side as foam broke over the bow, natural since the sudden increase in speed and the choppiness of the Mediterranean combated a wind gusting to force four.

'Excuse me,' said Angela, 'I don't feel well'.

* * *

Franco Pérez stood up from the breakfast table and wiped his neatly trimmed moustache.

'*Hola, Buenos días.*' He smiled. A special welcome to Conrad's group. I'm delighted you could join us at such short notice and that Mrs Grant wasn't left behind.

'I am Franco Pérez. On my right are Louis Ramos, Carla Flores, his assistant, and Paco Segovia. We have been commissioned by the King to oversee a number of housing development projects along the coastline east of Tangiers and ranging towards the capital of Morocco, Rabat.

'Some of you may know that Luis Ramos is working with Conrad's company on Bull Ring's developments along the Costa del Sol.' Franco paused to take a sip of his now cold coffee.

'Since leaving port, our itinerary has changed slightly. After berthing at Tangiers my team were scheduled to set off for Rabat; we will now be leaving for Marrakesh by helicopter from the helipad in the port. Conrad will brief you on your stay in Marrakesh. Hope you all have a pleasant trip and see you in a couple of days,' he concluded quickly.

An enthused Peter stood. 'Signor Pérez, I am sure my friends would like to join me in thanking you for your kind hospitality and including us in your business trip to Morocco.'

'My pleasure,' replied Pérez.

'From what I have heard thus far it all sounds suspicious to me,' Angela whispered to Peter.

Does she ever give up? thought Peter as he attempted to enjoy his full English breakfast, one thing he had missed lately.

Angela turned to Maria Carmen on her left. 'Maria, can you possibly enlighten me about Franco Pérez and Luis Ramos?'

'*Si, por supuesto* (of course) she replied. 'Signor Pérez is a successful lawyer with offices in Marbella with er, fingers in many pies. He has some connections with the courts in Marbella acting as defence lawyer for a broad range of clients.

'I also believe that Signor Hemmings and Pérez are friends. I wouldn't be surprised if they were somehow involved in business deals.' Maria, was trying hard to be cautious and not elaborate too much about her suspicions. She had witnessed Angela Grant in action over the past few days and purposely planted the clue knowing full well Mrs Grant would take the bait and investigate this liaison. 'No doubt she will report her findings to me,' Maria concluded.

'In respect of Luis Ramos,' she continued, 'Luis is one of the largest property developers in Spain, Bull Ring one of his major accounts.'

'Thank you very much, my dear, most enlightening; it has confirmed a few suspicions.' Angela leaned back, pleased with this exciting update on the enemies surrounding her. 'Just like writing my first detective thriller,' she whispered amused, and feeling the effects of the rolling ship.

* * *

The Sikorsky S-92 lifted off from the narrow helipad and headed south for Marrakesh.

Conrad released his safety harness and stood up to address his guests.

'I hope you are not offended, Maria and I have been asked by Franco Pérez to attend the various meetings with surveyors and planners in Marrakesh and Rabat.' He offered a mischievous smile, one of those I-know-what's-happening-and-you-don't sort of smiles.

Angela's thinking: Bastard, pull the other one. All you want is to get your leg over, dirty devil. So vehement were such thoughts she nearly blurted them out.

'After landing at the Palace you will be taken to your hotel . . . Let me see,' Conrad checked a wad of papers, 'ah yes, Hotel de Ville. A specially selected palace guide has been arranged to give you a tour of the city. I hope to see you sometime later this evening. Should we be held up in Rabat and I don't make it, you will be collected tomorrow at noon, and taken to the Palace for boarding the helicopter and onward flight to Tangiers for return by our boat to Spain. 'Are there any questions?'

'Yes,' replied Jim Connolly, 'hadn't you better leave your mobile number in case there are any unforeseen problems?'

'Good thinking, Jim.' Conrad beamed and reeled off his number before returning to his seat next to Maria.

Maria sounded upset when she said, 'I overheard the arrangements you were explaining to the other guests. Very presumptuous that I should be whisked off all over Morocco and alone with someone I have only just met. I was looking forward to seeing Marrakesh again.'

'I don't know what you mean,' Conrad feigned innocence. 'But it strikes me as an excellent idea that we should be on our own.' He laughed, and tried without success to take her hand.

'Actually Maria,' Conrad said seriously, 'Franco wishes me to accompany him. He needs help with setting up a marketing plan involving the sale of villas being constructed along the coast. A potential investment opportunity is there for me to consider; it is something to be discussed with the King's chief financier at the Palace.'

'Conrad, I cannot for the life of me understand why you should for one minute wish to get me involved in a property development scheme, and in a foreign country.'

'All negotiations involving planning and engineering in Morocco are in French,' he replied. 'Franco Pérez wants you as a member of his team, because you speak the language fluently.

'He needs an interpreter with your academic skills and attractive personality . . . Franco's assessment not mine. Have to say I agree with him.' Conrad tried to sound convincing.

'Flattery will get you everywhere,' Maria smiled. 'But he should have asked me himself,' she added swiftly.

'He asked me to sound you out first and if you accept he will have a word about the rewards.'

'Ah Maria,' he said changing the subject skilfully. 'Before you become involved in this slight diversion from your normal life, we should consider the question of integrity and trust between us. Who do you work for?' he asked pointedly.

'Well, that's a leading question I may not wish to answer.' Maria blinked. It was her way of saying this can be left for another time. Nevertheless, she did tell say,

'Apart from being a freelance model, I work as a legal secretary for a firm in

Torremolinos.' Her lying improved every time.

'Sounds good to me, no way are you involved with our competitors. Perhaps I could have a look at your portfolio.' Conrad smirked.

'Yes, I am sure you'd love that, but you won't get the chance.' *Because there isn't one*, she wanted to say.

*   *   *

The Sikorsky circled the magnificent gardens of the Royal Palace.

'You can quite see why Marrakesh is called the "Red City",' Peter enthused. 'Look Angela, all the buildings are pink and the streets are covered in red sand. A fantastic backdrop those snow peaked Atlas mountains in the distance don't you think?'

Angela didn't comment, just nodded.

The helicopter landed. Three long sleek black Mercedes' waited to whisk the party away to their different locations.

'*Bienvenu en Marrakesh, je m'appelle Amile Hassan. Je suis votre guide pour la visité*', a deep voice greeted as they settled into the plush leather seats of the Mercedes.

CHAPTER 13

The Hercules was a ghost boat apart from the officer of the watch.

Needless to say Conrad and Maria had not returned to Marrakesh the previous evening.

'Perhaps we'd better phone Conrad,' suggested Jim Connolly, 'we were due to leave Tangiers at 1400 and it's now 1530 hours.'

'Good idea Jim, you've got his number,' Peter replied.

Conrad's mobile rang. 'Hemmings,' he answered bluntly.

'Jim here. Is there a reason for our delay in leaving Tangiers?'

'Yes, I'm afraid so, we got caught up in an audience with the King at the very last minute,' Conrad lied. His audience had been with Maria on Rabat's golden sands. Bugger politics and houses, and worry.

He went on compounding untruths, saying: 'We'll be with you in about two hours. Why don't you take a trip into Tangiers, the centre is very close to our mooring?' he ended up suggesting.

'Excellent idea, see you later,' Jim said.

*　*　*

Franco Pérez had been summoned to the bridge by Captain Vouté, an experienced captain who had commanded French cruisers, before joining the Royal Moroccan navy. Tall and impressive, this man commanded as one would expect, his lean, kindly face also insisted he would not kowtow to anyone. On this boat, or any he commanded, he was master.

'Ah, Monsieur Pérez, *bon soir,* there is a severe gale warning for the western Mediterranean timed for around 2200 hours. Let me see –' he checked his watch '– it is now 1800 hours. Our ETA into Marbella, not Puerto Banús is 2000 hours and may prove too dangerous if we even attempt to achieve it.' Grey eyes settled on Pérez. 'What do you wish to do, monsieur, stay in port until the front passes or take a chance and leave immediately?'

'A difficult decision,' replied Franco thinking about the guests and an uncomfortable crossing. 'I need to be in Marbella for an important trial early tomorrow morning.' He avoided the man's eyes.

'Then why not take the helicopter,' suggested Vouté, 'I'm sure you could arrange special permission with the King's aide de compte.'

'Constructive thinking Captain, but I already tried that tactic. Unfortunately the Air Ministry in Rabat wouldn't listen to me. There is no option but to batten down the hatches and get going. After all this ship is built like a frigate and has water tight compartments.' His laugh didn't exactly promote any conviction.

For once Vouté bowed to his hirer and gave orders.

Hercules slipped her moorings and headed out into the choppy sea, the wind gusting to force five.

* * *

Later that evening, all a little tired yet happy after their sojourn ashore, assembled in the dining mess of the Hercules, a welcome glass of champagne for those who wanted it.

'Did you have an enjoyable time in Marrakesh?' Conrad asked his guests.

'Maria not joining us?' Peter asked.

'Afraid she's begged off; sends her apologies. We were having a nap. I thought it unfair to let you down so here I am.'

'Yes, well,' Jim followed up, 'our time visiting the various venues has been highly interesting and informative. That is until we lost Angela in one of the many souks. After a lengthy search our guide suggested we tried the Katoubia Mosque, the spiritual symbol and city landmark in the heart of Marrakesh; entry is forbidden to non-Muslims. Seems he had a hunch.

'Our guide enters the mosque,' Jim explained, 'and lo and behold there's our Saint Angela, wearing an enormous black headdress, kneeling and praying to Mecca.'

'Well,' said Angela, 'as a non-Muslim I've always wanted to pray in a mosque. Nor was I disappointed, except the air was very pungent. Hardly surprising with so many bodies jerking up and down praying to their god.'

Amused glances were evident; a few tittered at respective individual thoughts.

'Did you have a good time Conrad?' Angela attempted to reduce pressure on her somewhat blatant misdemeanour.

'Thanks for asking. Came down to mostly meetings and site visits. It's another reason Maria wants to rest.'

'Don't tell me you didn't find time to visit the infamous nudist beaches near Rabat?' Angela crackled with amusement, her suggestive look quite blatant.

For once in his life Conrad was totally lost for words.

Before any comment was forthcoming from anyone the figure of Franco Pérez appeared in the doorway. 'Ah, Conrad, could you spare a few minutes, we need to talk? Captain Vouté says we can use his day quarters on the upper deck, starboard side.'

Conrad collected Franco's urgency. 'OK, I'll just finish my coffee.'

'Well I'm going on deck to get some air, I still feel queasy,' Angela spluttered.

'I can offer some medication to help, I always come prepared.'

'Thanks Jim, I'll be fine.'

'Angela,' Peter stepped in, 'before you risk life and limb on deck in this weather, I suggest you put on your inflatable jacket, just in case you are swept overboard.' It wasn't meant as a joke, just sound advice.

* * *

Angela did reach the upper deck. On Peter's advice she'd sensibly donned her inflatable. On the port side was protection from the strengthening wind. The sea state looked scary, waves breaking across the starboard quarter. The growing ferocity didn't exactly aid her constitution.

'Slow ahead both engines, port twenty, steer 315 degrees,' Captain Vouté ordered, having decided to head for the shelter of Gibraltar's north facing harbour.

'Number One,' the Captain addressed his first officer, 'locate Monsieur Pérez, he should be in my cabin. Inform him we have altered course for Gibraltar. Tell him our satellite indicates storm force winds will be with us earlier than anticipated and we need to escape the eye of the storm before it is too late. Is that clear?'

'Yes, sir,' the lieutenant replied.

'OPS,' the Captain shouted down the intercom connected to the operations room, 'send a message to Gibraltar to this effect: "C in C requesting berthing facilities for Hercules. ETA 2000 hours, due to worsening sea state." And make certain you receive a reply.'

'Roger,' Ops confirmed.

Angela, buffeted by the increased blow, found herself beneath a large open porthole through which raised voices issued.

Uh, that's Conrad having a chew at Pérez.

Ever the nosey parker, a strategically placed fire hydrant beneath the porthole allowed Angela to obtain a footing on the 'T' shaped holding frame and raise herself to the lower part of the open port, thankfully unseen by the two men deep in conversation.

'Don't be a fool you need to do something,' a voice said loudly. Pérez.

'All right.' Conrad.

Pérez again: 'I have just spoken with Ernesto Carlos in London. He is extremely concerned. The police, he believes the serious fraud office, have contacted his personal assistant about the purchase of a large apartment block in Birmingham. They have requested details of all transactions taking place between the vendor and the purchaser. They will be interviewing Carlos tomorrow morning. Naturally I have advised our friend to have his lawyer present.' Edginess emphasised worry.

'Oh my God,' Conrad couldn't contain his thoughts, 'someone's blown the whistle.'

'I presume we are talking about the two million pounds transferred to our joint accounts in Spain by Carlos, contravening money laundering regulations,' Pérez was quick to establish.

'Correct,' Conrad confirmed.

'If I remember correctly, Conrad, you sold the apartments to Ernesto for two million pounds less than their value. You cooked the books, not to put too fine a point on it. And consequently the person who purchased Bull Ring Properties from you, Mr Young, lost out by two million pounds. You do realise, you idiot, that if the SFO discover these irregularities there will be an extradition order on your head! It means *all* your Spanish property will be confiscated, including our joint development in Elvira.' And that is mainly what worried the Spaniard. The old saying registered –

"always look after numero uno".

'Alhaurin is one hell hole prison, my friend.' Pérez clicked his tongue. 'Though I am hopeful I might be able to save you before you are sentenced and export you out of the country double quick.' Pérez's sigh indicated that his promise may prove difficult if it came to it.

There was a loud knock at the cabin door. 'Entra,' replied Pérez.

'Excusez moi, Monsieur Pérez,' said the captain's lieutenant, 'Capitain Vouté has asked me to inform you we have had to alter course for Gibraltar. The satellite predicts an earlier arrival of the storm. We require the shelter of Gibraltar's harbour as Marbella's narrow entrance is not suitable for manoeuvring in severe conditions.'

'Please thank Captain Vouté for keeping me informed.'

'Conrad,' Pérez shouted, 'we need to contact our members and tell them to make arrangements to off load the cargo in Gibraltar.'

In the excitement of hearing the incredulous revelation from Pérez, Angela had slipped from her position. Only the sudden roll of the ship to port had prevented her going head first into the cabin.

The sudden jolt brought Angela to her senses and she realised the immediate danger to herself if the two men discovered her attempt at playing James Bond, instead of playing with him!

Imperative then to contact someone who would understand the seriousness of her situation and take immediate action. Someone who would realise the mounting dangers facing her life. But on this voyage! Whom could she trust?

Then it tumbled: she knew just the man, Commander Varley. One drawback, and a big one, how on earth could she find him? More to the point, how could she leave this god dammed ship in the middle of a force ten gale?

It hit her in that second: *Julie Nash, she's the link.*

Stepping away from where there was a danger she may be overheard, she located her mobile, accessed Julie's number from the memory and hit send.

Julie relaxed in a deep bath when her mobile, always close by just in case, trilled out some recent pop melody.

'Julie Nash, how can I help?'

'Julie, Angela Grant here. Listen carefully as I don't have much time and I'm struggling trying to keep my balance in a force ten gale in the middle of the Mediterranean.'

'Sounds exciting.'

'Would you please make contact with Commander Varley, tell him I'm aboard the Hercules heading for the shelter of Gibraltar. Ask him to contact the Met, Serious Fraud Squad division, about a case involving Conrad Hemmings and Ernesto Carlos.

'Inform him I have just overheard a conversation between Hemmings and a Signor Pérez, concerning an illegal sale of property in the UK, and involving money laundering irregularities in Spain. And something else I am about to discover.'

Angela had failed to understand the significance of the 'cargo' mentioned by Pérez.

'I haven't got much time. Should they find out what I know, I think my life might be in danger.'

'Angela, yes I will do as you ask. Please be careful,' an alarmed Julie said.

She heard, what she assumed to be a huge wave striking the ship. Had she been able to see this, the wave had hit the vessel amidships on the port side, causing it to roll sideways. Worse, Angela lost her balance. The line went dead.

* * *

Thankfully the wave had struck the opposite side, and though Angela had been buffeted around she was OK. And she managed to retrieve her mobile from where she'd dropped it. She returned to her listening post but decided under these circumstances, to avoid a precarious stance on the hydrant.

Snatches of the two men's continuing conversation were easy enough for her to understand.

'. . . a further complication . . . need to consider.' From Franco.

'What . . .?' Conrad.

'You need . . . consider your position . . . carefully . . .. Discovery . . . Serious Fraud . . . of missing funds . . . contravening money laundering regs . . . will . . . damage your develop . . . in Spain.'

Outside wind gusted more fiercely. Angela risked the fire extinguisher: she wanted more to relate to Varley. She caught:

'Exposure by the media . . . ruinous to all of us, Ernesto included.'

To her Franco sounded as though he loathed every minute of this new development.

'What should I do?' Conrad, she knew was unaccustomed to ask for advice, but desperation was evident.

Franco said: 'Contact Carlos immediately, instruct him to put in place a holding plan; it will allow us time to put together a convincing story for the authorities.

'Finally, my friend, do make absolutely certain that no person is aware of our joint ventures, or it will mean the end of us all.'

Angela sneezed, she couldn't stop and in the process lost her balance, and clouted her head on the sharp side of the fire hydrant's support.

Inside the cabin Conrad heard a loud, to all intents snorting noise coming from outside, and close. Peering out of the porthole he blinked against the wind to see a figure dressed in a yellow jacket, sprawled on a sloping, spray washed deck and clinging to the guardrails for dear life.

'Excuse me Franco, must go.' Conrad panicked. More so because he really should be back with Maria. A shrewd lady that one.

Leaving the cabin, and gripping the support rail fixed to the outside bulkhead, he pulled his way around to the open porthole on the starboard side. Spray hampered his vision but not to the degree that he couldn't make out a person's body pushed and pulled along the deck as the pitching and rolling of the ship increased to alarming level.

He knelt by the heaving body, placed his arms around the figure in an attempt to prevent it going overboard.

He uttered a loud, surprised cry.

'Angela Grant, what the bloody hell are you doing here?' He pulled her into the lee of the bulkhead 'Let me guess. Espionage. Bloody eavesdropping on me and Pérez. Go on, bitch, admit it.' Even the crashing waves failed to drown his madness. Hoisting Angela up from the deck, he shook her violently.

'You realise my lovely Angel that 'espionage' is punishable by death, don't you?'

Still groggy from the clout on her head she managed, shouting, trying to shake off the monster she loathed, 'I was invigorated by the bracing air . . . I enjoyed listening to you two criminals.' Scared out of her wits by his vehemence, she still enjoyed baiting him, exposing his racket, both his and Franco.

'Don't play games with me "Angel". The outcome is simple. You take action to disseminate what you've heard and it will exterminate Pérez, Ernesto Carlos, *me* and Bull Ring Properties.'

This prospect scared him; he must act quickly.

The storm without became secondary to the growing unease inside her, but she spat, 'I don't care what happens to you or anybody connected with you. You're all criminals and need to be locked up. What a pleasure to expose your little gang . . . save the ones you're about to destroy.'

She'd said too much and knew it. In an effort to break free of him she dug her teeth into Conrad's fleshy cheek, making him howl in pain. Instinctively his arms tightened about her.

'If that's how you want to play you won't remember the result.'

The mounting storm had confined all crew members and the guests to their cabins, the decks were deserted. Struggling himself Conrad dragged the writhing, kicking body along the heaving deck, towards the iron stairway that led to the lower deck.

'STOP YOU BASTARD. THAT . . . HURTS. I'M BLEEDING.'

'Quit shouting, nobody can hear.' He stuffed a large red handkerchief into her mouth. By now they had reached the lower deck and its swimming platform; above them davits held a twin screw rescue launch.

Conrad lifted Angela's body in an attempted fireman's lift, unprepared for her resistance and strength. Bitch wouldn't let go. Her free hand found an opening in his shirt, her fingers wrapped around a pendant and chain about his neck; she pulled on it, at least enough to make him lose his grip.

His turn to call out as the links cut into his throat. The chain came loose, gripped tightly in her hand.

His grip did loosen, Angela suddenly released from Conrad's grip; at the same time a huge wave raced towards the platform. She managed to grab the side of the davit supporting the boat, as the wave hit the stern. Conrad lost his footing. Lifted high into the air he landed in the middle of the secured rubber launch.

'RIGHT,' he cried, jumping down from the boat onto the stern platform, 'THIS IS YOUR FINEST HOUR.'

Conrad, seething with hatred and intent on maiming Angela for life, pulled her from the davit, striking a heavy blow to her head.

Angela's world went instant black.

Heaving the deadweight body onto his broad shoulders, he waited for a gap between the waves. Standing on the bathing platform he tipped her into the boiling sea.

Devoid of any emotion, he stood and watched her body disappear into the abyss.

He turned away, failing to see a yellow survival jacket inflate, or the flash of the beacon.

CHAPTER 14

'Capitain Vouté ici,' came the voice over the ship's loudspeakers. 'If you look to starboard you will see the twinkling lights of Gibraltar.

'In a few minutes we will make a turn to starboard; this change in course will take us into Gibraltar's harbour giving us protection from the storm. We should reach the entrance in about twenty minutes. 'I am sorry you have experienced such a rough crossing. Merci.'

Peter catnapped in his cabin; his mind wouldn't shut down. It allowed the Captain's words to infiltrate. Angela's bed across the cabin was empty. Where was she?

Can't possibly have been on deck for the last two hours. At least he didn't want to accept she had.

Scared for her, he grabbed his sou'wester and hurried up companionway stairs to the upper deck. A cabin door opened behind him and out stepped Hemmings, long blond hair soaking wet, clothes dripping.

'Been for a swim?' Peter wouldn't know for some time how pertinent the joke sounded. He laughed at Conrad despite the need to find his wife.

'Nearly,' Hemmings said. 'Actually I've been saving someone from falling overboard. The body became trapped against the guard rails, huge waves shunting it up and down the slippery deck. Fortunately I arrived in time, otherwise there would have been a 'Man Overboard' rescue procedure taking place as we speak.

'Anyway, all's well that ends well,' he joked, 'the seaman is fine now.'

Conrad, haunted by the inhuman act he had just committed, recalled the scene in

Shakespeare's *Macbeth* at the juncture where Lady Macbeth says, *'there is blood on my hands'* and rightly since having murdered one of her husband's enemies.

'Well done,' said Peter. 'Terrible for anyone going overboard in these horrendous conditions, wouldn't stand a chance, would they Conrad?'

'You're right.' Conrad went to barge past Peter and avoid further discussion.

'Wait a second Conrad. I can't locate Angela, she didn't return to our cabin after her outing out there. I've searched the lower and upper. There was no watch keeper on the quarter deck to—'

'Excuse me,' Conrad interrupted, 'I haven't the foggiest where your darling wife might be.' How easily it tripped out.

'I suggest you visit the bridge, ask the Captain to send out a search party.' This time he managed to get past leaving Peter gob smacked.

*   *   *

'Ecouté, Captain Vouté ici,' the loud voice boomed over the ship's tannoy, 'we are missing one of our passengers, a lady, Madame Angela Grant. She was wearing a yellow life jacket and was last seen about an hour ago. I have instructed the first lieutenant to organise a search party and we will be heaving to until we find her.'

The ship's crew and guests searched in vain. Peter had been asked to return to the bridge where Vouté took Peter's arm. 'I'm very sorry monsieur, I hate to inform you, it possible your wife has been swept overboard!

'Under such circumstances I have no alternative but to set in motion the 'Rule of the Road 'procedures for Man Overboard.' Vouté looked shocked by the prospect of losing a life for the first time in his outstanding career as a naval commander.

A worried man, he was aware a board of enquiry would be convened into the accident, that statements would be taken from crew and passengers into the safety procedures implemented in such adverse conditions. No instructions had been given, meaning he could be found guilty of manslaughter.

'Operations,' the Captain shouted into the intercom, 'adopt Man Overboard procedures.' He tried to ignore the questions on Peter's face.

'Broadcast the May Day signal on all International distress frequencies, including Radio Channel 16. And contact C in C Gibraltar operations, on ship to shore frequency. Request helicopter assistance, giving our latest fix position. Also raise flag OSCAR and illuminate masthead navigation lights for man overboard. Over.'

'Willco, Roger and out,' assured a crackly voice.

'Number One,' the Captain continued, 'take a fix on our position and record the bearing in the log book. Then proceed with a Sector Search manoeuvre.'

'Aye, aye, sir.'

* * *

The Orsay, buffeted by enormous seas, was returning from the fishing grounds off the coast of Morocco, en route for Cadiz. The skipper, Pedro de Jesús, had decided to alter course and make for the shelter of Gibraltar's harbour.

Heavy seas had damaged the boat's communication systems which needed urgent repair, facilities lacking to send or receive messages.

The skipper, glued to his station in the wheelhouse amidst a fug of Havana cigar smoke, struggled to keep his boat on course as house-sized waves drove the rudder out of control, first to port then starboard.

Then, through a lull in the ever beating spray, his attention was drawn to a yellow object perched on the white crest of a mountainous wave. There and gone that quick, the yellow disappeared into a trough, only to magically reappear as the next roller raced towards the *Orsay.*

Pedro blinked several times; he cursed the weather. There! A red flashing light illuminating the yellow jacket, head covered by a hood.

The large swell brought the figure closer; vague, high-pitched and terrified shouts pummelled the night, snatched away.

'HELP . . . HELP . . . D-R-O-W-N-I-N-G . . .'

'All hands on deck,' ordered Jesús, bellowing down the pipe connecting wheelhouse to crew's quarters. 'Someone in water starboard side.'

A tired, motley crew clambered up the slippery stairway leading to the main deck; all wore safety harnesses. Although accustomed to stormy conditions, none had been involved in a rescue at sea before, so all looked nervous.

'Get in line starboard, throw the largest fishing net over the side and shine the search lights on the body,' the skipper shouted from his wheel house.

The helpless body swept closer, its right hand scrabbling desperately to grab the fine mesh netting, left hand clenched.

How long has the poor soul been out there, Jesús wondered. *Madre mia*, if hours, then the sea had definitely taken its toll. *Use the other hand*, he willed. From what he could see whoever it was had no strength in its frail body to grasp anything. Nearing exhaustion, hypothermia had to have set in, denying it any feeling in its extremities.

'COME ON, COME ON,' bellowed Antonio, the one crew member fluent in English. Well, at least he could try it. Most understood it, especially when in trouble. 'ONLY FEET TO GO. YOU CAN MAKE IT.' He stretched his long body over the side; other crewmen's hands gripped his legs as he removed his safety harness, praying it would allow him the extra foot to be able to seize the hand reaching out to him. Hampered by wind and spray and the roll of the boat, Antonio at last managed to grab the sleeve of the survival jacket and heave the dead weight towards him onto the netting. Hearing Pedro's loud shout, he knew something was wrong; this encouraged him to heave the body further up the netting.

'LOOK OUT,' shrieked Pedro, stunned and shaking with fear. 'Hold on. HOLD ON, ANTONIO otherwise it'll be TOO LATE.' Pedro's eyes went wider still as he watched . . .a 'Cape Horner' fifty foot wave about to engulf them. Pedro crashed through the gears and went full astern on both engines, immediately wrenching the wheel ninety degrees to port, in an attempt to steer alongside the threat.

'My ship has a history of survival and this wave is not going to win!' Pedro said through gritted teeth and crossed himself.

The *Orsay* surfed on the crest of the fifty footer, the lights of Tangier visible from this extraordinary vantage point, for they were now heading south, in the opposite direction. Antonio still clung to the body at his side, both suspended in space high above the water, only the stern and bows making contact with the sea.

'Right,' Pedro muttered to himself, 'it is time to win this game and take action. Save us a person.' At this time he didn't know if said person was alive or dead.

In a split second he turned the wheel hard to port and stopped both engines.

The crest of the Cape Horner rumbled on allowing the boat to slide astern into the stillness of the trough far below its foaming crest where the sea was less savage. The boat upright once more, this allowed the crew to haul in the nets holding their mate and one other who, please merciful God, was alive.

'Well done Skipper, we knew you would save the day,' a member of a very frightened crew shouted.

On the deck now, Antonio, a qualified staff nurse, employed in Cadiz hospital, explained to his uncle: 'Our patient is female, shivering, nearly unconscious, breathing irregular. She's suffering from severe hypothermia, possibly concussion. Has a large cut on her forehead.'

Definitely no fisherman, on board as a guest of his uncle, skipper Pedro, Antonio had done what his oath dictated, he'd saved a life.

'Good thing I asked you along for the ride,' Pedro laughed. 'Tell me, what can we do apart from keep her warm and get her into hospital?'

'We need to open the airway allowing the patient to breathe properly, if we don't act quickly she will die. Let's get her to a cabin where I can work.'

And between them they did, into a cabin stinking of men and cigarettes. Did it matter? Here Angela was stripped of her wet clothes and wrapped in blankets.

'Pedro, contact air sea rescue at Gibraltar, she needs professional medical attention. This lull in the storm might allow you to re-connect the satellite search and rescue system.'

'Sure, Antonio, I give it a try.'

Antonio started a sequence of twenty compressions and two rescue breaths.

After the second set, the patient attempted to move her head, chapped lips suddenly started to move as if wanting to say something.

'Thank God the pulse and breathing are more regular,' he sighed.

Pedro looked on and noticed the tightly clenched left hand appear from beneath the blanket. He pointed this out to Antonio.

'Perhaps the tendons are damaged and the severe cold has made them stiff; the hand cannot move.' Antonio gripped the frozen hand. 'I must attempt to open the fingers otherwise frost bite will set in.'

He noticed a small golden chain link swing between the fingers.

In his attempt to prise them open, the patient uttered a blood curdling demand.

'NO. NO,' she shouted trying to push him away, 'Leave me alone!'

'Well,' said Antonio, 'at least I've got you talking. At least I know you are English.

Don't worry I won't interfere with the secret you hide in your hand.'

The stranger on the bed drifted into her own deep.

*   *   *

Pedro looked up from the wheelhouse as he attempted to repair the satellite. From above the distinctive sound of chopper blades alerted him, the strong beams of the helicopter's search light illuminating the deck.

He pulled an emergency flare gun from the locker, aimed it in a direction he was sure the chopper crew wouldn't miss, its incandescent red and yellow starfish pattern lighting up its fuselage. Almost instantly the chopper reduced height to hover directly above the already stationery, but bobbing boat.

Rope ladder lowered, a swaying air crew petty officer landed on deck.

'What's the problem?' He tried to make himself heard above the wind, now lessened. 'We've been trying to contact you on the emergency frequency?'

'All our communication systems have been destroyed by the storm,' a still panicked Pedro told him, 'otherwise we would have been in contact earlier.

'We have an emergency on board, and must thank God that you have arrived in time to save a life. Come quickly, sir, we have a very sick lady . . . she been in the water for some hours. If she doesn't reach hospital . . .' Pedro shrugged, the answer obvious.' He tugged at the P O's life jacket, guiding him below to the makeshift sick bay.

The crewman returned immediately. With the rescue team radioed, a stretcher was lowered; within seconds the patient was in the helicopter with Antonio.

* * *

Following two days in Gibraltar's General Hospital intensive care unit, Angela awoke from the coma and asked for water. Since being delivered here her left hand had remained closed. Antonio and the ward's Sister-in-Charge, a buxom, pleasant faced woman, stood by her.

Antonio said quietly, 'Now you are with us once again we need information if you feel up to it. Please tell us your name and how you managed to be in the water.'

An extremely disorientated Angela said, 'I . . .I don't know . . . know my name.

Can't remember anything.' Sea water had tightened her throat, her voice was gravelly.

'The cut on your forehead, how did that happen?'

'What cut?' She tried to touch the bandage; the sister prevented her, telling her not to disturb it.

'What about the gold piece you have in your hand, where did you get it? Why won't you let go?'

Angela looked down, and slowly opened her hand to allow Antonio, a complete stranger, to take the revealed gold pendant attached to its chain.

'May I have a look?' asked Sister to receive a nodded "yes".

'The clasp is twisted. It looks as if it has been wrenched from someone,' the sister said. Checking closely she added, 'There appear to be stains on the chain which could be blood.' She glanced at Antonio, both shocked at the conclusion.

'See,' Sister held it out to him, 'there appear to be tiny shreds of hair between links. Perhaps I am right and the chain has been pulled from someone's neck.'

Antonio sensed the pendant must be the link to the near drowning of the patient. 'Second and not least,' he offered, 'how could someone receive a large head wound without some kind of struggle?' Maybe a fall, but his gut feeling told him the two events were connected. 'I'm thinking there must be a third clue to the fate of this unfortunate lady,' he said.

'May I?' He took the pendant from the sister and turned it over. On the reverse two engraved initials, though barely decipherable did prove legible enough.

Antonio bent over the patient and whispered in her ear, 'Who is C H?'

Blank looks passed from one to the other.

CHAPTER 15

Commander Varley and his beautiful wife, Patricia, relaxed on their balcony enjoying the ambience of the palm tree grove below as lingering sun's rays dipped below the impressive foliage.

'Cheers.' They chinked goblets filled with an ice cold *Esmeralda* wine.

'A perfect end to a relaxing day.' Varley took his wife's hand.

His Apple i-phone rang. 'I spoke too soon, my dear,' he said reluctant to pick up.

'Varley. Who do you say you are? Ah yes. Julie Nash, how could I forget you?'

Varley, never one for compliments, made an exception.

'We met briefly at the fun packed evening full of fireworks and gun battles,' he laughed, more relaxed, the pressures from the Met faded though not quite into oblivion. Unfortunately, euphoria wouldn't last.

'You did well to track me down, my number is only known by special branch. So, Julie, how can I help?'

'I've received a strange phone call from Angela Grant. You may know that Peter and Angela will be your neighbours in Mijas.'

'Yes, delightful couple, she is a doctor of medicine.'

'That's right. The Grant's and Connolly's have been Conrad Hemmings's guests on a short trip to Morocco. Franco Pérez made the visit possible, apparently he has ties with the King—'

'You mean Mohammed V, the present King of Morocco?'

'I presume so. Angela said they were aboard the Hercules in the Straits of Gibraltar, battling against a terrible storm. The captain had altered course seeking shelter in Gibraltar.

'Apparently Angela overheard a conversation between Hemmings and Pérez concerning the illegal sale of property in the UK. Something about money laundering irregularities. She was going to look into it but couldn't elaborate.'

Varley shifted, glanced at his wife, feeling less sure of himself. 'Interesting so far Julie, please continue.' He reached for his wine, maybe for a little sustenance.

Julie said, 'She's convinced her life will be in danger should Hemmings discover her covert operation. She sounded extremely scared. Obviously concerned I called her mobile shortly after our conversation. No reply.'

On a sigh she added, 'That's all I know.' Pause, then: 'What are we going to do Commander?'

Varley mulled it over. 'Thanks for the contact. Don't you worry Julie, I'll start things moving and let you know when I have news on Angela. In the meantime keep it to yourself, understood?'

'Yes,' Julie said. 'Thank you for your help.'

'Patricia darling,' Varley said to his wife, 'I'm afraid it's going to be a long night.'

'If you make certain we have the keys to our villa to-morrow, I might just forgive you,' she teased.

Varley dialled Cummings, the M15 station commander in Gibraltar.

'Cummings.' Recognisable, sophisticated and educated. 'Ah, Varley. And don't worry about disturbing me, I often keep late hours as you well know.'

'Andrew, I need your help. I'm meant to be on holiday trying to finalise a deal on the purchase of a property in Mijas.'

Varley and Cummings had become firm friends at Bramshill Police Training College in the UK whilst engaged in senior police officer training prior to their transfers to M I5, and over which they'd normally have a few laughs, but not tonight.

'Sounds a sensible idea, just watch out for the unscrupulous developers,' Cummings said.

'I don't have much time to explain on the phone. Fact is I've received a tip off from a reliable source concerning friends of mine, Doctor and Mr Grant. From the conversation I'm bound to guess they're in some kind of trouble. Could be completely wrong but I daren't take the chance.

Both are guests aboard the HM Hercules journeying from Morocco. The captain diverted from Marbella to Gib due to a storm in the straits.

'I am about to contact CEISD and arrange a helicopter to drop me at the harbour's helipad. O K if we meet you outside the police checkpoint in about an hour?'

Don't think I've much option, Cummings mused, *not every day a senior M15 Commander makes a request.*

'Fine,' he said, 'I look forward to seeing you again. Been a long time!'

*   *   *

Varley dialled CEISD.

'*Hola,*' the signora replied.

'*Quiero hablar á Inspector Valdez, por favour. Me allmo Commander Varley.*'

'*Un momento signor,*' she replied.

'*Valdez aqui.* We speak again Commander. A a good thing I'm on the night shift. How can I help at this late hour?'

'It's a lengthy story and I will try not to waste your time,' Varley said. 'No doubt CEISD are aware of Franco Pérez. I understand he acts as defence lawyer for most of the drug barons and corrupt town hall officials.'

'Indeed you are correct,' Valdez confirmed. 'We are aware of Signor Pérez's activities with the underworld and have been keeping a close watch on his little jaunts to Morocco.' Valdez touched on the trip to Tangiers with Conrad Hemmings and guests.

'You are kept well informed, I'm impressed. Now, please listen. I am concerned about a Doctor Grant, she is one of Hemmings's guests. Apparently she overheard a confidential meeting between Hemmings and Pérez, the contents of which could send them to Alhaurín.

'Doctor Grant needs protection. Hemmings is dangerous and will stop at nothing should he discover her, shall I say, infringement on his privacy. Therefore I need a big favour, Nacho. Can you arrange for a police helicopter to airlift me to Gibraltar immediately?'

'Circumstances of this nature will permit this. Give me a while to contact the boss; a colleague will phone you within a half hour with arrangements. And good luck Philip. Do let me know the outcome.'

Valdez was naturally curious about Conrad Hemmings, more so his involvement with Pérez. Perhaps CEISD would need to plant surveillance on his movements. Face it, any links with Pérez's gang world would prove very useful.

* * *

A sombre, tense mood infiltrated the Hercules, more evident since the search for the missing person had been called off by the rescue services.

Peter Grant, overcome with grief, feared the worst, already convinced his wife had been drowned. He'd since said to Jim Connolly that he intended following her by throwing himself over the side and drowning, which prompted Jim's concern for his safety and a need to keep him sedated.

* * *

Pérez and Hemmings stood on the port side of the quarter deck looking at the glowing lights of Gibraltar edging closer.

The officer of the watch paced the deck.

'Conrad,' said Franco, 'I have asked myself many times how on earth you managed to get soaking wet during the storm, thus prompting a shower and change of clothing. I overheard Mrs Grant's husband asking if you'd been for a swim. Then you made up some cock and bull story about saving a crew member from going overboard. What did actually happen?'

'I said I was outside the captain's cabin when a freak wave struck me and washed me down the sloping deck. The guard rails prevented me falling into the sea. The explanation I offered about saving a rating was a bit tongue in cheek.' Although he'd aimed for flippancy Conrad was worried.

'Do you mean to tell me, my friend,' Franco muttered, still unconvinced, 'that the ship's log will tell me that we were hit by this alleged freak wave, endangering the lives of the ship and crew? If true please to explain why more people weren't nearly drowned, injured or lost overboard?'

'Conrad, you're avoiding the truth. I know it, and so do you. How did you get that red mark on your neck for starters? Looks as though someone has tried to garrotte you?' Franco peered closer. 'Interesting. You used to wear a gold necklace with a medallion. I've seen you play with the chain, put it in your mouth. Where is the medallion now?' Franco, familiar with the cross examination of witnesses knew exactly the line of questioning to follow to promote maximum anxiety and confusion to the *accused.*

Conrad's hand absently went to his throat. 'Hadn't actually noticed it was missing, probably left it in the shower.' His smile was sewn on.

Another lie, Franco more than ever determined to gain a confession from this unpredictable, and definitely unreliable witness. Gone was any apparent friendship since this was not the same Conrad he'd agreed to accept as a partner and invest in his property venture.

He's changed into a ruthless and callous individual. If I allow him to continue with such deceit and destruction then my self-made empire will come crashing down, and damned soon. Such disturbing thoughts railed, to the degree that Franco knew that something has to be done.

'You've never liked Doctor Grant, have you?' said Franco. 'I've heard about the mountain incident . . .' He spoke of the coach carrying Bull Ring clients that were almost killed by some madman in a Bentley almost ramming their coach. 'But for the coach driver's skills they would have plunged into a ravine near Estepona. Angela Grant, I gather, provided first aid to one of your employees, Julie Nash. Then—'

'I don't know what you are talking about,' Conrad interjected. 'I am not aware of attempting to write off any clients in the mountains. It seems someone who doesn't like me insists on spreading rumours to to discredit me.'

'Allow me to continue,' insisted Franco. 'What about the slanging match you and your Chairman had with Mrs Grant in front of many guests in Kon Tiki's ballroom? I understand you had a tantrum and referred to her as 'Angel' Grant.'

Conrad waived it. 'A silly joke made after she called me 'Conman' Hemmings.'

Appropriate, Pérez thought. How he sounded like a spoiled child.

'I'm sure there are—' Conrad's mobile rang before he was able to finish the attempted assassination of his friend.

Franco knew from experience, unless he was able to extract the truth, there was no point in defending clients in the dock, however heinous the crimes committed.

Franco left him to it, and wandered off with a brief wave.

'Hello, Ernesto Carlos here. How are you Conrad? Haven't seen you in a long time.'

'I'm aboard a ship in the Med with Franco. We've just been through a terrible storm,' Conrad explained.

'Glad I'm not with you, but I soon will be.'

'What do you mean Ernesto, you'll soon be with us?' Conrad sounded shocked.

'I expect Franco has mentioned the Fraud Office are sending people to my office in the morning. Just letting you know I won't be there when they arrive; neither will any incriminating evidence, you'll be pleased to know.

'And at this precise moment I'm at Gatwick airport waiting for a flight to Malaga.'

'You are coming to Spain? What on earth for?' Conrad could have jumped overboard right now after his cross examination from Franco, never mind this bomb shell from Carlos.

'I'm sure you'll be delighted to know, I am coming to see you and Franco, we have to sort out the repercussions following the discovery of our little liaisons. If we don't do it immediately we'll all be cell mates in Alhaurín prison for a long time.

'Tell Franco we need to use his offices in Marbella for a meeting. Shall we say tomorrow afternoon, three o'clock?

'I have the perfect solution to prevent HMRC, the UK and Spanish police, in fact anyone with access to our past transactions from using the evidence against us.

'Conrad, you there? I take it by your silence that we agree? That's all, see you to-morrow. My flight's been called.'

* * *

Conrad felt he couldn't get his breath; he leaned on the taffrail as the Hercules rounded the breakwater into the calmer waters of Gibraltar's harbour.

My God, what a mess and more to come.

The sweet, seductive odour of Ma Griffe surrounded him. Suddenly he couldn't move, his arms pinned by his side.

Someone seeking revenge for my misdemeanours, about to throw me overboard!

He felt warm breath on his neck. *Perhaps I'm being seduced at last!*

Long manicured, dexterous hands slipped slowly from around his waist before sliding down his thighs.

'Conrad, I've missed you,' Maria said softly and bit his ear lobe.

'Hey, that hurt,' he said joking, 'but it was very pleasant.' He turned slowly to face his seductress.

'Where have you been Maria?' Taking her hands in his he leaned towards her and kissed both cheeks.

'Below deck in my cabin feeling ill; better now and ready for anything.'

'Yes, I can see you are,' he laughed, 'Though I am not sure in my present state of mind I'd be good for anything.'

He found warmth and sympathy in her sparkling eyes.

'I feel lonely and misunderstood about so many things. I see you as someone who would sympathise and understand. I enjoy being with you and would like to know you better.' At least, he admitted, he was being truthful for once.

'I feel flattered and wanted,' she replied. 'Let's plan something after we've disembarked.'

* * *

Varley and Cummings bounded up the gangway, their path blocked by a burly officer.

'Can I help you gentlemen?' the lieutenant asked abruptly.

'Good evening. Yes officer, we would like to see your Captain.' Varley was trying to be polite.

'I am afraid that's not possible, Captain Vouté is busy with port officials. Nor are you welcome aboard.'

'We'll see about that.' Varley shot the guy one of his laser stares. 'I am Commander Varley, my colleague is Chief Superintendent Cummings of MI5. We will wait as long as it takes to see your captain.' Varley more than exerted his authority and sensing something wrong, was about to show his identity card.

The officer's reply was cut short by a voice behind him.

'Philip what are you doing here?' Peter Grant was supported by Jim Connolly as he staggered to the gangway.

'Officer, let these people aboard now, they are my friends high ranking police officers.' He took a chance on Cummings.

The surly lieutenant saluted and reluctantly gave ground.

Varley studied Peter. 'Hell,' he muttered, 'you look terrible, what on earth is wrong? Maybe best we find somewhere to talk where we cannot be overheard.'

They went below deck to the deserted dining mess. As they walked Varley said, 'Sorry, this is a colleague of mine, Andrew Cummings, based here in Gibraltar.'

Varley and Cummings had realised that Peter Grant seemed incapable of saying anything coherent in his present condition. Fortunate then that Jim Connolly, neuro surgeon and friend, was present.

'Answering that Philip,' Connolly whispered, 'we think Angela was washed overboard somewhere in the middle of the straits during a horrendous storm. The captain radioed all rescue services and an extensive search ensued. Poor Angela didn't stand a chance in such seas. I doubt the yellow survival jacket she wore would have saved her.'

On hearing this, Varley hugged a still trembling Peter.

'Peter, dear friend, I am so sorry to hear this. A terrible tragedy.' He paused, then said, 'But I don't think it was an accident.'

Connolly looked shocked, and so did Peter. 'How do you know that?' he said.

'You asked me earlier why we are both here.' Varley indicated Cummings.' Julie Nash received a call from Angela, just after the captain had decided to alter course for Gibraltar. Angela had obviously decided for whatever reason to stay on deck.'

'That's correct,' said Connolly. 'We were all together here in this dining mess; Franco Pérez appeared in the doorway and asked Conrad to join him for a meeting in the Captain's day cabin.

'Shortly after he left to join Pérez, Angela said she was feeling queasy and wanted some fresh air. I offered her medication which she refused. That was the last time my wife and I saw her, before retiring to our cabins.'

Peter, feeling helpless and hopeless, wanted to do his bit. Damn it, he couldn't bloody mope all the time, he was a doer, so get on and do!

But Varley interrupted anything he was about to say with: 'Thanks for that Jim. It appears Angela was indeed on deck sheltering beneath one of the open portholes outside the Captain's cabin. She overheard Pérez and Hemmings in some heated exchanges, the content of which must have been upsetting to her. At this point I assume she decided to phone Julie, at least tell someone before they discovered she'd been eavesdropping.'

Peter's stress racked up, except this time he sounded angry, and did offer, 'When will my wife cease her obsession to become involved in other people's affairs?' It's the same thing with colleagues in hospital; and she follows the same disastrous strategy in her private life. Why can't she be more accepting of life and people?'

'Indeed,' said Varley. 'This time she appears to have gone too far and Conrad-bloody-Hemmings, a shite that will stop at nothing, has killed her!'

Peter, hearing this, turned away, more shocked and defeated. For sure both Varley's and Jim's somewhat ruthless explanations had hammered the final nail in Angela's coffin.

Cummings, recognising Varley's *faux pas* tried to defend it by stating: 'Until we have a body there is no reason to believe Angela is dead.. The straits of Gibraltar is a very busy shipping lane, it's possible she could have been rescued.'

'I understand.' Peter faced them once more. 'Thanks for trying to console me. But let's be honest it doesn't look very hopeful. Anyway, what did Angela overhear to make Hemmings turn killer?'

Varley chipped in, 'At this moment we don't have a single shred of evidence that would help start our investigations.' Said because he wished to remain evasive about revealing any aspects of the meeting between Hemmings and Pérez,

'Andrew Cummings and I will be having a word with Hemmings before he—'

'Excuse me. Captain Vouté had been standing unnoticed at the entrance to the dining mess, quite how long no one knew.

'I heard that you hoped to have a word with Hemmings. Sirs, it is impossible since he and Pérez left my ship with the lovely Maria Carmen ten minutes ago.'

CHAPTER 16

Bill Young strode confidently into the magnificent oak panelled boardroom where windows overlooked a series of small islands surrounded by reed beds, bull rushes and tall grasses. Here, a large expanse of water embraced breeding areas that attracted migrant birds en route from the Arctic Circle to Africa.

Bill, a keen, indeed dedicated ornithologist, had designed the bird sanctuary as a tribute to Peter Scott, not least the man's dedication to Slimbridge.

Floor to ceiling viewing glass offered a panoramic view of the hundred or so different species of birds.

Marvellous! Bill shivered with a pride hard won these days.

Thoughts meandered, Bill happy to think he'd designed a paradise enabling him to retreat from the twenty five years in the cut throat motor industry.

Is there no peace or justice in this crazy world crammed with deceit, dishonesty and crime? Right now I'm being forced into saving my company from total annihilation and can't even prosecute the perpetrator, Mr -effing- Conman -bloody- Hemmings.

A knock at the equally magnificent oak panelled door interrupted.

'Come in.' Bill hated being disturbed despite its inevitability.

* * *

Bill Young had called an emergency meeting with Simon Peters and Matthew Larking, senior partner with Symonds & Reed.

The revelations by Manuel Gomez, Bull Ring's lawyer in Spain, had sent shock waves through him; inevitable than that the reverberations would be felt throughout the company.

How could he possibly agree with Gomez's strategy to use Hemmings as a pawn in a game that might lead to the prosecution of drug barons and dubious lawyer, Franco Pérez? Come to that, how did Gomez think the two million pounds Hemmings had stolen would be recovered?

Didn't take a deal of thought to realise Gomez was more interested in feathering his own nest, and becoming Spain's chief prosecutor, rather than saving his new client from extinction. Bill Young was certainly a realist, and one highly aware the key to Gomez's future lay with him.

Instincts insisted Hemmings was important to the company's survival, at least for the moment, until eventually someone would place a noose around his neck. Or the crazy sod placed one around his own.

*   *   *

'Gentlemen,' Bill said through a forced smile, usual ebullient mood conspicuous by its absence. 'Good morning and thank you for attending this crisis meeting. Please help yourselves to coffee, it's nice and fresh.'

Over some subdued china cup clattering, Bill went on: ' As you are both aware the company has serious liquidity problems, cash flow severely affected to the point that suppliers are beginning to exert pressure on payment terms. Barclays have already made a request to see us and discuss new lending facilities.'

Bill sat at the table, sipped coffee, and risked another look through the window, aching to be one of the many birds on the wing.

No chance, It was back to the snake pit for him. 'A shortfall of £2 million shows in our balance sheet, due to the fraud by Hemmings. This gives us minimal chance of raising a loan from any of the major banks. We don't have any collateral to support any further borrowing. Before we attempt to find a solution, give me your thoughts.'

Bill finished his coffee, and enjoyed it. At least what he'd said made him realise he still had some clout, the bit still firmly between his teeth. Face it, Bill hated being dumped on.

'Well,' said Simon, 'it is a very bleak picture. What makes matters worse is that Hemmings appears to have raided the cash account. An additional £500K was transferred to an unidentifiable account after he revalued the assets in the balance sheet. Always possible he used the money to pay off the mortgage on the large block of apartments sold to Carlos. My jury is still out on that one.'

'Just a minute Simon,' Bill interrupted now more than a little shocked . . . again! 'You're telling me I have been swindled out of another half a million pounds? How much more has gone undetected? No real surprise the bloody cash flow has reached crisis level.'

He stood, again drawn to the viewing window. At precisely the same time a large flock of Canada geese landed to build their nests for the breeding season, Bill seeing only creditors demanding recompense for mortgages that never materialised, such demands equally as loud.

'I'm thinking there's little point in going on, that we need to find a buyer. With the buoyant Spanish market I should get a good price and recoup the £2.5 million lost.' He bit back tears, blinked them away, not about to appear the wimp.

'Wait Bill, really no need to think about selling this successful company in panic mode due to a *small* deficiency. We can—'

'What, Simon?' Bill shouted at Simon's reflection impressed in the viewing window. 'What is a *large* deficiency? £20 million? Thirty? Care to put a figure on it, Christ man, to me even £500,000 is a large deficiency.

'I've worked freaking hard in my lifetime; my success and ability to raise over £20 million to purchase this company was made possible because I didn't make mistakes or lose money. Every frigging penny counts. Do I make myself clear?'

'Sorry, Bill.' Simon felt suitably chastised. 'I didn't mean to offend. I understand your success in life has enabled you to purchase this successful and growing company.' He shuffled in the leather chair. 'However, I do have some positive proposals that will, I hope, help us solve the liquidity crisis.'

Bill rejoined them at the table, helped himself to more coffee. 'Go on.'

'On a high note, sales in Spain have exceeded all expectations. Properties in Estepona, Casares, Duquesa and Mijas have all been sold, except a few apartments. I estimate sales values are in excess of £50 million, of which our share will be £30 million. Currently we are holding reserves from clients of £40 million, the majority of this money being used to make stage payments to Ramos, the developers.' Simon shuffled papers ready to continue, before Larking interrupted.

'Sounds fine Simon, but fails to solve the cash flow problem. The properties may have been sold but as I understand the situation, completion cannot take place until occupation licenses are agreed and issued by the Town Halls in each district.

'We know issuing of licenses will be a lengthy process not helped since there is already a back log; this is due mainly to the corruption in the town halls involving the mayors and planning control officers.'

Bill Young, groaning inwardly, listened intently to Larking's concerns, highly aware of the implications. Impulsively he jabbed a finger towards his wild life sanctuary.

'Look Matthew, Simon, here quickly!' Waving madly, 'See there, two kingfishers. Amazing I've never seen them in my habitat before.' He looked sheepish. 'Sorry about the diversion but worth it, don't you think?'

The two men had remained seated.

'Yes, well . . .To business. When Gomez requested we should delay charges against Hemmings he convinced me he would be asking the British and Spanish foreign offices to defer extradition procedures.

'In return for this co-operation not to take legal action, he guaranteed there would be no delays in obtaining habitation licenses. That he personally would negotiate the final inspection procedure on all our developments with the Town Hall planners.'

'Certainly improve the liquidity,' Larking agreed. 'But there is a slight flaw in the plan. Solicitors in UK will not permit their clients to complete on contracts unless occupation licenses have been signed. Most of them are conditioned to follow the rules governing the exchange and completion of house purchases in the UK.'

'Simon,' Bill sounded exasperated. 'I thought a clause in our sales contract stipulated clients would use the services of Fernandez Sanches, the company's lawyers in Marbella?'

'Quite correct.' Simon sorted his papers again. 'Ah, here we are Clause 34 of the contract is conditional. He quoted: "The customer agrees to use the services of Fernandez Sanches (*Abagado*) *67 Avenue Ricardo Soriano Marbella for: obtaining statutory NIE number; preparation of completion documents for each property and mortgage deeds; annual wealth tax and income tax computations".*

'Spanish lawyers are unconcerned by missing occupation licenses at the time of completion. This arrangement is key to our cash flow, as completion triggers automatic payments from the banks and mortgage companies.'

'Thanks Simon. Erm, before we continue help yourself to more refreshments. Looks like we're in for a lengthy meeting. Oh and Simon, would you please arrange some sandwiches. Shall we reconvene in say ten minutes?'

*　*　*

Bill reached for the phone and dialled his secretary.

'Pamela, would you please get hold of Manuel Gomez in Marbella.' He then went to draw water from the cooler.

The boardroom phone rang. His secretary.

'Mr Young, Gomez's personal assistant, Maria is on the line, would you have a word with her, she sounds very distraught.'

'Of course. Are you all right Pamela, you sound upset?'

'Not really, just a bit shocked, Maria will explain.'

Oh my God, he's thinking, *not another disaster!*

Maria's softly spoken voice interrupted his thoughts. 'Signor Young, I am very sorry it is not possible to speak with Signor Gomez,' her voice seethed with emotion, Bill thinking: She's crying.

Matthew and Simon came through the door with sandwiches, pre-wrapped of course. Bill clicked the hands free mode switch and replaced the receiver. He indicated for the other two to listen.

'Maria, what is wrong? Please tell me.'

'Oh Signor, a terrible, terrible thing has happened. Manuel has been shot many times and is lying in intensive care fighting for his life. The next 24 hours are critical.'

Bill paled, he shot glances at the others, also shocked, Simon poised with a sandwich halfway to his mouth. The sandwich fell on the table.

Although severely upset by such shattering news, which indeed was another disaster, Bill tried to sound less agitated.

'My dear,' he said, 'I am so very sorry, how awful, who would want to murder such a personable and successful person? Can you say what happened?'

Calmer now, she managed to explain: 'Manuel Gomez was asked to stand in for the Chief Prosecutor in a case in which he'd personally been involved in bringing the criminals to the courts. It was an important trial for the police and for Manuel. It involved a large gang who had been caught smuggling 20 million Euros worth of hashish and marijuana from Morocco into Puerto Banús.' Maria faltered again, hardly able to continue; her deep breaths like white noise on the line.

'Sorry, it is so upsetting, Signor Young. Anyway, Manuel fought hard and won the day with convictions against the drug baron Gennadios Petrov, head of Malysherkaya, and twenty members of his Russian gang.'

'Maria, Simon here. I'm in a meeting with Bill and our auditors. I overheard what you said about Manuel. Be assured I will do everything to help.'

'Thank you,' she replied. 'Manuel was walking to the office in the Avenue Ricardo, I've been told. He had been given police protection after the important trial, fearing there would be an attempt on his life.

'A black BMW – '

'Aren't they always? mused Bill.'

' – with bullet proof windows, drew alongside the curb opposite the office entrance. Two surveillance police officers, following a short distance behind, anticipated the next move by whom they rightly assumed to be assassins. They shouted to Manuel to get inside the office door immediately. The police fired at the tyres of the BMW, puncturing the two near side wheels. At precisely the same moment a hooded man inside the car opened the passenger window and fired many rounds from an AK-47 into Manuel's retreating back. . . He . . . he'd made it halfway through the door and then slumped forward.

'The four gang members, realising their car had been immobilised, ran down the avenue. One of the officers phoned for back up and medical assistance; the second officer chased the four men. What happened next I can't say. I'm . . . sorry I have to go.' Sobbing hysterically she hung up.

'My God, poor Manuel, *and* poor Maria having to deal with such a *bloody* tragedy,' Simon whispered his appetite gone.

'Just as I thought we were getting somewhere with our liquidity crisis, another disastrous bombshell slams in. Bang goes my deal with Gomez in obtaining early release of licenses. Clients will have to wait months before they can enjoy stable electricity and water supplies; communal areas and swimming pools will be unusable.'

Despite all, Bill gestured and said, 'Would you pass me a ham roll, Simon, I'm starving. Crises make me hungry! And do tuck in the pair of you. Oh, would you get me a coffee Matthew, preferably laced with cognac!

'Realise gentlemen,' Bill spluttered through a mouth full of ham and bread, 'our rental programme will be non-existent. Clients will be unable to let their properties if the main supplies are unstable. Make no mistake, it is a certainty that electricity will be unstable, fuse boxes will be overloaded and trip out. This will continue until villas are connected to the Spanish grid, as and when the occupation license is in place, *not before.*'

Simon ate grudgingly; he was worried. 'I didn't realise the serious implications if a community lacks the habitation license. As you say Bill this is very serious to our rental business and will adversely affect our cash flow.'

'Wait a minute,' Matthew interrupted, 'Maria said Gomez was in the intensive care unit, please don't let us write him off yet. That guy sounds like a survivor.' At least he prayed that way.

'I don't think we can count on an optimistic outlook for him, and we do we need to take action now.' Bill paced, still chewing and drinking.

'Simon, I want you to pack your bags and get over to Spain immediately, oversee the operation. Liaise with Maria and appoint another partner in Manuel's firm to act as our legal representative. I'll also leave you to liaise with Conrad.

'On a more positive note, and still thinking on the hoof, we can start proceedings against Hemmings, since Gomez is out of the way, so to speak.'

CHAPTER 17

Ernesto Carlos found himself outside a solid oak portal resembling an entrance to a Spanish castle. *Franco Pérez* it said on a gold plaque.

He tugged the bell rope, his small hands hardly sufficient to grip the rope's thickness.

The inner door swung back with a resounding thud, each rusty joint of this medieval masterpiece creaking with time and use.

Franco has built another Alhambra. Such thoughts went with Carlos as he stepped into the mosaic tiled courtyard, filled with the noise of cascading blue water from the fountain.

Pérez smiled down at him from the top of the long spiral staircase.

'An amazing sight,' Ernesto shouted, overcome and unable to contain his excitement: 'The water features, the canal and the beautiful, beautiful water lilies, it is indeed another Royal Palace in Granada.'

'Come and join me my friend, the view is even more spectacular from here.'

'Magnificent, you are right.' Ernesto laughed. Once on the landing, Ernesto allowed Franco to take his arm and lead him to his opulent office.

Inside the room Conrad Hemmings stood to greet his friend. 'Ernesto how good to see you again.' His false smile already glued in place, Conrad was acutely aware this would be a far from enjoyable meeting.

Ernesto Carlos, small in stature, dapper in every way, immaculately dressed in dark pin striped suit, complemented by black and white tanned shoes, returned the smile in the same way – merely a token. His trim, heavily waxed upturned Poirot moustache complimented his bright red bow tie for shape though hardly shade. Myopia forced him to wear thick lenses contained by gold rimmed frames. Underneath said façade, a man of steel; ruthless, demanding man, he possessed qualities of an interrogator, one who could easily be taken for another Lavrentiy Beria, head of the Russian KGB.

'When last we spoke you were returning from Morocco with Franco. Was it a good trip apart from the storm?' Carlos's penetrating gaze dissected Conrad.

Conrad squirmed and nodded, 'Most enjoyable, thanks.'

'Well, nearly enjoyable,' Franco butted in. 'We only lost one lady overboard during the storm.'

'My God how terrible anyone I would know?' Ernesto always inquisitive about everything, then asked: 'What is her name? Or perhaps I should re-phrase it and enquire, what *was* her name?'

'Actually one of my clients, Doctor Grant,' said Conrad. 'We don't know for certain if she is alive or dead. I'm expecting she will turn up on a Spanish beach, more alive than dead knowing our Doctor 'Angel' Grant.' His sarcasm sounded obvious.

'A doctor? And one you don't admire.' Carlos's astuteness collected Conrad's negative vibes.

'You must have a very good reason to leave England in such a hurry, 'Franco said, quick to change tactics. 'Something that is most unlike you, Ernesto. Why are you here?'

So. Conrad had failed to brief Pérez on the phone call he had received from Ernesto whilst aboard the Hercules. The fellow was too interested in developing the relationship with Maria, Frankly who would blame him, certainly not Ernesto.

Hadn't Conrad already whisked her off the Hercules and spent precious time with her in his luxurious penthouse? And never without good selfish reason. Good idea to take advantage of her sympathy for himself, a poor misunderstood Mr Hemmings!

'In answer to your question, Franco,' put in Ernesto, 'I deduce Conrad failed to discuss our chat when you were rolling about the Med in your little boat.

'He also failed to inform you the Fraud Squad wanted to interview me this morning and probably issue a search warrant for missing documents.' Ernesto tweaked an eyebrow. 'I had the foresight to retrieve all the relevant documents and transactions, even to scanning and downloading information onto a hard drive, which now resides in my briefcase.'

Highly pleased, Ernesto Carlos removed his thick prism glasses and set to cleaning them with a large red silk pocket handkerchief.

A knock sounded at the door. Franco looked at his watch: Four o'clock.

'Entra,' he shouted. To the others he said, 'I have taken the liberty to order you an English cream tea, which my maid has prepared for you.'

'Thanks very much, looks delicious,' they all said as Carmina placed the tray on the table.

*   *   *

'Ernesto,' Pérez wiped the remains of a scone from his face, 'you haven't answered my question. Why have you decided to travel all this way to tell us the Fraud Office will demand information from you? How am I involved with your police problem concerning the transfer of sensitive material and disappearance of the originals?'

Ernesto Carlos looked about to burst a blood vessel. Heaving up his small frame, he stood to attention and slammed both fists onto the solid oak table with such force, his scone complete with creamy jam took off and landed in Conrad's lap.

'WE ARE ALL IN IT TOGETHER FOR ONE REASON OR ANOTHER,' Carlos shouted pointing at Franco and then Conrad, oblivious of the accident, and the stain on Conrad's white trousers.

A bill for cleaning fees I think! Conrad didn't interrupt Carlos's flow.

'Conrad,' he continued somewhat calmer, 'with help from me you have stolen two million pounds from your company. It wouldn't surprise me if you have spent the money and bought a luxury penthouse overlooking the harbour in Puerto Banús. Tell me, is your Rolls Royce strategically parked on the quayside for everyone to admire?'

Conrad smirked; one one-upmanship came into play as he said, 'Actually, it's a Bentley. Good try Ernesto. How did you know about the penthouse?'

'An inspired guess; I know all about your extravagant life style. So: Now we have set the scene, or you might say laid the foundation stone to our meeting, let us seek solutions.' Carlos realising his mouth watering scone had mysteriously disappeared, noticed the bright red stain on Conrad's trousers. He never said a word.

'Wait a minute,' Franco said rubbing tired eyes, 'let's set the record straight. You, Ernesto Carlos, are equally guilty of fraud, having knowingly purchased property for two million pounds below its official valuation price. Need I add that you also contravened money laundering regulations. A minimum jail sentence of twenty five years could be imposed for these crimes.'

'My friends,' said Ernesto, 'please, there is no point in wasting time arguing about our misdeeds. I requested this meeting in an attempt to agree a plan resolving any further investigations into our private affairs.'

'How on earth are you going to achieve such an impossible goal?' Conrad asked. 'I mean Bull Ring's accounts have been thoroughly audited by our new whiz kid accountant, Simon Peters. I have recently received notice of a leak from within the company informing me Peters has managed to unveil my accounting deceptions.

'The deprecation of fixed assets, the property revaluation, the entries in the Suspense Account, the double entry in the accounts, the reduction of Fixed Assets in the Balance Sheet. Irrespective of the illegality involved, I developed a water tight audit trail system that would convince auditors, accountants and fraud officers that the accounts were in order.

'I am bound to agree with Ernesto, further investigations into our personal affairs is bound to happen.'

Conrad re-filled his cup with the Darjeeling.

'Well my friend,' Ernesto replied, 'sounds as if you consider your position is untenable. My situation is equally tenuous—'

'We are all accessories,' Franco interrupted, 'as lawyers, Ernesto and I understand the seriousness of the consequences if we are exposed. Although I was not involved in the property deal, the investment Conrad made in the Elvira development would be traced to the original transfer of funds.' He laughed: it lacked any motion, since Franco himself was running a little scared. He went on, 'In this instance, Conrad was unable to use his creative accounting skills and provide a watertight audit trail.

'The ball's in your court Ernesto.' Franco sighed and metaphorically pointed the finger. 'Let's pray you can put us out of our misery.'

'Firstly,' Ernesto smiled, 'may I have another cup of Darjeeling and a scone. I can't understand how the first one . . . disappeared!'

'I can,' Hemmings replied. 'During your outburst, your thumping the table, your scone took off and landed on my trousers'.

'My God, I'm so sorry. Please send the cleaning bill.' Taking an enormous bite from his second scone, he said, 'Delicious,' and winked.

'Somehow,' Ernesto went on once he'd emptied his mouth, 'we have to infiltrate computer data systems to ensure we destroy relevant files, folders and back up storage devices from hard drives to magnetic tapes. Such destruction can be made similar to the damage resulting from a large fire. Nothing will be recoverable.

'One thing however, a fire cannot usually destroy servers used by organisations such as the Police, Accountancy firms, Solicitors et cetera … they are protected by fire proof cabinets. We have to infiltrate these highly sophisticated and criminal proof devices from the inside.'

Franco jumped from his chair, waving his arms in all directions, shouting, 'YOU MUST BE OFF YOUR ROCKER.' It sounded funny coming from the Spaniard. 'Are you suggesting we commit the crime of the century by accessing main frames, mini computers, desk top's, servers, automatic back up devices . . .?' He was out of breath, but hurried on in his effort to encompass every known recording device know to man.

'Systems where data protection is top priority; systems with special password access, systems requiring the source code to access the files?

Your farcical dream is tantamount to infiltrating Fort Knox and stealing gold bullion bars.'

Franco still remained on his feet gesticulating at Ernesto.

'How on earth could you come all this way, wasting our time on some crappy, stupid, fanciful idea to destroy a few unclassified computer files?'

Franco's anger really bulged. Picking up his Royal Worcester cup and saucer he hurled the collectable pieces to smash in the fireplace.

Ernesto removed his gold rimmed frames, yet again, seemingly unperturbed by the outburst from Franco. Fully understanding the concerns of his friends, he decided it was time to play the ace card, and pray it might offset further tantrums from Franco, indeed Conrad.

'Gentlemen, I won't waste time justifying Franco's outburst. By the end of my speech you will be eating out of my hands, and wondering what all the fuss is about.

'After graduating as a lawyer in Barcelona, where as you know we met Franco, I travelled to London, deciding to incorporate my investment company and studying for a computing degree at London University. And a wise decision it turned out to be.

'I met some extremely clever computer buffs, software engineers, programmers, system analysts, and wait for it, '*hackers*'. Yes, computer hackers.

'Carlos Investments employs some of these whiz kids; they know about accessing source codes . . . And seeing as we're in to lists, Franco, also web design, system engineering, complex server installations, password strategy, networking management. Which, my friends, is only the tip of the iceberg.'

'It is no wonder your investment business has expanded so rapidly with help from your hacking friends,' Franco laughed.

Ernesto ignored the dig. 'The majority of buffs are motivated by breaking into computer networks as a challenge, seldom for monetary gain. The media refers to these cyber criminal hackers as 'crackers'.'

'Excuse me,' Conrad spluttered, finding Carlos's solution preposterous. 'Are you seriously proposing that these so called *hackers* or *crackers*, whatever the terminology, are prepared to commit serious crimes on our behalf, thus relieving us from warrants being issued for our arrest? I mean, just how much is this 'hacking' activity going to cost, should we agree to proceed?' Conrad demanded.

'It will be pocket money,' Ernesto replied. These technocrats are more interested in the enjoyment, the challenge and satisfaction it gives them, breaking codes and gaining access to undiscovered worlds. Don't worry, most are millionaire celebrities; their services highly sought after by Government Agencies and Corporate businesses worldwide.'

'That's all right then.' Conrad nodded approval.

Ernesto Carlos checked his watch. It read 1600 hours. He reached for his mobile.

'Excuse me a moment gentlemen.' He accessed the address book and pressed the green send button.

'Adrian, hello. Ernesto Carlos. We've reached the appropriate point in our meeting for your input.'

'Fine,' said a voice, 'I'm standing outside some sort of castle gate staring at a large gold plaque with FRANCO PÉREZ AVICADO upon it. Am I in the right place?'

'Indeed you are. I'll be right down to let you in,' said Ernesto.

'Who is this Adrian person?' Franco asked surprised. 'And why is he invited to this meeting?'

'Adrian Teneman is a computer programmer, software engineer and network specialist. Also the founder member of a hacker group called *Trojan Horse*, and he works for Carlos investments. I brought him to Spain with me last night.'

Ernesto left the room.

* * *

Carlos's slight frame was eclipsed by the tall, lanky figure of Teneman, as they returned and entered Pérez's office. Straw coloured hair, swept back and tied with a large toggle revealed a long narrow fox-like face out of which stared dazzling blue, piercing but quite shifty eyes, this anatomy of a Mensa programmer completed by a large multi coloured 'T' shirt and black shorts. Gold rings smothered nicotine stained fingers.

Epitome of an eccentric computer buff, Conrad concluded.

'It is a pleasure to meet with you all,' smiled Teneman, offering his hand to the strangers in turn. 'Hopefully you will find my involvement in your exciting lives very rewarding.' His soft tones belied his appearance. 'Ernesto has briefed me on your problems; he has been very good to me over the years and I wish to repay his friendship.'

'Ernesto,' Franco interrupted, 'why didn't you include us in this undercover operation?' He sounded upset.

'In order to reach a satisfactory conclusion, I considered it imperative to leave Adrian out of the equation. Everything will be explained.'

'Do you mind if I smoke?' Adrian removed a grubby pouch of Old Holborn, and a packet of Rizla's from his shorts. One rolled and placed behind his ringed ear, he repeated the exercise and lit the second one.

Franco and Conrad watched the operation and looked at each other in amazement, such dexterity beyond their capabilities.

Blowing smoke in almost straight lines, Adrian continued, 'My programming comrades have access to the source codes covering all software programmes we have created over many years. We are experts in *Password Cracking,* a process of recovering passwords from data either stored or transmitted by any computer systems.

'When writing programmes, say for the Metropolitan Police, CPS, or perhaps international firms of accountants we use a technique called "Trojan Horse". This allows us to set up a back door into a computer system. The programmer, the technical term used is "intruder", can gain access later without the security codes being broken.

'The name "Trojan" refers of course to the horse from the Trojan War with conceptually similar functions of deceiving defenders into bringing an intruder inside.

'We are able to—'

'Wait please,' Franco said, 'this is a different language to me. I need a break, shall we say five minutes, I've ordered more tea.'

'Excellent idea, could we have another batch of Carmina's delicious scones? I'm sure Adrian will enjoy one.' Ernesto smiled, knowing he would too.

* * *

'Continue please Adrian, it is time to reveal the pièce de résistance.' Ernesto looked anxious.

'I'll try.' Adrian consumed his second cream scone.

'Gentlemen,' he said, 'you will be pleased to know my team have managed to hack into a number of key sites where information is held concerning Franco Pérez, Conrad Hemmings, Ernesto Carlos and Carlos Investments.' He paused for effect, and to check the reaction, quite naturally one of surprise. 'Using the techniques described we have infiltrated top security computer data systems.

'As instructed,' he checked his notes, 'we have gained access to the sites of the Metropolitan Police, Special Fraud Office, M15, Crown Prosecution Service, HMRC, the Land Registry, Symonds & Reeds *and* Bull Ring Properties That's about it for starters.' Rubbing his hands with glee he contemplated another scone.

'Thank you Adrian for your invaluable input and help.' Carlos smiled in triumph.

'Finally gentlemen, I am pleased to confirm the following. All evidence previously available to the Crown Prosecution Service, has been completely destroyed by Adrian's team. This means we cannot be brought to trial nor can extradition notices be served on anyone.'

Ernesto punched the air. 'THANK GOD WE CANNOT BE PROSECUTED'

The conspirators stood, joined hands and danced around the table like overgrown schoolboys.

Adrian looked on, smiled, and engulfed his forth scone.

CHAPTER 18

Andrew Cummings, returning to his office after the usual weekly meeting with the Chief Constable, noticed a copy of the *Gibraltar Times* on his desk. Checking the publication date he was curious as to why someone would take the trouble to deliver a back copy to his office.

The headlines explained all:

DROWNING FEMALE RESCUED IN THE STRAITS OF GIBRALTAR

Cummings read:

"Pedro de Jesús captain of the Orsay, *a Spanish fishing vessel registered in Cadiz, and whilst returning from the fishing grounds off the coast of Morocco encountered mountainous seas in the Straits.* Orsay's *communication system, badly damaged, and needing repair, forced him to head for the shelter of Gibraltar's harbour."*

Cummings glanced at the picture of the captain puffing a large cigar, and with every right from what he had read.

"Signor de Jesús contacted the Gibraltar Times, giving an account of rescuing a drowning lady during a hurricane Force 12. The captain's report highlights the bravery of his crew and that of the rescue helicopter in conditions allegedly not experienced in over 50 years."

This reporter learned about keeping a boat afloat, in thirty feet high waves... the captain's attention drawn to an object, its red flashing light illuminating a yellow jacket swept towards the *Orsay*. And of the desperate screams of drowning... Of a crew using fishing nets... how one went into the water to haul what was a drowning lady onto the boat's deck. – a body motionless, breathing laboured. Verey lights from the *Orsay* alerted a helicopter luckily in the area it having responded to a May Day call from another boat. Woman heaved onto deck, transferred to helicopter, followed by the rescuing crewman and the petty officer... soon heading for Gibraltar.

According to General Hospital doctors, the woman is suffering from severe hypothermia and a deep cut to her forehead that confirms concussion.

Now conscious and out of intensive care, the Jane Doe wears a wedding ring. Aged between 40-50, there is some memory loss. Police are hoping she will eventually be alert enough to offer her name, plus details of what must be assumed, an accident.

I appeal to anyone, who can help us in identifying this lady, to contact me, Rachel Ellis, at the *Gibraltar Times* news desk.

*   *   *

Picking up his phone Cummings dialled the Met.

'Varley here.'

'Hello Philip, Andrew from Gib.'

'Hey, it's good to hear from you. Must be important.'

'Recall the disappearance of Angela Grant? Good. We have a lead. The Gibraltar Times recently published an article re a married woman, mid-forties, saved from drowning during storms . . .' Andrew told him the rest.

'Yes Andrew,' Varley said. 'The reported event links very nicely with Angela's sudden disappearance from the Hercules. How is she now?'

'If it is Angela, she nearly didn't make it. Severe hypothermia. Received a nasty knock on the head. Total memory loss I'm afraid.'

'Oh Christ,' Cummings heard Varley moan. 'That's the worst possible news I wanted to hear if we are to be successful in nailing Hemmings to the flag pole.' A brief silence followed then: 'Andrew, I suggest you visit this unfortunate woman as soon as possible. I will contact Peter Grant, explain the new evidence and ask him to e-mail a picture of his wife to you. You never know he might decide to leave for Gibraltar immediately in the even she is his wife.'

'When will I see you again Philip?'

'Bull Ring Properties have informed me of the completion date on our villa in Mijas. This will apply to Peter and Angela, since we'll be neighbours. We should be in Spain within the next few days.'

* * *

Cummings opened the e-mail attachment from Peter Grant to reveal a picture of a voluptuous, middle-aged lady wearing a bikini, relaxing beside a pool complex.

Instantly he dialled the news desk rewarded with: 'Rachel Ellis speaking, how may I help?'

'Hello Ms Ellis, Andrew Cummings M15. May I ask if you've received any response to your tragic report on the drowning woman rescued in the Straits?'

'Interesting question sir,' she replied, 'I had a strange call two days ago from a man; he wouldn't give his name. He'd read my article in the Times and requested to know if the victim was still suffering from memory loss. And did I have a photograph I could e-mail to him?'

'And do you have such a photo?'

'No and if I possessed one, no way would I send a photo of an unknown woman to a stranger, especially one who declined to divulge their name. I did give him a vague description, told him she was suffering from concussion and possible memory loss.'

Cummings clicked on the icon enlarging the photo attachment.

'You'll be extremely interested in seeing the photo staring at me from my laptop,

Ms Ellis. You may well know the exact location from its background.'

'Fantastic, perhaps we should arrange to meet at the General Hospital,' she suggested.

'Let's say noon to-morrow. I'll leave you to seek the necessary permission to see Doctor Angela Grant,' insisted Cummings.

'My God, a doctor. How on earth do you know her name?' Rachel was shocked by such sudden developments.

'That's another story,' said Varley, not about to divulge further information. 'See you to-morrow.'

* * *

Hemmings too, read the same headlines in the *Gibraltar Times*.

Reading on he realised that his worst enemy might be alive, perhaps not well yet alive enough to say a few things. Disastrous then that Angela Grant had survived against all the odds; bitch had got lucky, something about which he should make amends otherwise, as invincible as he regarded himself, this Mr Hemmings would be in court for attempted murder.

Reaching for the phone, he dialled the newspaper's news desk.

'Rachel Ellis, how may I help?'

'I was interested in your article about the lady nearly drowning in the Straits. A very graphic description and well written.'

'Thank you very much. What exactly is your connection with the lady?'

'Depends,' Conrad said guardedly, 'if you could e-mail me a photograph of the unfortunate woman, it might help.'

'I'm afraid that won't be possible,' she replied so tersely Conrad could hear her feathers ruffle. Not someone to give info' ad lib.

'Unfortunate. Is it possible you could confirm if the lady continues to suffer from memory loss.'

'As far as I know her condition remains the same.' Rachel was uneasy, worried she might divulge confidential information.

'Could you give me your name and number, that way I can update you on any progress?'

Conrad slammed down the phone.

* * *

Accessing the internet, Conrad typed the words *Memory Loss* into Google. Scrolling down he found *"Memory loss can be caused by a traumatic brain injury, of which concussion is a form."*

He performed the same function for *Concussion* and read: *"Symptoms usually go away within three weeks . . ."*

Wavy lines appeared on the computer screen, words grew blurred, a hard day attending to complaints from clients completing on their properties taking it's toll. He slumped where he sat, exhausted, his mind refusing to shut down.

There is no time for delaying my next move, since my beloved Dr Grant has survived a battering. The blow I inflicted on her head is not life threatening; she will recover her memory. Yet only circumstantial evidence exists that she was attacked and thrown overboard. My next disappearing act for Dr Angela Grant will be conclusive. No mistakes.

He's thinking to visit the General Hospital posing as Peter Grant; a Personal ID easy. His lovely *Angel* will be delighted her husband has arrived to whisk her away from her prison. They would drive north of Marbella, to the uninhabited and beautiful Antequara National Park surrounded by deep ravines and lakes, spend a few days in a chalet, owned by Miguel, a business colleague of his. A chloroform pad and a bottle of the stuff in his briefcase and Grant would be comatose in seconds. Why he could picture her dying moments as his grip tightened around her neck. No problems in disposing of the body, trussed and placed in a large sail bag. Mustn't forget to attach two eight kilo weights, *all the better to sink you with, my dear.*

Conrad awoke with a jerk, a wailing police siren invading vicious planning, and even though admitted, shocked by the detail of murderous intent.

Computer turned off he headed for the deserted front office, and pulled a personal file from a cabinet drawer.

'Here we are: Mr Peter and Dr Angela Grant.' Opening the folder, locating a copy of Peter Grant's passport, Conrad placed the photo page, with its personal details in the scanner and transferred the page into his laptop. In 'My Documents' he found a recent photograph of himself and superimposed it on Peter Grant's image.

'Voila', he laughed. 'We have another Peter Grant. Perhaps my dream will come true after all!'

*   *   *

Reaching the fifth floor the lift doors opened to reveal a tall, balding doctor, about his neck, all smiles shaking hands, pleased to see them.

'Who is your friend, Sarah?' he inquired about Cummings.

'Inspector Andrew Cummings M15.'

'Sir, I am John Hernandez, consultant neurologist. 'I have been monitoring the progress of our mystery lady since she was admitted. She is a lovely person, resilient, highly spirited and extremely intelligent. I could do with her on my staff.' Added with a chuckle.

To Rachel he said, 'You will be pleased to know that her total loss of memory has improved since your last visit.'

Walking slowly down the long corridor, he held their attention. 'You obviously know about the concussion,' he said to Andrew.

'How do you think this happened?' Cummings wanted to know.

'Difficult to say. The blow to the head, falling heavily when she disappeared overboard. 'We have carried out neuro-psychological tests for memory functions. Everything appears normal; CT and MRI scans are not showing any brain damage, which is good news for her recovery. She has no recollection of the accident, the fishing boat rescue or the helicopter transfer.

'That said, following a series of tests the lady remembers her name. She tells us she is Angela Grant, a Doctor of Medicine in Bath, England; also the names of her husband, parents, school, achievements et cetera.'

At the end of the corridor Hernandez paused for a moment outside room 215, *Dr Angela Grant* on the name plaque.

'If you are ready, we can go in.'

Cummings expected to see a frail figure slumped in a chair but no, Hernandez was right, here indeed was a sprightly, attractive lady greeting them with enthusiasm.

'Hello Rachel, good to see you again.' Grinning she kissed her on both cheeks.

'And who is your attractive friend?' she said waving at Cummings.

'Andrew Cummings is the Superintendent in charge of the M15 division in Gibraltar.'

'How exciting. What interest would a poor old lady, suffering from a slight memory disorder have in common with M15?'

'There are two reasons for my being here Dr Grant. Firstly—' Cummings pulled the e-mail photo from his pocket.

'By showing you this seductive, attractive lady posing in a bikini, sent to me by your husband who hoped and I quote, "the shock would reverse your memory loss".' Cummings made it sound flippant, a slow smile emerging.

'My God.' Angela grabbed the photo. 'Certainly me showing off my curvaceous figure. It was taken by Peter at the Kon Tiki Hotel.'

'It's good that you remember the detail.' Rachel beamed.

Cummings said: 'The second reason for my presence is linked to the ongoing investigations covering your unfortunate and life threatening disaster at sea.'

'Unfortunately Superintendent, I can't provide evidence of the accident. Perhaps I'll receive another blow and be normal again.' Angela made it sound amusing although she didn't look it.

* * *

Once at the hospital's main entrance Conrad walked into the reception area to be greeted with a charming smile from the dark, vivacious receptionist looking cool in her blue uniform.

'Good morning, how may I help you, sir?'

'I'm here to see a patient who was admitted suffering with hypothermia and concussion following an accident at sea. There was an article in the local paper. I am sure you will be kind enough to assist.'

'I do know of the lady, sir. She is making a good recovery. Let me see.' Checking her computer screen she smiled up at Conrad. 'Yes, the lady in question is on the 5th floor, Room215. She has two visitors with her.'

'Thank you for your help.' Conrad went to the lifts.

Having summoned the lift, he became conscious of a person standing quite close.

'Hello Mr Hemmings, you visiting someone?' Peter Grant's startled eyes looked into his.

'Oh, er hi. Peter Grant, right?' All he could say, shocked by this appearance. 'I'm visiting an old family friend on the fifth.' Immediate recovery was definitely his forte.

'Interesting, I'm visiting Angela, my wife on the same floor.'

'Oh, I didn't know Dr Grant had been admitted.' His gaze settled on the floor indicator above.

The door opened. Both stepped into an empty lift and travelled in silence. At the fifth floor, they bade farewell; Hemmings turning left, Peter right in the direction of Angela's room.

Strange, thought Peter positive he'd heard the receptionist giving instructions to Hemmings concerning the fifth floor and Angela's room.

Shocked to see me as well. And why say he was visiting an old friend?

Peter bet diamonds Conrad intended visiting Angela.

Something cold skittered down his back, Peter concerned for his wife's safety.

* * *

Tall, athletic Peter Grant entered the room, pushing past Cummings to reach his wife who stood by the bed testing her legs.

Always over the top, wanting to prove something, Peter threw his arms around her still weakened frame, and buried his head in her cleavage, unwilling to let go.

'My darling, I've missed you. When I heard . . . Jesus, you don't realise how it scared me. I thought we'd never see each other again.'

Talk about melodrama, she thought and said: 'Good to see you again Peter,' her sarcasm intended and devoid of any emotion or feeling for him. She eased away from his grasp.

Cummings was surprised by such cool response, more so since it was in complete contrast to Peter's obvious delight in finding his wife alive.

'You remember the last time we saw each other?' she said, returning to settle in her bedside chair. 'You ordered me to wear my inflatable jacket before going on deck in that terrible storm. You saved my life, Peter dear. For that I will be eternally grateful.'

Opening the bedside drawer she retrieved a pendant attached to a gold chain; holding the pendant tightly, she undid the clasp on a black handbag and dropped the object into the gap.

'There, now it's time to go home, husband.'

CHAPTER 19

Simon Peters packed his bags and headed for Birmingham International airport.

Once in the executive departure lounge he opened the address book on his Blackberry, accessed Gomez's personal number and pressed send.

Maria, standing on Gomez's treasured balcony, watering can in hand, tending to his rare species of exotic plants, heard his phone ring.

'Hola, soy Maria Carmen.'

'Hola, buenos dias, soy Simon Peters, qué tal?'

'I'm fine thanks Simon, how can I help?'

'Tell me about Manuel. I hate to ask, but is he alive?'

'Thank God yes! He is improving daily and out of intensive care. The bullets missed the main arteries. The police told me they'd issued him a bullet proof vest after the trial; this saved his life.'

'Great to hear. Listen Maria I'm in the departure lounge and leaving for Malaga in a few minutes. Something urgent has arisen. In Manuel's absence I need to discuss important developments as soon as possible, preferably today. Let's see, can we meet at your office at 3.30 this afternoon? And would you arrange for one of your partners to attend the meeting please?'

'Nothing wrong I hope.' She sounded put out, thinking this odd.

'I'd rather explain when we meet,' he insisted.

Still unsure what more could she say but: 'OK, see you this afternoon Simon.'

Maria hesitated before returning to her plant watering duties. Grabbing Gomez's bright red phone she dialled Conrad's mobile.

An automated voice asked her to leave a message.

Exasperated she rattled out, 'Conrad, I need to talk. Received call from Simon Peters. He's on a flight to Malaga and wants to see me this afternoon to discuss *important developments*. Do you know anything about his visit? Speak with you soon. Take care.'

*   *   *

Bill Young opened his e-mail inbox. Messages with attachments filled the screen. More monthly reports from managers to read, which he really didn't wish to.

One message, recently sent, and marked *Urgent, Level 1 Security* did beg his attention.

Bill, somewhat puzzled as to why he should receive such high level government security mail, clicked on the message.

From: David Wiltshire –Serious Fraud Office, London
To: Bill Young; Matthew Larking; Cdr VarleyM15
Cc HMRC (Rm 296);F O London(Rm 505); F O Madrid (Gonzales)
Subject: Hemmings (Bull Ring); Carlos (Carlos Investments); Pérez (Marbella)

Gentlemen,

You are all aware of pending prosecutions against the defendants named above.
1. Warrants for their arrest have been agreed by CPS and the FO.
2. Criminal actions include:
Fraudulent re-valuation and sale of company assets in excess of £2 million
Falsification of company accounts
Money laundering activities involving Spanish banks
Illegal purchase of property in Spain involving stolen funds

In agreement with the FO's in the UK and Spain, arrest warrants were delayed. Spanish prosecutor, convinced the friendship and partnership of Hemmings and Pérez could provide a breakthrough in tracking down and prosecuting drug barons, and prevent £20 billion worth of drugs being shipped annually into Spain for consumption in Europe, was behind the delay, with the best intentions.

Gentlemen, following serious developments, explained below, the SFO has reached agreement with the UK and Spanish FO's that the three suspects should be brought to justice immediately.

We have discovered a serious breach in Government security systems, involving computer installations in HMRC, Met Police and the Land Registry. Bull Ring Properties, Symonds & Reed, have been targeted thus emphasising all company accounts be checked immediately.

The SFO are convinced one of the trio, Ernesto Carlos, a computer genius, hired computer hackers to destroy all files linked with Hemmings, Carlos and Pérez. Network systems, have been accessed, IP addresses vanished, bugs planted, hard drives and tape back-ups destroyed. Data files are totally irrecoverable.

This illegal entry into top level security Government sites has prompted the Home Office to set up an enquiry. The Minister for Security is convinced the hackers have used the exercise as a test run for hacking into Government departments in the UK and USA.

The SFO will continue to prosecute the perpetrators, regardless of the fact that essential prosecution material has been destroyed.

My sincere apologies for these unfortunate and unforeseen developments.

Finally, gentlemen, you are instructed to destroy this e-mail NOW!

Sincerely
David Wiltshire

Bill's phone rang as he was in the process of deleting and binning the sensitive mail from Wiltshire.

'Yes Pamela.'

'All OK Mr Young?' his secretary said, 'You sound upset.'

'I am, but I can't say anything. Who's on the phone?'

'Matthew Larking. He says it's urgent.'

'OK.' Bill completed the deletion. 'Matthew, hi. No doubt you're phoning to discuss the enthralling thriller story unfolding before us, involving the new breed of hackers, or should that be 'crackers'?' Bill tittered. 'Maybe we all are!'

'Indeed,' Matthew said. 'Poor Bill, you must be feeling anger and remorse about everything. I've dealt with many accounting malpractices in my time. Hacking into Government sites is one thing, tapping into private company accounts is unknown and does present auditors with serious problems.'

Larking was reeling from the implications as he'd read the mail from the SFO.

Should its contents be leaked to the media it would mean financial institutions responsible for auditing the accounts of both public and private companies, throughout the world, would be in serious trouble.

Blast it, how could he sign off end of year company accounts if entries had been deleted? He was positive HMRC, involved as maybe in the 'hacking' scandal, would need convincing evidence before agreeing the final accounts.

'Matthew, you still there, you've gone very quiet?'

'Yes, just thinking how to audit your 'falsified' accounts," Larking said. 'Calculate the tax and obtain approval from HMRC.'

'I'll leave that one to you. Let me say I do acknowledge what you're saying. 'I'm annoyed with m'self for being persuaded by Gomez to postpone action against Hemmings, all because of Gomez's bloody ego trip to be appointed Chief Prosecutor. Seems he's more interested in the drug barons than the demise of Bull Ring. How do we persuade Town Halls to get off their arses and give us habitation licenses without Gomez's intervention?'

Bill Young's turn to fall momentarily quiet as he attempted to find some peace out of the turmoil surrounding his life. Phone in hand he strolled to the viewing glass and its soothing picture of his bird sanctuary.

'I fully understand your feelings Bill,' Matthew came back, but hear this: Somehow we have to move on if we are to save your company and—'

'Matthew,' Bill shouted , 'we wouldn't be having this discussion if I'd followed my gut feeling, and proceeded with destroying Hemmings and saving my company in the process.'

'Bill,' Matthew shot back, ' I need to contact Simon immediately. We need to audit the nominal ledger and balance sheet, to establish the files our hacker friend has deleted. Simon is the only person who has the passwords to access these accounts. I'll be in touch when I know the damage.'

'Don't worry, we already know the damage. And action cannot be brought against

Hemmings,' Bill said effectively ending the conversation.

More birds announced their arrival from wherever, Bill mesmerised by the aerobatics as they circled the lake to land gracefully like mini Concords.

CHAPTER 20

Simon guided his trolley down the slope leading to the car rental area in Malaga airport and turned on his Blackberry to read a message from Andrew asking him to ring urgently. He pressed the return call option, too late. His phone vibrated.

'Hello Simon, Conrad Hemmings. Hope I'm not disturbing you.'

Simon flinched at the cynicism in Hemmings's tone. 'Conrad, what can I do for you?'

'Well Simon, I understand you've arranged a meeting with Maria Carmen and one of the partners. Just wondering why I haven't been invited. After all my position as Operations Director surely entitles me to be included in discussions involving, "important developments" don't you think?'

His attitude rankled Simon. Did this guy ever change?

Simon realised he needed to think quickly before replying to the monster. Had to be a mole in the camp – Maria Carmen? Pretty good guess, he thought, but no proof. Only Bill and Matthew knew he was in Spain, sent there by Bill to sort out the immediate license issue problem following the attempted murder of Gomez.

Although instructed to liaise with Hemmings, he had no intention of involving the enemy. Simon would control operations in Spain.

'There's nothing important to discuss that requires your immediate involvement Conrad,' he said. Not giving him chance to answer back, Simon went on: 'I want to review the budgets and cash flow forecast. In order to achieve this I require an update from the lawyers on the completion of properties, coupled with projections. Naturally in Gomez's absence, a partner is required to provide me with the information.'

'I'm afraid I don't believe a bloody word you're saying,' Conrad retaliated. 'All you had to do was pick up the phone and speak to me about your frigging budgets and forecasts without even setting foot on Spanish soil.' Conrad was beside himself, shouting and . . .*losing it?*

Simon held his phone at arm's length and let Conrad rant, much to the amusement of the crowd around him.

'You're a sodding awful liar Simon, and I will not tolerate your inconsiderate behaviour towards me. I will be at your meeting and don't worry I will let dear uncle Bill know exactly what I think of your conduct.'

'Go for it Conrad, much good it will do you.' Simon laughed loudly thinking it may be the final insult.

* * *

Simon's phone bleeped as he walked through Kon Tiki's hotel foyer.

'Hello Matthew, sorry I didn't return your call. Explain later.'

'OK Simon, now listen. The SFO have sent us a highly sensitive e-mail relating to the disappearance of computer files. I want you to check Bull Ring's nominal ledger and balance sheet and verify that Hemmings's fraudulent account entries have not been wiped. You're the only person with all the passwords to the accounts.'

'My God,' Simon shouted, 'what do you mean *wiped?* Everything is backed up in Head Office and you have copies of the accounts.'

'Sorry I can't elaborate further except to say the situation is extremely serious and Government departments have been involved. Come back to me once you've undertaken your search.'

'Wait a minute Matthew, I haven't told you about the conversation I had with

Hemmings just now. Bastard phoned me at the airport.'

'Sorry. no time for another Hemmings scheme, I've a call on hold from HMRC.'

* * *

Simon, reeling from Matthew's phone call, checked in at reception and confirmed his room was wired for internet access.

Turning on his Sony laptop, he pressed the WEB button on his keyboard.

Entering www.castlenet.com into the browser; the service provider's screen appeared.

He next typed MATTHEW LARKING, as the user name, followed by PIXIE, the user's password. Simon, overwrought, waited for the server connection to be made.

PASSWORD ERROR appeared on the screen.

Damnation. He was certain that was Matthew's password. 'Better check, maybe a numeral missing.'

Typing in the user name, he decided to amend the password.

This time he entered PIXIE 1 and waited. Connection was confirmed and Matthew Larking's e-mail's lit the screen.

Scrolling down the "inbox" there was no sign of mail from the Serious Fraud Office.

Let me see, he thought, *a highly confidential message from a Government department and part of the Crown Prosecution Service would instruct the recipient to delete the e-mail immediately once read. Could be Matthew might have neglected to execute the second deletion.*

Opening "deleted items" he was rewarded to see the first message appearing had been sent by the Serious Fraud Office.

Simon clicked on the e-mail. He realised the seriousness of his actions if discovered. Hacking into Larking's personal mail would be treated as gross misconduct, and result in his being dismissed.

Two paragraphs caught his attention.

The first: We have discovered a serious breach in Government security systems, involving computer installations in HMRC, Met Police and the Land Registry. Bull Ring Properties, Symonds & Reed have also been targeted; company accounts need to be checked immediately.

The second: The SFO are convinced one of the trio, Ernesto Carlos, a computer genius, having connections with computer buffs, hired some of his hacker friends to destroy all files linked to Hemmings, Carlos and Pérez. Network systems, have been accessed, IP addresses vanished, bugs planted, hard drives and tape back ups destroyed; data files totally irrecoverable.

Simon saved the entire e-mail into his documents folder; realising his decision to print a hard copy from his portable printer just happened to be contravening the last sentence from David Wiltshire's final instruction: Destroy this e-mail NOW!

If challenged about the possession of the highly sensitive document, his defence was simple, that *a Government Department had leaked the information sending the e-mail to his address. Perfect.*

CHAPTER 21

Simon located the offices of Fernandez Sanches to be greeted in the foyer by a pretty receptionist. They certainly knew how to select their front of office staff in Spain!

'Hola, buenos dias, I've come to see Maria Carmen.' He offered a smile and hoped she applauded his Spanish.

'Buenos dias, you must be Simon Peters. Please take the lift to the first floor, Maria will be waiting.'

Barely out of the lift door, a beaming Maria appeared; she kissed Simon on both cheeks. 'Hola, good to see you again.'

And can you ever be trusted, my little vixen? he wondered.

Entering Gomez's empty office he glanced towards the balcony. The glass doors were open to allow a glimpse of Gomez's garden of paradise. A black wheel chair straddled the threshold, all he could see of its occupant just long black hair tied back.

'Signor Gomez, Simon esta aquí,' whispered Maria.

White hands gripped the chair wheels, allowing the figure to execute a 180 degree turn.

'Signor Gomez!' Simon sounded more than pleasantly surprised. 'I cannot believe this. How wonderful to see you again.'

Looking tired and drawn from his ordeal, Manuel managed a smile.

'Thank you Simon, it feels good to be home amongst my plants, and working on the Bull Ring portfolio again.'

Walking to the balcony Simon admired the many and varied rarities of Gomez's exotic plants.

'I can't imagine anyone other than Manuel Gomez being able to give the loving tender care and attention your magnificent specimens deserve. Don't you agree Maria?'

She nodded.

'Obviously God decided it was not the right time for me to shirk my gardening duties,' he chuckled. 'I'm extremely fortunate to be on this earth. I am thankful also to the bullet proof vest, that alone saved my life. There is one thing. I shall take great pleasure in helping to identify the gang who did this to me.' He gestured to the swathes of bandages covering his body.

'Anyway enough about me. Maria mentioned you phoned requesting a meeting. To involve another partner is hardly the solution so I persuaded my doctors to allow me a few hours in the office'

He smirked at his own cunning 'Tell me, Simon, am I correct in thinking Bill Young's decision in sending you to Spain relates to occupation licenses?'

'Well, that and other issues.'

'Maria, would you please organise some tea for Simon, and water for me please. It's medication time.'

'Oh, Maria before you go,' Simon said trying not to sound suspicious, 'where is Conrad? He phoned me at the airport. He sounded upset, asking why he hadn't been invited to the meeting to discuss *important developments*. It was the phrase I used when I spoke with you.' He noticed how quickly she avoided his gaze.

'He ended our heated conversation by saying he would be delighted to see me again!' A white lie always helped.

'I'm afraid I don't know what you are talking about. I will get the drinks.' Maria blushed and hurried from the room.

'Well my friend, you obviously touched a sensitive nerve. Something I should know about?' Gomez enquired. He judged something in Simon's attitude, a tension unnoticed before. 'Why are you really here Simon?'

'Back in England I was in a meeting with Bill and Matthew Larking when Maria called. She told us about you, the assassination attempt after your successful prosecution against a gang of drug dealers. How you weren't expected to survive.

'Bill decided that with you out of the way, Hemmings could be removed from office and repatriated to the UK. It seem the SFO have sufficient evidence to prosecute him, alongside Pérez and Ernesto Carlos.

'The agreement reached between you and Mr Young not to prosecute, using Hemmings as a pawn to catch bigger fish, was an act of humanity on his part. Hopefully preventing billions of pounds worth of drugs being shipped into Europe.'

Simon looked weary as he awaited a response.

'Yes, you are right. In return for his generous co-operation I guaranteed there would be no problems in obtaining the various licenses for your developments.

'Simon allow me to et you into a little secret.' Gomez beckoned his guest nearer. 'Having diced with death, my family have persuaded me it would be irresponsible of me to allow them to have a second stab at ending my life. I have decided to withdraw from my prosecutor's duties of bringing drug traffickers to justice.

'I have little doubt Bill Young will be delighted by the news. I will do everything in my powers to support any actions against our three musketeers and more importantly, concentrate on the Town Halls to improve the time delays in granting licenses.'

'This is brilliant news, Manuel.' Simon visibly relaxed. 'Seeing you alive is a bonus I never expected. I will say I was convinced you would continue to focus your efforts solely on the ring of drug barons, as if nothing else mattered. Thank God you have decided to review your grandiose ambitions of becoming Chief Prosecutor and—'

'Wait a minute Simon, that's not quite what I meant.'

'Manuel, whatever you mean, there is something else you need to know. Just before your accident, one of our clients, Dr Angela Grant, returning from a trip to Morocco, organised by Hemmings and Pérez, was lost overboard in the Straits. She is by all counts on the mend but appears to have lost her memory.'

'I recall someone in hospital reading an article to me. As you say a lady was washed overboard and a fishing boat from Cadiz saved her from drowning. At least I haven't lost my memory, thank the Lord.'

Simon settled on a garden seat, agreeing the day's events were catching up, but he couldn't afford to be 'off base' yet, too much to consider and to undertake.

'Manuel, you will also remember Commander Varley, the M15 officer involved in the shooting incident on the evening La Manga restaurant caught fire. He's of the opinion that Hemmings could be involved in the attempted murder of Angela Grant. Also recall the venomous exchanges between Hemmings and Doctor Grant in Kon Tiki's ballroom, prior to our departure for La Manga. The two loathe each other.'

'Yes, I had noticed animosity between them. Let me see , , ,' Gomez flicked papers on his lap. 'Here. The Varleys' and the Grants' complete on their Mijas properties this week. Good for your cash flow at last!' His smile was genuine at that.

Maria, bearing a laden tray, more or less whispered into the room, to catch the tail end of their dialogue. Although outside noises from the balcony drowned Simon's quiet voice, she did hear Conrad's name mentioned, something about *attempted murder* and *they loathe each other.* Outraged by the castigation of her beloved Conrad, an honest, respected, successful and charming person, she coughed loudly.

Simon jumped. He turned quickly perturbed she may have overheard something she shouldn't.

'Thank you Maria,' Gomez said accepting his medication and the water. They watched her leave before resuming.

'Excellent cup of Ceylon,' Gomez said. 'A good pot brew makes such a difference.' Simon nodded in agreement.

'What other drama has happened in my absence, Simon? Any ideas?'

'You won't thank me for saying it, but I'm convinced Maria and Hemmings are in some kind of relationship.'

Silence and a pained expression said it all. 'Simon I find your opinion very hard to believe. My lovely Maria, known since she graduated, suddenly falling for a divorcee, a criminal, a conman, and what is more a gigolo twice her age. Unbelievable. How do you know about this relationship?'

'I have been informed by reliable sources that Hemmings and Maria staged a disappearing act and split up from the rest of the Bull Ring guests on a visit to Morocco apparently organised by Hemmings.'

'Wait a minute,' Gomez appeared about to exploded and tried to raise himself from the wheel chair. 'Maria never went to Morocco. I remember her requesting a few days leave last month to visit her sick mother in Granada.'

'I'm sorry Manuel, she lied. There is more evidence of their collaboration, relationship, friendship, whatever you wish to call the affair. Maria tipped Hemmings off about this meeting . . .the "sensitive nerve" I touched. Remember, I asked Maria why he hadn't turned up at the meeting, She was the only person who could have known, and guessed correctly that I didn't want Hemmings involved.'

'Have we reached the end of the agenda for this meeting yet?' Gomez sighed beginning to feel weary, and looking it since realising the truth of what Simon had imparted.

'Nearly,' Simon replied. 'I have one other item for discussion, then we'll call the ambulance to take you home. Tell me, have you come across David Wiltshire in your dealings with the criminal world?'

'I know David. He's head of the Serious Fraud Office. He contacted me about a month ago giving me insider information on Conrad Hemmings and his fraudulent ways.'

Simon opened his briefcase and extracted a folder. 'You might be interested in reading this.' He placed the copied e-mail onto Gomez's lap.

Gomez scanned it and looked both surprised and shocked. 'How on earth did you get hold of this copy? You are not one of the addressees.'

'Good question, let's say it was leaked via Matthew Larking's mail box.'

'You're admitting you illegally hacked into someone's mail to obtain confidential information. Doesn't it make you feel like one of the hackers?

'Larking explained the e-mail's contents and without any prompting informed me Government files, and probably Bull Ring's had been destroyed. I do not consider my actions were out or order.'

'Let's move on Simon, I'm tired. The main purpose of your visit is to discuss occupation licenses. I have spoken with Town Hall planners and given the assurance that licenses will be in place for your completions to be finalised on Mijas, Duquesa and Estrella over the next month. How does that sound?'

'Excellent,' he replied relieved in many ways that Gomez was in the driving seat again, and helping solve his cash flow problems.

'Manuel, what about the relationship of Hemmings and Maria?'

'Maria presents me with a problem. Could be her so-called relationship with Hemmings may be beneficial. Needless to say I'll need to watch her closely.

'As for Hemmings, well I think Angela Grant's drowning stunt could possibly provide circumstantial evidence leading to a conviction, should she regain her memory that is. Commander Varley's involvement is crucial.

'Simon, our strategy is simple. We monitor Hemmings and remain silent about the hacking fraud. But, wait for it, we leak the SFO's highly sensitive e-mail to the media, sending the file to the press office at Reuters. I will arrange the material to be sent from a friend of mine in Gibraltar, the tracing of whom will be impossible. Eventually the media will hunt down Hemmings, Pérez and Carlos, placing pressure on them to reveal their side of the story and incriminate themselves.'

'Manuel you devious devil, and you dare to accuse me of being a criminal!'

'Fighting crime over many years has taught me one thing, if nothing else. How the criminal mind works. How else could I be a successful prosecutor?'

'What next?' asked Simon, pouring another cup of tepid Ceylon.

'Please ask Maria to call my private ambulance, it's been a long day.'

CHAPTER 22

From the balcony of No 10 Buena Vista, Julie Nash looked in awe at the magnificent view of the African coastline just visible on the horizon, opposite a tower of black stone-Gibraltar- and slightly to the right as the seagull flies. Mesmerised by the beauty and tranquillity, the light touch on her arm was hardly the surprise: Peter Grant was as he planted a kiss on her lips, before she had time to properly turn and face him.

'Peter, wonderful to see you.' Julie responded to the warmth of his passion.

A pity then that the tall gaunt figure of Angela emerged through the patio doors and interrupted their embrace.

'Angela,' Julie exclaimed, 'I certainly didn't anticipate seeing you today and so soon after your terrible accident.'

'I discharged myself from hospital when I discovered we were completing on our property.' She said nothing about Peter's embracing Julie; in fact Julie doubted she had seen anything.

'But Angela, you can't be fully recovered.'

'I'm fine, apart from my memory loss.'

'Have to say it's good to see you alive; hopefully this idyllic setting will help you regain your memory. Now, allow me to show you around your fabulous new home.' Julie added a follow me look, aimed primarily at Peter.

'Suits me,' said Peter, 'lead the way.'

In a kitchen washed with shadows, Angela pressed the switch for the ceiling lights. Nothing happened. Even the fridge's interior light failed as she opened the door on the silhouetted and welcoming bottle of Monopole champagne.

'Julie,' Angela queried, 'why no electricity?'

'Perhaps the fuses have tripped.' Julie shook her head and laughed. 'This is Spain you know.'

Peter eventually found the fuse box in the garage, its trip switch in the OFF position. Back at the front door and seeking the incoming supply he pulled a face at the sad state of the mains supply box, its door open, bunches of wires dangling somewhat dangerously on the outside of the cabinet.

'Julie,' he shouted. 'Check this out. It's obvious we haven't been connected to the mains; I'm guessing all properties must be linked to the builder's emergency power supply. The electricity has to be unstable. It must have tripped due to an overload which will happen unless we are properly connected.'

'I'll phone Miguel the site foreman immediately.' Julie paused to catch her breath after racing up the stairs.

'Wait. Before you do that let me check the water supply.' Peter hurried off to the cloakroom. He turned on the cold water tap, nothing. I guessed as much. Builders have to be using tankers to fill the underground tanks. Either the water level is too low to boost the pressure or the holding tanks are empty. Bloody marvellous.'

As an afterthought Peter shouted, 'Phone Hemmings and get him up here now. Then contact Gomez and ask him why the bloody habitation license for our development hasn't been signed off by Mijas Town Hall?'

'I think we may have a problem,' Julie sounded worried, 'Signor Gomez is recuperating in hospital.'

'Well then get Luis Ramos, our developer on the case and sort out this unholy mess.' Peter was seething and continued to pace and rant.

'You must realise, Julie that Bull Ring Properties are in breach of contract allowing clients to complete on contracts if there is no license. EEC Health and Safety regulations specify owners cannot rent out their properties if electricity and water supplies are not connected to the mains network.'

'Stupid Spanish lawyers allowing clients to complete without licenses! Hell, solicitors in the UK would be in breach of clients contracts if they allowed such malpractices.'

Julie, half listening to Peter's tirade, was au fait with Bull Ring's legal position and the accuracy of his assessment. She dialled into her mobile.

'Hemmings?' She sounded surprised, and so did he hearing her.

'Julie!' Totally non-committal he said, 'What's the problem?'

Julie went straight in, none too pleased when she told him, 'The Mijas development is not connected to main supplies. The electric has tripped and there is no water. I am in the process of handing over properties to the Grants and Varleys. Bottom line, what are you going to do?'

'Nothing I can do if the license is not in place.'

'Conrad, be sensible for once. You need to get over here now, otherwise you'll have a court case on your hands.'

'Julie, calm down, it's not the end of the world. I'm leaving Casares now. Get the builders to sort the supplies and I'll talk to Ramos about the license. Gomez is out of action and obviously our lawyers, Fernandez Sanches, haven't chased the town hall. Be with you soon. Try not to worry, Conrad will sort it.'

Julie heard what she might term a sinister laugh.

*   *   *

'Julie,' Angela shouted from downstairs. 'Where are the air conditioning units for the bedrooms?'

'There's been a delay with the suppliers, they should be installed soon.'

'That's not good enough. We paid Bull Ring months ago and were promised installation would happen before completion. Total disaster! Find your Operations Director whoever he is, and get him over here like now!'

'My dear,' Julie said, a look attached that hinted she knew quite a bit more about Angela, 'you've become very involved with him over the past few weeks.'

Angela never wavered saying, 'Nothing scandalous I hope.'

'Let's say you're not the best of friends. Not to worry, Conrad is on his way. Perhaps his appearance will trigger something off in your brain and help you remember Mr *CONMAN* Hemmings, as you often referred to him in public.'

'Did I?' replied Angela, 'I don't remember saying any such thing.'

Julie walked off. Out of sight of the others and having done her best to keep up, found her act overwhelming; she plonked down on the stairs and cried, now more than concerned about the three properties she had purchased and the probable disasters confronting her. Not only that, but didn't action with Peter earlier lend credence to why Angela had never said anything about his kissing her.

Had Angela something to hide? Something hidden in a convenient loss of memory? Tasteless to think so, But Julie, out on her own in a way, decided she'd trust no one.

* * *

'Hello Peter, I heard all the shouting and wondered if you were being attacked.' Varley stood watching, an amused air about him, as his new neighbour inspected the damaged fuse box.

'Good to see you.' Peter shook Varley's hand. 'I don't think you're going to appreciate the problems facing us, bearing in mind this is only day one of our new adventure.'

'Let's hear the worst,' Varley prompted, already resigned.

Peter obliged.

'I cannot believe that after months of negotiating and planning we've been so badly let down by the incompetence of Bull Ring Properties, and that effing Louis Ramos. There's no water connected, neither is the electricity. It's inconceivable that builder's emergency supplies are connected to over forty homes. Interruptions will be frequent.

D'you know Philip, there is no town hall license in place.'

Philip responded with, 'We need Hemmings here *right now*'.

This M15 Commander was not used to cock-ups.

* * *

Following Julie's cry for help, Hemmings jumped into his Bentley and sped down the mountain. About to exit the Casares development, his mobile rang. *Another problem*, he sighed, pulling into a passing place.

'Hemmings, who's speaking?'

'Monsieur 'Emmings,' a soft voice with a strong French accent replied, 'you will not remember me, we met briefly on the 'Ercules.''

' I don't remember meeting any Frenchman, except of course Captain Vouté, who speaks impeccable English.'

'Ah, oui, Capitaine Vouté, he is well known to me.'

'Get to the bloody point, Frenchie, I have some urgent business in Mijas,' Conrad said brusquely.

'You can call me François, if you like. It's Conrad isn't it?'

'You cheeky sod.' Hemmings, always suspicious, was about to end the call.

'You remember the big storm, n'est pas?' The Frenchman sounded like he enjoyed every minute of what could only be delaying tactics. 'A lady, oui, swept overboard?

Let's say, this is the story all are meant to believe.'

'That's the truth,' said Hemmings, 'she was swept overboard by a freak wave. Even Captain Vouté agreed.'

'It's fortunate for you she survived, and very fortunate the poor lady suffers from memory loss,' the Frenchman said amiably.

'What the hell are you talking about? Why are you telling me everything I already know?' Hemmings tried his best not to shout. 'The lady you are referring to is Doctor Angela Grant, a client and close friend of mine.' Some joke.

'Monsieur 'Emmings,' the Frenchman sounded a tad more excited, 'I'll come to the point and let you out of your misery. That night my watch had just ended on the boat and I decided to have a Gitane. I made for the shelter of the quarter deck, situated directly above the boat deck.

'I heard some shouting below and noticed two figures in a brawl, the lady was wearing a yellow survival jacket, and trying desperately to escape from a tall man, who it appeared was attempting to strangle her. She pulled something from the man's chest, a pendant I think—'

'Listen my friend,' Hemmings interrupted, 'I'm not listening to any more of this crap, I have to go.'

'I advise not to until I've finished, you might regret the consequences.'

'To continue . . . good sir,' he said, 'the attacker hit the lady on the head; she fell backwards obviously unconscious. He heaved her dead weight onto his shoulders and threw her into the ocean I saw her engulfed by a large wave.'

A prolonged pause heralded: 'The person who carried out this heinous crime was you, monsieur.'

'Ridiculous.' Hemmings went into immediate denial, almost as if he'd decided it convenient to lose his memory. 'There are no witnesses to support your fantasy and anyway I was nowhere near the boating deck.'

'Fortunately, monsieur my mobile phone was turned on and I managed to take quite a few shots of the brawl, also a lovely picture of the lady being thrown into the boiling sea. Please excuse my literary attempts but I 'ave to say I am enjoying hearing you squirm. And I 'ave copies should you like to see them.'

Hemmings gripped the phone until his knuckles bled white. 'What do you want?' he asked trying to maintain some calm.

'Money would be nice, and lots of it.' The Frenchman's laugh sent a chill through Conrad.

'We'll see about that,' he retaliated. 'I hate and despise blackmailers. This is a matter for the police. Anyway I don't have any money!' Despite sudden bravado Hemmings was frightened.

'You're a good liar as well as a possible murderer,' Frenchie said. 'I also know you are a very rich man. With the evidence in my possession, involving the police would be suicidal. Face it, you would be arrested immediately, with a threatening life sentence pending.'

'At the moment *Froggie* I don't care a sod where I spend the rest of my life. Agreeing to a blackmail threat is the last thing on my 'to do' list.' Conrad was furious.

'There is no need to make a hasty decision,' the Frenchman assured, 'I will send you an e-mail to your mobile giving details of my proposals, together with the photos of your attempted murder of the good doctor.'

* * *

Angela, continued her tour of the villa. Opening the master bedroom door, she paused. Strange why the door should be hard to open.

Attention drawn to the diagonal cracks in the lintel above the glass doors leading to a terrace, she noticed how the cracks reached the plaster wall to the right. *Those cracks, she told herself, are wider than the thickness of a 10p coin. That's not right.* She tried to open the glass doors and found them locked.

Returning to the stairwell, she heard before noticing Julie sitting on the stairs, head bowed and sobbing.

'I guess you're upset about all the shenanigans Julie, but I need your help. I want the keys to the doors leading onto the terrace. The outside wall should be checked. And please ask Peter to come, wherever he happens to be.'

'Not another problem,' Julie said despairingly, I can't bear it,' Nevertheless she stumbled off to get the keys.

'Yes, my dear,' Peter said joining his wife. 'Julie insisted you want me to look at something. OK if Philip joins the party?'

Angela acknowledged Philip with a curt nod.

'Peter,' she said pointing to the lintel and adjoining wall, 'check out those diagonal cracks in the plaster?'

Close up to the wall he said, 'Yes, they're quite common my dear, probably caused by changes in temperature. Julie, open the doors, let's have a look at the brickwork outside.'

'I need some help,' said Julie, 'the doors are sticking.'

'That's definitely not a good sign.' Varley shoved his large frame against the doors and forced an opening through which they all managed to squeeze through onto the terrace.

'My God.' Peter was even more shocked to see large diagonal cracks in the plaster

on the corner of the house. 'Look, you can even see the concrete breeze blocks are cracked.'

'Understatement I know, but I'm afraid you have serious subsidence problem,' Philip said. 'Gotta say I'm stunned by the enormity of the damage.'

'I remember now ' Julie had been pondering matters and exclaimed, 'before the foundations were laid, this was an area of forestation; the pine trees were obviously planted to stop landslides. Now the trees have been destroyed it is conceivable there is soil erosion. The foundations are bound to require immediate and urgent attention.'

'Oh Christ,' moaned Angela, 'yet another disaster. Didn't I tell you Peter we should never, never, never have bought a property in Spain built by unskilled, cheap labour from countries in the Eastern Bloc.

'I can't take any more. I need a strong drink.' She disappeared to fulfil the need.

*   *   *

'Evening all,' Conrad laughed, suddenly appearing on the bedroom terrace with Miguel the site foreman in tow. A man all smiles, and large traditional, very dark moustache.

'I heard some strong language from someone; what seems to be the problem?' Conrad sounded oblivious of the seriousness confronting him.

'Well,' said Peter, 'apart from no water, no electricity and no license we—'

'Wait a minute,' Conrad interrupted, a hand on Miguel's shoulder. 'My friend Miguel is fixing the power and water supplies and I have been in contact with Ramos, about the license. Don't worry my friends, everything will be sorted.'

'Sounds great,' Peter said with some determination to be heard,' but what about the sodding subsidence problem we've just discovered? Take a look for yourself.' He pointed. 'See the enormous cracks in the plaster and brickwork.'

'¿Qué te parece?' (*What do you think?*) Conrad whispered turning to the Spaniard, whose brow resembled wavy lines in concrete as he twiddled that magnificent handlebar moustache.

Miguel prodded the large cracks with a steel rod he'd brought in with him perhaps anticipated. Bricks and mortar tumbled out, the gaps much larger.

'Looks interesting.' Conrad's acidic laugh rolled out. 'But then we can easily fill those gaps, eh Miguel?'

Miguel wasn't listening, he'd squeezed through the gap in the glass doors and back into the bedroom. He prodded the cracks on the inside wall, regretting the exercise as large chunks of falling plaster covered his face and clothes; these diagonal cracks grew wider.

Miguel spoke no English and turned to Julie for help as translator.

'Lo siento,' said Miguel.

'Miguel says he's sorry,' Julie said. 'There is a major problem with subsidence of the building. The whole house is very dangerous and needs to be underpinned, otherwise it will fall into the ravine below. It is not safe for anyone to live here until the work is completed. This could take a month; after that no problems.'

'Isn't that marvellous!' shouted Peter. 'Means you'll have to find us another villa, Conrad.'

'It can be done,' Hemmings said. 'Don't let's get so up tight. We'll discuss this over refreshments.'

'Good luck,' smiled Philip. 'Excuse me whilst I go and inspect my house for subsidence. Miguel.' he beckoned the man and both made a hurried exit.

'Don't be too far away, we may need you,' Peter called to the disappearing figure.

* * *

Angela relaxed beneath a large umbrella on the terrace; she clutched a large glass of red wine, lemonade and ice, and enjoying the peace and ambience of the location. To hell with the cracks, and the house. In fact to hell with everything.

On her left the last rays of the sun were fast disappearing over the mountains. In the distance Fuengirola's twinkling lights began to illuminate the town.

Her idyll was shattered by the sound of voices from the kitchen.

'This should do the trick for a sundowner,' Peter said to the others pouring the same mixture of wine and lemonade Angela had prepared into three glasses filled with ice.

'Bring your drinks through to the terrace,' he invited, 'Angela will be keen to hear an update on the state of play.'

Peter found his wife slowly getting sozzled in the sunset. 'Hello, sweetheart.' He kissed her. 'You can wake up now we have some news.'

Angela swivelled in her chair. Beyond Peter she saw Conrad approaching.

'Ah, Dr Grant, isn't it?' We haven't met for some time, at least not since your unfortunate accident at sea. Do you remember me, Conrad Hemmings?' He oozed charm, and extended a hand to Angela who ignored the gesture.

'Nice to meet you Mr Hemmings,' she said quietly, completely unfazed by his presence. 'Sorry, but I can't recall seeing you before today.'

'Oh well,' Conrad laughed, 'perhaps we can renew our acquaintance and remain friends.'

'Perhaps,' she whispered then out of the blue said, 'Tell me Mr Hemmings, what are you going to do about our house falling down?'

'Miguel, our site foreman,' Conrad quickly replied, 'has recommended we underpin the building immediately. You'll be able to use your property in a very short time.'

'Conrad,' said Peter, 'underpinning is a serious issue, the house will need propping while the foundations are strengthened, itself a lengthy process. Manuel already said this. Do you realise this place will be like a building site? We insist all rooms are cleared of fixtures, fittings and furnishings.'

'I really don't think we need to be so drastic, it's not such a major operation.' Conrad was becoming dismissive of any existing problem.

'Mr Hemmings, let me tell you exactly what your bloody company are going to do,' Angela stated firmly, red face fused with a certain rage and determination.

Why should this *arrogant* man dare to presume nothing was seriously wrong?

'You will phone Bill Young now, explain the situation and inform him we want a refund of the £150,000 we have paid Bull Ring Properties; you will also instruct him to get the mortgage deed for £140,000 cancelled. This property with all fixtures and fittings, Mr Hemmings, will once more revert to you.

'Peter and I are not prepared to take the risk that underpinning will provide a long term solution. We might never be able to sell the property or even give it away.'

'Well said, my dear.' Peter applauded, the sound somewhat mocking of Conrad's predicament. 'You are regaining your fighting instincts; it's so refreshing to see you in such an aggressive mood. Just like old times at last.'

'Wait a minute,' Conrad demanded, arms waving to gain attention, a large fist skittling a half filled glass of wine from the table, pieces skidding across the highly polished marble floor.

'Hold it one second!' He transfixed Angela with a blowtorch gaze. 'Dr *Angel* Grant you are an imbecile and a bloody idiot; you can't dictate settlement terms to me woman! Money back is out of the—'

Angela jumped out of her chair.

'What did you call me? Dr *ANGEL* Grant? I've heard someone call me that name before. I remember at the Kon Tiki hotel having an argument with Bill Young about the viability of your company . . . about corruption in town halls granting of habitation licenses. Don't you remember Mr Con—'

Angela, suddenly ceased her tirade. Stared intently at Hemmings and then fled the terrace.

'Sorry about the outburst from the wife, Conrad,' uttered a now concerned and equally confused Peter. 'Don't know what came over her. Never seen her so pumped up since the accident. What do you think happened Julie?'

Julie, who had remained quiet watching proceedings with interest said, 'I'm certain she's regaining part of her memory. The brain has received some kind shock and is gradually beginning to function normally, plus the—'

'Excuse me everyone, and thanks for the drink. Sorry about the slight accident.'

An unperturbed Conrad eyed the broken glass on the floor. 'Must be off. Will let you know Bill Young's comments re your situation.'

'Oh no you don't, Mr *CONMAN* Hemmings, I haven't finished with you.' Angela stood at the terrace entrance, she meant business.

'I definitely remember the scene in the Kon Tiki, when you called me ANGEL Grant. And I recall what happened aboard the Hercules when you caught me eavesdropping. Yes Mr Hemmings, you went berserk!

'Do you remember dragging me along the pitching deck, down the stairway onto the boat deck, me struggling against you, grabbing your pendant and chain. Talk about a madman, you struck me on the head. That's all I remember.'

Angela snivelled and then sobbed, this ordeal she'd prompted just starting.

'My *dear* Angela,' Conrad laughed. 'I've read a lot of Clive Cussler novels in my time. The drama, suspense and excitement you've created in your vivid description of a 'drowning lady' beats them all. You are not well. Totally irrational.

'Now I really must leave you.' Conrad nodded and turned on his heels.

Philip Varley had heard the shouting and abandoned his property inspection, now more than concerned for Angela in her present state of mind. He took up a position, out of sight, adjacent to the terrace area.

Angela blocked Hemmings's path. Tears streaming down her face she reached into the pocket of the dress to slowly extract a gold pendant and chain.

'Remember this Hemmings?' She determined to provoke a reaction from the man who attempted to retain ineffable calm.

'This pendant . . .' Angela let it dangle on its chain for Hemmings to see, 'has never left me since I pulled it from you.' She glared like Medusa might. *'Now do you remember?'*

Oh the gall of the man, the quiet insufferable manner when he said, 'Never seen this chain in my life. It certainly doesn't belong to me.'

'Take a closer look, at the initials engraved on the pendant.' Angela held the piece in front of his ever shifting eyes, Conrad glancing first at her, then the others, almost an appeal there which he daren't voice.

'Shall I read the engraving out? I think I will, for the benefit of the audience.' She took her time, revelling in the moment of recollected glory.

'It says "C H." That stands for "CONRAD HEMMINGS." What further proof do you need?' Angela handing the pendant to Varley, who moments before had emerged from his hiding place and hurried to her side.

'Conrad Hemmings,' said Varley, 'I am detaining you—'

'Don't bother to see me out.' Conrad dashed from the terrace, and towards the open front door to jump into his Bentley.

CHAPTER 23

Peter's mobile vibrated, he didn't recognise the caller's number.

'Hello Mr Grant, Pamela, Mr Young's secretary. Bill would like a word.'

'Peter, how are things?' Bill's deep voice came through.

'Talk of the devil,' Peter said, 'I was about to phone you.'

'Nothing serious I hope, apart from your little *house moving* problem.' The attempt at a joke nosedived. He cut to the chase, stating: 'Julie's given me an update on the action we need to take. Very unfortunate your property needs underpinning, you have my sympathy.'

'Thanks. Changing the subject, did Julie Nash update you on the scene between Hemmings and my wife?' Peter despite his determination to sound on top of things, sounded drained.

'Not a word. Why, something I should know? I spoke with Hemmings earlier and he seemed fine.'

'Let's say you need to keep an eye on him before it's too late and he commits another felony.'

'Sorry Peter,' Bill sounded put out, 'I didn't phone to discuss one of my main board directors, but merely, and solely, your problem. Here's what I propose.

'I fully understand your new home is not fit for its purpose and right now there is no chance of achieving a return on your investment through rental income. What I propose is offering you a property which has just come back on the market, on the first phase development situated just above you. Julie says the views are even more spectacular.

'I have arranged for Julie to take you there now. How does that sound?'

'If we did accept I presume there will be no extra costs and the title deeds will be transferred.' Peter tried not to sound unimpressed by the offer of another move.

'It's not quite as easy as that,' Bill said. 'The financing of properties in Spain is a complicated process as you well know. Developers, builders, banks, town halls, lawyers. Need I say more?'

'Quit stalling Bill. What's the bad news you are obviously afraid to divulge?' Things hidden behind a certain smokescreen began to emerge.

'Cash flow problems, simple as that,' Bill eventually admitted. 'We cannot refund or transfer the £150,000 covering the deposit, including extras paid to this company until another buyer is found for your present home. There is no problem transferring the mortgage when ownership is confirmed on the new house, but this means, unfortunately, that you will have to re-finance the £150,000 shortfall.'

Bill Young awaited Peter's verbal attack.

Peter said: 'Either I need a hearing aid or static on the line is playing tricks with my hearing. Bill, are you seriously proposing we take out another loan, before we can move out of this crumbling house?' Peter couldn't prevent his tone rising.

In part because she'd heard the conversation Angela grabbed the phone.

As uptight as Peter, banter, excuses, and what she deduced were lies, dictated it was her turn.

'You listen to me Mr Young, I am not impressed by your offer. I insist you will have to repay all our money or we'll sue Bull Ring Properties.'

As though he'd expected this, Bill said calmly, 'Please do take us to court, Dr Grant, and much good will it do you. Understand we don't have the funds to repay your deposit, thanks mainly to Mr Hemmings embezzling over two mill' from my company.'

'Uh! And there you were seconds ago protecting Hemmings, a valued director! I think not Mr Young, not any more. You and your gang of directors never change. You are a devious, crooked bunch of convincing liars who do not deserve to be in business. Personally I don't think you will be trading for much longer. Nor is it a concern of ours that your golden boy Hemmings is guilty of embezzlement.

'We'll definitely see you in court.' Angela shoved the phone back to Peter.

'Fine. Fine,' said Bill, aware he had Peter back. 'I can understand you're both upset. I will contact Simon and see if arrangements can be made to transfer the funds you have already paid.'

'Well, well Bill,' Peter's sigh whooshed out, 'I think you finally realise we mean business. Perhaps the only person we'll see in court is Mr Hemmings on charges for the attempted murder of my wife.' Peter grinned, realising that by playing his trump card would end the call.

'I need to speak with Gomez *now*,' a flustered Bill said before hanging up.

CHAPTER 24

Wheels screeching, the stink of burning rubber, and Conrad at the wheel of his Bentley, didn't exactly brighten a very angry M15 Commander, waving his arms and shouting for the maniac to stop.

Varley dialled his mobile.

'Hola,' the signora replied.

'Inspector Valdez,' Varley commanded, eventually being put through.

'Valdez aquí.'

'Nacho, Philip Varley.'

'Ah Philip, I was beginning to wonder if you'd returned from the helicopter trip I arranged.'

'I've moved on since then. Our last little episode has taken another twist. Need your assistance again.'

'What is it this time? A second request for a police helicopter will cost your Government a small fortune.' He tried to keep it light deciding it wouldn't last long.

'Not quite Nacho, slightly more serious. You remember the doctor who nearly drowned in the Straits and lost her memory. I suspected foul play, yet without evidence we had nothing to follow up.

'I can tell you that Dr Grant regained her memory. I was present at the meeting when she identified the would-be murderer.'

Varley could mentally picture arched eyebrows at this as Nacho said, 'Incredible. You are actually stating they have met face to face?'

'Indeed, I have just witnessed the dramatic moment when our much recovered "victim" accused this man of attempted murder, following her identification of him.'

He told Nacho of the pendant, and the struggle before he hurled her into the sea.

The top security phone started to flash intermittently.

'Philip,' he said to Varley, 'I'll phone back. Urgent incoming call to answer.'

*   *   *

The Inspector picked up the red phone.

'Qué quieres? he asked.

'Me llamo, Francois,' a French sounding voice answered.

'Ah, a Frenchman!' Obvious yes, but he wondered if the caller was using a false name plus accent.

'Oui, monsieur, c'est ca,' the man confirmed. 'I 'ave important information that will interest you.'

'Continué mon ami,' Valdez said. Yes, his French was improving.

'I 'ave photographs showing a . . . a lady being thrown into . . . the sea by a . . . big man,' the words stuttered as he tried to ensure he used them to good effect.

'Did you take these pictures on the Hercules? Valdez asked.

He was stunned by the question. 'Mais oui, Inspector. How did you know about the 'Ercules?'

'This is the CEISD monsieur, we know everything. Can you identify this man who you allegedly witnessed throwing the lady into the sea?'

'Absolutement, I know this man. I 'ave spoken with 'im. I give 'im opportunity to buy my pictures. Alas 'e is not interested.' The English was deteriorating with excitement.

'So you're a blackmailer Monsieur François. How much did you want?' Nacho was worried yet tried to sound blasé.

'Non, non Inspector, I'm a seaman. An opportunity arose,' he shouted to emphasise his point.

'I think, my friend that we'd better meet and look at your evidence, before you commit another crime. We don't want you to end up in Alhaúrin now do we, François?'

Valdez gave details of a rendezvous to the Frenchman and then redialled Varley's number.

CHAPTER 25

Maria arrived at the gated entrance to the luxury block of apartments in Puerto Banús; leaning from her BMW Z4, she pressed the illuminated button for Conrad's penthouse suite.

Intent on his attempt to decipher a text message from the Frenchman the sound startled Conrad.

'Hola Conrad,' Maria's seductive voice oozed through the intercom.

Someone he'd longed to hear, he brightened. 'Hi Maria, you know your way up.' He pressed the switch to open the gates.

Beemer parked on ground floor cobbles within the secured compound, Maria made her way to the balcony terrace. Conrad relaxed in a recliner reading texts and inputting into his mobile. Always the joker she crept forward and placed both arms around him. Again startled, he relaxed into her as she kissed his forehead, both now responding to passion, Conrad especially by caressing every inch of bare skin he could find.

Text and phone forgotten he whispered, 'Maria, I never want to let you go. I think myself fortunate to have you. I can never erase the image of you dangling your beautiful long legs in the cooling waters of the fountain.'

He'd tugged her onto his knee and lightly, playfully touched her nose.

'Remember our first meeting in the Plaza del Toros when I was lost?'

'How could I ever forget?' She kissed him, this time more passionately.

They parted, he looked troubled. 'Despite what we have Maria, I need your help again.'

'Oh my poor darling, I detected a little melancholy. Tell Maria all about it.' By adopting complacency it was something she guessed he needed right now.

'How long have you got?'

'All night if you want.' Maria's sexy voice, her innuendo complemented the look in her gorgeous eyes.

'You remember Angela Grant being washed overboard on our return from Morocco? And you are aware Dr Grant lost her memory in the accident, until today!' All said without enthusiasm.

'Regaining her memory can only be good surely.'

Conrad ignored the comment. He eased her from his knee and sat her beside him on the chaise lounge. 'Whilst in Casares I received a call from Julie Nash. There is a major subsidence problem with the Grant's house in Mijas. Naturally I dropped everything and was leaving the development when my phone rang.

'Some bloody Frenchman I didn't know.' He lapsed into a rather good, he thought, imitation, '*Monsieur 'Emmings, you vill not remember me, we met briefly on the 'Ercules.*'

He'd mimicked his caller to the letter, how could he forget the wretched man? 'Maria, this François as he called himself told me he's a member of the Hercules ship's crew. Bloody idiot accused me of throwing a lady overboard, even telling me he had pictures of a struggle on the ship's deck between a large man and a woman.

'These pictures, *if they exist,* could be anyone. I mean how do we know this man is genuine? I cannot recall meeting him.' He switched on his puppy dog expression reserved for such occasions and said, 'Is that something you agree, my love?'

'Complete pack of lies.' Maria sounded adamant. 'You were asleep with me . . . weren't you? We were both shattered after the trip. I . . .'

There it was, that pinch of doubt, there in her look had he cared to notice.

'Yes,' he said guardedly. 'For some of the time. Then I left for a meeting with Franco.' He smirked. 'Hey, you haven't heard the best part. This Froggie is trying to blackmail me; he's demanding 50,000 Euros. Says he'll prevent his evidence reaching the police.'

'That . . . God how terrible.' Maria grabbed his hand. 'Darling, we must contact Signor Gomez, he will know what to do.'

He smiled warmly. Wasn't this what he'd expected from her? Quieter, yet with emphasis, he said, 'No Maria, I don't wish to involve anyone at this stage. I will not agree to the demands of this blackmailer; let him go to the police, I don't care any more.' For once he sounded resigned.

'Good for you, my darling. It is difficult to find anyone guilty of attempted murder if there is no evidence.' On the surface Maria too seemed more relaxed, and quite pleased with his decision not to pay the ransom.

Easy to think this, yet deep inside she couldn't help but wonder about the gaps in Conrad's movements after leaving their cabin.

'I'll make some tea and I've bought you a treat.' She smiled and pecked his cheek.

'Thank you, sounds exciting.'

Conrad's position was extremely tenuous now that Angela Grant's memory had returned. Something he had decided, rather than being hounded by Varley and his MI5 friends, would be to sell his penthouse. Since speaking to Franco, good old Franco, his friend for life, things were floating on a slightly less tempestuous sea. Hadn't Franco persuaded one of his drug baron friends to purchase the apartment, and make Conrad a healthy profit? Subsequent to this he, Conrad, would carefully consider other business arrangements with his friends, this part of his operation involving transfer of assets to Brazil.

This important thinking time was carved by a high pitched scream issuing from the direction of the kitchen. Another of Maria's childish tantrums which he didn't need right then.

'Conrad, why are there packing cases everywhere? I can't find the kettle or the tea, and the fridge is empty. What's going on?'

Gone was her seductive treaties of earlier, mounting distress bubbling over in tears.

He joined her. 'Calm down, babe. Nothing to worry about.' He held her close, making soothing gestures he didn't feel like.

'Listen, Maria, and carefully, I have a plan!' At least it quieted her. 'How would you like to spend the rest of your life with me in Rio de Janeiro?

'There is nothing left for me here. I've sold the penthouse and my Bentley. I'm bored, need a new life, hopefully with you. And what could be better than somewhere exciting like Rio?'

Soulful, still damp eyes settled on him. 'But Conrad you haven't completed the company's development in Spain. Besides how can you afford to part from such a good life style in the Costa del Sol, disappear to a foreign country, all without a job and no income?'

'Maria, I've had enough of company procedures, the red tape, others forever checking up on my movements. I have friends in Rio; they will help us start a property business. Don't worry I have money. My darling, *we* would make a good partnership.

'I love you Maria Carmen, I will make you very happy.' The passion sounded genuine for once.

'Then how can I refuse you. I want to remain with you for the rest of our lives.' She laughed and kissed him passionately.

Breaking from the kiss Conrad, always in a hurry Conrad, and why not right at that moment, said, 'There's little time to lose. I will stay in Estepona, friends have lent me their apartment. Don't worry about your wardrobe, Maria, I'll buy you a new outfit in Brazil.' He was beginning to feel better already. Screw the business, and its people!

'What about Bill Young and all your staff, have you told them?'

I've told everyone I am taking two weeks holiday in South Africa. It is as much as they need to know. And Maria, you will need my new mobile number. I think the Frenchman will contact me again, now I've turned down his offer.'

Maria grew more concerned by the sudden turn of events. Why would Conrad want to hide from his business colleagues and friends? Not so naïve as she made out, she had the presence of mind to think many things lately. Surely a director of a large organisation would wish to leave on good terms, and this, to her, warned that making an excuse to take a holiday in the middle of serious problems, was inexcusable.

Instincts told her something was extremely wrong.

It wouldn't surprise me if Conrad is involved with his friend Pérez in drug trafficking. That's it, he needs to disappear now before CEISD expose the gang of drug dealers.

For Maria, Gomez would know what to do.

CHAPTER 26

Reaching the top of Milsom Street, Peter looked at the window festooned with images of luxury villas. Six months earlier he had been mesmerised by the large sign that had pretentiously declared THE SPANISH DREAM.

And he realised the temptation of a new life had ruined him.

Back in England, Bath bugged him after the views and excitement already experienced, but to him Bath and his big house was home right now.

He crossed the road into Edgar Buildings. Strange, but he found he missed the sight of Julie's attractive and seductive figure staring out of the large window; indeed the way she'd beckoned him to enter the open door.

Poor Julie, another life in ruins, like many of her clients who had crossed this *threshold, seduced by the "dream".*

Once in Gay Street he walked up the slope, and entered Number One, his accountant's office.

'Good morning,' he greeted the receptionist, she busy inputting data on her terminal.

'Peter Grant isn't it?' she said without looking up. 'Go on up, Mr Parker is expecting you.'

'Thank you, sorry to trouble you.' Sarcasm remained as Peter stormed up the stairs.

Thank god a different attitude met him as Alan pumped his hand, peter certainly in no mood for complacency.

Despite such thinking, he got a bit anyway when Alan said, 'You're looking well, the Spanish venture is suiting you. How can I help?'

Never one for pleasantries, Alan was the eponymous accountant with attitude. It's how Peter saw him at any rate; always immaculate in attire, and precise in thought, and a reasonable match.

'Well, a slight problem I'm afraid,' he said, peeved that Alan looked at his watch, a habit of his when starting the charge clock that ticked away at the exorbitant rate of £120 per hour.

'The villa we purchased is the victim of subsidence,' Peter told him. 'Bull Ring Properties have agreed to re-market the property and offered us a similar house on another development. Drawback is the bastards have refused to refund the £150,000 we paid them until they've sold our first property.'

'There's a thing. I do understand your dilemma.' Alan stared out of the window. 'I assume it will be difficult for Bull Ring to find another buyer until any underpinning is complete. I assume that will be done pronto? Good. And I'm guessing you will be waiting a long time for your money.'

He flopped in his leather desk chair, so new you could still smell the soft hide it was made from. *Yeah, a hundred and fifty smackers an hour!* 'The alternative,' he said, rubbing his hands as if about to come up with a drawer full of glee to appease Peter, 'and the simple solution, is to sue the company for breach of contract, recover your money through the courts and get out of Spain.'

Peter's hope diminished. 'Yes, I've already investigated that possibility. Fact there is Bull Ring have major cash flow problems and I'm convinced they could go under, very soon.'

'Peter, before you arrived and since our call to set up the meeting, I decided to carry out searches on the company,' Alan said. 'Doesn't look very promising either. The audited accounts for 2007/8 have not been filed with Companies House, they are way overdue and Bull Ring are subject to a penalty charge for late filing of their accounts.

'I've had experience of companies using delaying tactics to offset publishing a set of accounts denoting they are insolvent.

'Look, I'll contact Bull Ring's financial director, ask for a set of draft accounts, and explain your flimsy position.'

The smile was there, the way Peter saw it, half-hearted. 'There is another problem,' he said, aware the charge clock was ticking away. 'Solbank have advised us that we cannot legally own the second property until the £150,000 is paid. If we default, the mortgage is withdrawn and a penalty charge of £20,000 becomes applicable.'

Alan no longer fiddled annoyingly with his gold pen. "My God, what a mess, there seems to be no easy way out.' Thinking rapidly, eyes flicking to the desk, his pen, then to Peter, he said, 'You have sufficient equity in your beautiful house to re-mortgage another £100,000, but this will take you to the limit. The remaining £50,000 will be taken from your company's capital account as a Director's loan.'

'Dandy! Thanks for the encouraging news.' Peter despaired. 'Alan, let me say that I intend my next course of action is to pay Bull Ring's head office, in Tamworth, a visit. There I will have great pleasure in nailing its Chairman to the ceiling.'

'Peter, before you go to such extremes on Mr Young, there is something I need to discuss . . . as a friend.' Alan checked the time and noted it.

'I assume there is no charge for this off the record chat.' Peter laughed.

Alan ignored the remark. 'What I am about to say is none of my business, just don't want to see you hurt.'

'What on earth do you mean? I've had about all the hurt I can. Who, or what else is there?'

'I was visiting a client in the Royal United, poor guy recovering from a kidney transplant. Returning to the car park, I noticed Angela sitting on a bench, but she wasn't alone. I met Jim Connolly, y'know the brain surgeon, at one of your fabulous parties, so I was not mistaken by—'

'Hold it. Connolly? You trying to tell me something is going on between Angela and Jim Connolly, one of my best friends?

'Yes, afraid so. They were clawing each other like animals, no holds barred. People in the staff car park were staring in disbelief.

Peter fell silent; he stared about the office, walked to the window, and finally stated: 'I might have guessed there was someone else. Angela's avoided all bodily contact with me for some months. I didn't discuss this with her, thinking the drowning accident had affected her hormonal cycle. Now I understand. How naïve I've been.

Peter stared ahead, seeing nothing other than Angela and Connolly together.

* * *

Peter and Angela Grant, relaxing in their beautiful terraced garden, were enjoying a large glass of Mersault d'Or, and likewise drinking in the sunset over the Royal Crescent.

'How did the meeting go with your accountant?' Angela asked.

Peter savoured the vintage wine, uncertain how to phrase any answer, since being dogged by Alan's account of Angela's alleged affair, one he guessed she would deny anyway.

'Fine,' he replied, 'except Alan advises us to re-mortgage our house for £100,000 and the remaining £50,000 needed, will be taken out of the Company as a Director's loan.' Sufficient, trite enough and innocent.

'Beg your pardon Peter, what are you talking about?' Angela tried not to raise her voice. 'You surely remember Bill Young giving his assurance that the £150,000 would

be transferred to purchase the second house.'

'Wishful thinking on your part, my dear.' Peter attempted friendly.' Simon Peters phoned me to say the transfer cannot take place at present as there are no funds available.'

Angela stood up, notable eyes flaring yet again. 'You didn't tell me that. Now we have to deal with another "conman" . . . Mr Bloody Young. That bugger deliberately lied, aware there never was any cash to repay the Grants.'

The house phone rang. Peter hurried inside, relieved to have a break before the inevitable next scene he knew was scheduled to explode.

He picked up the hall phone and heard a click. Angela was listening in.

'Hi Peter, Julie Nash, have you a moment?'

'Depends what you're going to tell me, I've had enough upsets for one day. Then they say everything goes in threes.' He fought to remain calm.

'What's the good news then, my darling Julie?'

'I thought you should know your Mijas property, the one suffering from subsidence, was re-advertised on our web page, following your agreement to purchase the other villa. You'll never believe within two hours we had a cash buyer. The new purchaser has paid the £150,000 and their mortgage has been agreed by Solbank. My new client, by a strange coincidence, happens to live in Bath. I have been instructed by marketing not to mention anything about the slippage problem.

'I realise I shouldn't be telling you all this, but my loyalty to the company disappeared when I discovered the commission owing to me, in excess of £50,000 has not been paid.

'Even worse, there are problems completing on one of my properties on the Estrella development and no chance of recovering my £100,000 without some kind of legal action. Now that's off my chest , my suggestion to you, Peter dearest, is to make moves to recover your money immediately, before it's too late.'

Peter heard a click, Angela had replaced her receiver. She waited for him in the kitchen.

'That's it,' Angela shouted. 'Now I've heard everything! We'll never get our sodding money back. You know I never wanted a property in Spain. What's more I will refuse to re-mortgage our lovely home. You may do what you like with your bloody Director's loan, it's none of my business.

'You, Peter, have ruined us financially. I want a divorce for diminished responsibility and possibly there will be a case for infidelity with the Nash girl, from the endearing remarks I've just heard.'

'Rubbish, Julie is just a good friend,' Peter retaliated, pissed off by her self-denying attitude.

'Well, I'm not concerned about your excuses, Peter Grant. As long as I never see you or Spain ever again in my lifetime, that's fine with me. I've had enough; I'm off to live with a friend.'

Peter followed his distressed wife into the hall and noticed a row of suitcases in the corner. Angela started to wheel them towards the front door.

'Hold it a minute.' His tone did halt her. 'Your little scene was all planned. You have astutely used the financial issue to your advantage. Angela, you want to leave me because, my once precious light of my life, are having an affair with Jim Connolly.'

A second's gawking before she recovered herself enough to say, 'You can't prove that!' She tugged the last case through the door.

'Don't worry sweetie, there are witnesses who saw the sexual passion between the two of you, would you believe in the hospital staff car park! Good enough reason for curtailing sexual favours to me. Oh hell, to think your clandestine meetings with Jim probably started in Morocco.

'I guess the real reason you are leaving me, and our daughters, is because you have a lover you craved, and has bugger all to do with bloody diminished responsibility. Am I right?'

Angela stared at Peter, eyes brimming tears.

'See you in court,' he said, and slammed the front door in her face.

CHAPTER 27

Peter Grant had pulled into the M5 motorway services near Worcester; he walked to the restaurant. His cell phone rang.

'Hi Alan.' He recognised the number. 'Lovely day. On my way to Tamworth.'

'Morning Peter. From how you sound tells me you've managed to sort out that lovely wife of yours, and you're opting for a second honeymoon.'

'Quite the opposite. Angela has left me and wants a divorce on the grounds of irresponsible behaviour. Strange, yet I'm relieved in a way. OK, guess it still hurts. Can you believe after thirty years of marriage, she blames me for the breakdown, and her shacking up with one of my so-called friends. Bloody doctors.'

'I'm upset for you, Pete. I'm always here if you want to talk.'

'Thanks Alan.' Peter, despite said condolences and all that shit, wondered how much the call from his accountant friend would be costing him.

'Right now other news isn't good,' Alan said. 'I've received a copy of Bull Ring's draft accounts for 2007/8, showing a Net Loss of over £2 million. The profit brought forward, showing in the P&L reserve account, is a staggering loss of £10 million.

'The balance sheet does not make for enjoyable reading. Current Liabilities exceed Current Assets by thirty percent. Basically the company is insolvent, its shares worthless.'

'Bloody hell,' Peter said stunned. 'No wonder they haven't filed their accounts. To think so many clients haven't a clue about the reality of the situation and could lose their deposits and properties.'

'You are right of course,' said Alan, 'the company have serious problems. Symonds and Reed could be held accountable under the Companies Acts, for permitting an insolvent organisation to trade.

'Somehow you'll need to put pressure on Bill Young. Make him aware you have evidence proving the company is insolvent and threaten to take out an injunction against the company. You and your lawyer will need to move quickly before a major creditor issues a writ, freezing the assets.

'Nor will they be able to refund your £150,000.' Alan paused. No response. 'Peter, do you understand the angle of attack? And—'

The line went dead.

* * *

Bill Young, about to sit down at his desk, noticed a copy of the Sun newspaper staring at him.

'Pamela,' he shouted, 'any reason why I should be reading a copy of my most least favourite newspaper?

'Yes Mr Young,' her pretty face appeared in the doorway, 'take a look at the picture on the inside page and I don't mean the Page 3 girls!'

Bill spread the paper across his desk, turned the page and failed to contain what could be termed shock.

'Good heavens, that's Hemmings with his partners in crime, Carlos and Pérez.' Bill flopped into his chair with a bump.

'Anything wrong?'said Pamela, already anticipating her boss's look of incredulity.

'Pam,' he said quietly, no hint of annoyance apparent, 'Get me Commander Varley.'

As he waited for her to do it Bill Young read the headline:

HACKERS TARGET GOVERNMENT SITES.

The article gave an account of a leaked e-mail to the media. The reporter outlined the contents, focussed on the criminal activities of Hemmings, Carlos and Pérez., highlighted the embarrassing dilemma of the CPS. All incriminating evidence against the criminals had been destroyed by the hackers.

The report ended by giving an assurance that the Sun would help in exposing the three musketeers and help the CPS bring them to justice.

Bill's phone rang. 'Sorry to disturb your Page Three reading,' Pamela chuckled. 'I have Commander Varley for you.'

'Hello Philip, sorry to disturb your holiday.'

'No problem, Bill,' Varley said. 'I'm still trying to sort out the sodding mess made by your company. Now that Hemmings has gone to ground there's no one out here to make decisions.'

'Apologies and meant, Philip. Let me see what I can do this end. Changing the subject, have you seen the newspapers?'

'No,' said Philip, 'but I have received a call from the SFO informing me of the leaked e-mail, presumably to the media. Is this the reason for the call?

'Yes, thought I should acquaint you with developments,' Bill said.

'From experience, I think the media will flush out our criminals and make our task easier.' Philip sounded flippant. 'I should also mention I have a meeting arranged with Gomez and Inspector Valdez to discuss strategic plans in bringing charges against Hemmings on two counts.'

'Good luck Philip. Hear from you soon?'

'You most certainly will be hearing from me very soon if you fail to sort out my completion problem. I don't want to be joining the re-location queue. Sort it Bill!'

Philip hung up.

Bill Young sauntered to his favourite window overlooking the sanctuary, sadly unable to find comfort in seeing a flock of Canada geese arriving from the Arctic.

A knock at the door disturbed him further.

'Sorry to bother you again Mr Young,' Pamela said. 'I have Peter Grant on the line for the fourth time insisting you see him to-day. I can't take his foul language for much longer. What are you going to do about him?'

'Oh,' he said trying to conjure another excuse, 'tell him I'm tied up with the auditors for the next few days. He only wants to discuss his re-location problem.'

'I know, better still . . .' he laughed, '. . .arrange the appointment to see me, this will keep him quiet. When he arrives, reception is to say that I am in a Board Meeting and cannot be disturbed under any circumstances. Arrange for Chris Hancock in operations to have a word with him. I'll leave the arrangements with you.' He smirked at the brainwave. 'Thanks Pamela that should do the trick, yes?'

'I'm not convinced. Our Mr Grant can be very persistent.' Pamela was worried, especially since she would be taking the flak.

CHAPTER 28

Peter Grant found a parking space in the visitor's car park. He couldn't help failing to notice a glossy light blue Rolls Bentley, its registration number BY 2000, parked in the Chairman's slot.

'No fobbing me off this time.'

The receptionist had seen Peter arrive. She dialled Pamela's number.

'Good morning sir,' the receptionist said smiling as Peter entered her domain. 'Mr Peter Grant, I presume.'

'How on earth did you guess?'

'Intuition?' She smiled sweetly. 'How may I help?'

'As you seem to know me so well, you will have guessed I am here to see Mr Young.'

'I'm afraid Mr Young is in a board meeting and cannot be disturbed. Chris Hancock, our Operations Manager will see you inst—'

'Now listen young lady, I'm not here to play games. Your Chairman agreed to see me and I am not leaving this building until he comes down those stairs and hears what I have to say. Is that quite clear?'

'I'm only following instructions,' she said attempting to maintain both decorum and determination. 'It's not my fault your appointment has changed.' She grabbed a Kleenex from a box in her drawer.

Pamela, anticipating Peter's reaction and hearing the shouting from reception, appeared on the balcony.

'Morning Mr Grant,' she called. 'I'm so sorry Mr Young is unable to see you. He sends his apologies and hopefully Mr Hancock will answer your queries on the re-location issues.'

Peter jogged up the stairs anxious to get this sorted; he stopped halfway to glare at Pamela.

'I have just driven 120 miles,' he said maintaining an even temper. 'I have wasted four phone calls trying to make an appointment. I get lucky and a meeting is arranged. Now you're telling me, though not in so many words, to get stuffed.'

Peter reached into his jacket pocket and tugged out a long piece of chain on the end of which was a shining pair of handcuffs.

'You can tell your bloody Chairman,' he bellowed, winding the chain around both sides of the stairs spindles, threading both ends through the handcuffs and placing the cuffs around his wrists, 'if he persists in avoiding me I will lock these handcuffs and stay here all night if necessary. The stairs will become a no go area and your staff will be unable to leave the building. SO. Would you be so kind and advise Mr William Young of my plan. Or might it be better to send him a text?' He rattled the chain against the railings, enjoying the sound. And the threat.

Simon Young heard Peter's booming voice and the accompanying rattle from the stairs and hurried along the corridor to see Pamela waving a large bundle of papers.

'There is really no need to be so stupid Mr Grant, your childish, school boy actions won't help you one iota,' she shouted, shocked by Peter's ridiculous behaviour.

Peter noticed Simon's timely arrival on the scene.

'Ah Simon,' he said, ignoring Pamela's short tirade. 'Perhaps you can help to solve the impasse we have reached.'

'I have no idea what *impasse* you are talking about. From what I can see it looks as if you mean business with those handcuffs. Do tell me more.'

Pamela and Simon were joined on the balcony by other members of staff, lured there by raucous sounds.

'Your bloody chairman refuses to see me,' Peter said. 'I suggest you get him here now. Unless of course you would prefer me to discuss the confidential nature of my visit with your staff who, I have little doubt, will be more than interested in what I have to say about Bull Ring Properties.'

This probably rattled Simon more than the apparent comical sight that had first met him. 'OK Peter,' he said in his attempt to placate the man and reduce the possible outcome, 'I'll see what I can do.' He left the gathering, heading for the chairman's office and saw the portly figure of Bill Young disappear into the Gents. He followed.

'Morning Bill.'

'Ah, hello Simon,' Bill jumped at Peter's being there. 'I thought you weren't due to return from Spain until later.'

'Correct,' Simon shouted through the noise of the hand dryer. 'I changed my plans, I have urgent matters I need to discuss with you.'

Bill Young was more interested in returning to his office sanctuary rather than being subjected to a session of further disasters.

'Bill, before you disappear we have an immediate problem only you can resolve.'

'No time now Simon, I have to prepare for the board meeting.' Bill pushed past Simon and nearly made it to his office.

'Listen Bill, there is a major disturbance in reception and only you can intervene and sort out the charade.' Simon paused for effect, angry at his superior's negative stance and fixed Bill with a stare that emphasised: 'Otherwise there could be serious repercussions.'

'Disturbance? Why can't security sort it?'

'Not a security issue. Peter Grant is out there threatening to expose confidential information about the company to our personnel. He is on the verge of handcuffing himself to the stairs unless you agree to see him. Be reasonable, we cannot afford another major disaster . . . now can we Mr Chairman? You have to see him; you have no alternative.'

Bill flopped against the wall. There really was no escaping his responsibilities.

'Wheel him up,' he said eventually. 'One thing though, I want you present in the meeting.'

Bill was resigned to the ignominy of admitting defeat.

* * *

'Peter,' Simon shouted from the balcony, 'Bill Young will see you now.'

'About bloody time.' Peter unwound the chain from the spindles and joined Simon.

'Morning Peter,' Bill said through a manufactured smile. 'Sorry to keep you waiting. Fortunately I was able to re-schedule the Board meeting.'

'Making up stories for me doesn't fit,' Peter said trying to free the stubborn, though not fully fastened handcuffs from around his wrists. This much to the amusement of Simon, who had never witnessed such a bizarre scene in a chairman's office before. Nor anywhere as far as it went.

'You have been avoiding me because you can't face the truth about your company.

Isn't that right Mr Chairman?'

Bill was furious, and stalked to his sanctuary window. 'Get to the point, before I throw you out, Peter.' Certainly no love lost.

'As you know,' Peter said unperturbed by the threat, 'your company is insolvent and in law should be placed in administration. All your assets would be frozen and eventually distributed to the creditors, always assuming there was anything to distribute.'

'How the hell do you know the state of the company's finances? There are no published accounts to prove your libellous statement.' Bill continued to stare at his birds.

'Mr Young, you must think my accountant naïve or plain bloody stupid. Simon here was very co-operative and sent Alan Parker draft accounts for 2007/8, accounts that should have been filed at Companies House six months ago.

Bill whirled and levelled a dark gaze at Simon. On his lips to say 'turncoat' he remained quiet and simply staring.

'The current assets are substantially less than current liabilities,' Peter went on, 'and the accounts show a trading net loss of two million pounds. That tells me, and several others that your company is in serious financial trouble.'

'I have nothing to say.' Bill sounded stunned by the fact an ordinary client was telling him the state of the finances, and not his auditors. A fact then that he would need answers from Symonds and Reed.

'Peter,' he said, more subdued, 'just come to the point will you.'

'Quite simple,' Peter said. 'As you are not in a position to repay my debt. To date, I have taken legal advice on recovering the £150,000. Bull Ring Properties are to be served an injunction. Should the company default, which is more than likely, a charge would normally be raised on a large asset, for example the buildings. Unfortunately your company cannot supply the collateral required for such charge to be levied.

'Given said circumstances the courts will place a lien on a Director's main residence . . . and I don't mean the ones in Spain.' Peter paused to enjoy his little joke.

'The courts can't do that . . . can they Simon?' Bill was beside himself.

'I'm afraid raising a charge is possible,' Simon told him. 'But Bill, don't worry unduly there is always the appeal procedure. We'll go the House of Lords if necessary.' Simon knew this was not a reality but that Bill needed positive news.

'One final point, Mr Young,' said Peter. 'Simon Peters is on loan from your auditors and is an ex officio director of Bull Ring Properties. If a charge were to be made on a Director's residence, it would be registered on your country mansion. You would need to sell it in order to repay my debt, be—'

'Get out of my sight Mr Grant. Don't let me see you again,' Bill said with all the determination he could without falling back on the urge to chuck himself through the big window.

'Oh but you will be seeing me again, in court, Mr Chairman. 'Goodbye for now gentlemen.'

Peter released the handcuffs and dragged them and the chain along the wooden floor for maximum noise effect before slamming the boardroom door.

CHAPTER 29

Maria tapped on Gomez's door.

'Entra,' he called.

'Signor Gomez, your visitors are in reception.'

'Please send them up. And would you organise refreshments?'

'Of course.' She hesitated. 'Before I leave you signor, I have something important I should tell you.'

'Venga, dime cuál es el problema!' he said.

'Well, over the months I have developed a relationship with Conrad Hemmings.' Maria blushed.

'I did hear something. I hope it's not too serious, for your sake my dear.'

If being honest would counter her white lie she said, 'Conrad has asked me to give up everything and go to Brazil. At first I was tempted by this unexpected and exciting offer. It . . . it sounded genuine, that is until I discovered he has sold his penthouse.'

'Where is he now?' asked Gomez, aware that the unpredictable criminal mind of Hemmings would resort to anything

'He's somewhere in Estepona waiting for me to join him before we leave for Brazil. At least that's what he thinks.' Maria sounded uncertain.

'You seem to have changed your mind about the man.' Gomez offered an understanding smile, thankful Maria had come to her senses without any real effort from him. 'I cannot see how a director of operations overseeing a large property company in Spain can absolve himself of all personal responsibilities and simply disappear overnight.'

'He's hiding something.' Maria paced, obviously concerned. 'I'm suspicious of his motives. Oh sir, I don't like it; I believe he's involved with drug gangs I think are run by his friend, Franco Pérez. Conrad is wanting to get out quickly.' Scared eyes begged: 'Please, tell me what you think, signor?'

'That you are jumping to conclusions, my dear. There is no way Hemmings could be involved with the drug world. That is something I should know.' Gomez was doing his best to convince Maria, all the time unable to divulge the reasons behind Conrad's rapid departure.

'Don't worry Maria, Mr Hemmings will not worry you again, I promise.' The smile again. 'Now please show in my guests.'

* * *

Gomez stepped onto the balcony to control growing agitation. He wondered about Maria, mainly because he had not cautioned her about getting too close to Hemmings. He needed to be careful, she could well become a threat.

'Ah there you are Gomez, not hiding from us I trust. Varley stepped onto the balcony with Valdez.

'Good to see you both. Refreshments are on the way.' Manuel shook their hands. 'Please gentlemen, be comfortable. 'Over to you Nacho, assuming you do have an update on the Hemmings situation.'

They settled in comfortable balcony chairs.

'I have interviewed the Frenchman,' Nacho told Gomez. 'He has made a statement on the drowning incident. In my opinion pictures in his cell phone provide the evidence to incriminate Signor Hemmings for the attempted murder of Dr Grant.'

Gomez nodded. 'That sounds a positive step forward Nacho, but I discern one problem using your evidence.'

'What on earth could stand in the way of issuing a warrant?' Philip asked, surprised by Gomez's remark.

'Quite simple,' he said. 'Spanish law will require a positive identification from Angela Grant before we take further action against Hemmings. Grant will be asked to testify that these images represent a true likeness of Hemmings and herself of course, being the victim.'

'That's bloody ridiculous,' said Philip trying to pull rank. 'Are you suggesting that we fly the defendant to Spain in order to testify the validity of some excellent pictures. There's no disputing the characters involved, I've seen them.' Varley stood, wandered to the balcony rail, briefly took in the view of the courtyard then turned to Gomez. 'You ignore the fact that we possess the pendant belonging to Hemmings. Nacho has ordered DNA sampling tests as we speak. Tell me, what more could the prosecuting counsel wish for?'

'That is quite correct, Philip, 'but not quite sufficient enough to nail Hemmings, yet.' Manuel, maintaining a quiet calm, smiled. He enjoyed the control.

'Nacho, I suggest you let me have the Frenchman's mobile. I will download the pictures and mail them to David Wiltshire at SFO. In my opinion he will be the best person to arrange a statement from the doctor.' He eyed them both. 'Opinions, gentlemen?'

'Sounds a reasonable solution if there is no alternative,' said Nacho, 'but like Philip

I am not convinced we need the Grant lady involved.'

Maria quietly came on to the balcony to deliver a tray of refreshments, unable to avoid overhearing parts of the conversation.

'My friends,' Manuel invited, at the same time nodding to Maria as she left, 'please help yourselves to coffee, or a cold orange juice. Philip be so good as to pour me a cup of black coffee.' With Maria out of the way he knew that the discussion could move forward.

After a sip of his favourite Brazilian coffee, Gomez said, 'Philip, please to give us an update on the money laundering activities of our three friends now the media has exposed them?'

Philip raised his own coffee cup in a gesture of "cheers". 'The good news for everyone is that the hackers who infiltrated various government departments and destroying vital evidence were restricted from placing their 'worms' in UK and Spanish bank files. Fortunately they had not written the source codes for the banks and were unable to retrieve the passwords.

'We will have evidence to convict the criminals once documentation has been passed to my office.' Philip again raised his cup, looking mighty chipper with himself.

'I think that brings an end to our meeting, except for one item,' Manuel said with a tweaked eyebrow prompt at Nacho, 'the Frenchman's mobile.'

'Oh si, I nearly forget.' Nacho reached into his jacket. He placed the mobile and connecting computer cable on Manuel's desk, reluctant to part with incriminating evidence, notwithstanding that Gomez would be appointed chief prosecutor.

'And Manuel,' Nacho said, 'don't forget to return the mobile with the photos intact. No deletions please.'

Gomez ignored the remark, treating it as an insult.

Coffee finished, the three reasonably confident things were moving favourably in their respective directions, Manuel said, 'Thank you for coming, gentlemen.'

* * *

Gomez's phone rang.

'Hello Maria, anything wrong?'

'Signor Young wants to speak with you now you are free.'

A moment, a click then: 'Hola Bill, trust you are well.'

'Far from it but thanks for asking. Once you hear my exhilarating and stunning news you will understand why.'

'Try me,' said Manuel.

'Bull Ring Properties have just been served a court injunction for the immediate payment of £150,000 to Mr Peter Grant.' Bill sounded deeply shocked.

'Lo siento,' Manuel muttered.

'Manuel, there is no way the company can find such a large sum of money in seven days. Bull Ring is insolvent and if payment cannot be made, the courts will take out a charge on my house. Not only that, the banks have refused to increase our overdraft facility and are likely to foreclose very soon.'

Bill had the bit between his teeth. '*And* it is more than likely the company will be forced into administration meaning I will have no alternative but to sell my Jacobean mansion to pay off Mr High 'n' Mighty Grant.'

Manuel commiserated. 'That's terrible for you and your family. Surely there's some way in which I can help you avoid such a disaster? The repercussions over here in Spain will be catastrophic.'

Manuel maintained an unusual calm demeanour, maybe since he'd already anticipated the fate of Bull Ring some months before. He awaited Bill's response.

'Well yes, Manuel, there is a way out, if we can reach an agreement. You are holding a large amount of clients deposits, Simon calculates £50 million, for release to the developers on completion of three developments.

'In order to save Bull Ring from going into liquidation could you release say £10 million from those accounts until the completion funds are received?'

Well aware of ways at his disposal to siphon funds, not necessarily legal, but feasible, Manuel Gomez also knew that with Bull Ring on the verge of ceasing to trade and his own ambitious plans, maybe now was the right time to transfer a few million of clients deposits into offshore accounts.

'I would like to help,' he said calmly, but sadly such a transfer would contravene clients confidentially and would likely put me in prison.' *As if such a thing could be envisaged!*

'Worth a try?' Bill sounded hopeful. 'If you think of anything let me know.'

* * *

Gomez turned on François the Frenchman's mobile and plugged the connecting cable into his Apple laptop. With the photo mode on the mobile opened he retrieved nine images and saved them in the MY PICTURES folder on his computer.

Selecting each individually Gomez complimented the photographer on such high definition of scenes revealing Angela Grant and Hemmings clawing at one another. The image of the doctor being thrown overboard was astounding. A pity then that a few shots were blurred by heavy spray from huge waves, and did make it difficult to identify either figure.

He saved three pictures on the lap top and binned the rest. That done he also saved the same three images in the Frenchman's mobile and deleted the remainder.

Address book opened in Live Mail, he highlighted *David Wiltshire* and attached the photos before starting to input text.

David
You have been made aware of the attempted murder of Dr Angela Grant.
　The CEISD have received pictures of the incident on board HM Hercules.
　As required by Spanish law, Dr Grant is required to identify the attacker and herself as the victim.
　Dr Grant's confirmation is required in a sworn statement, before the attachments can be used as evidence in the Spanish courts.
　Would you please forward the affidavit on completion.
　Gracias
　Manuel Gomez

*　*　*

Gomez stepped onto his balcony and punched in Hemmings's new number, sent to him earlier.

'I take it that's you Manuel,' Conrad said.

'Si Manuel aquí. Cómo va todo?'

'I beg your pardon, no intiendo,' Conrad said.

'I was asking, how's life?' Manuel laughed.

'Could be better but no doubt you are going to surprise me with some good news.' For once lately, Conrad sounded in ebullient mood.

'We need to meet. I propose coming over to your hiding place this evening. I have a preference for Krug.' He laughed enjoying the thought of sipping his vintage nectar.

CHAPTER 30

Gomez encountered no problems in locating Conrad's temporary residence, in the block owned by Franco Pérez.

Nearing his destination he noticed what he knew to be an unmarked police car tailing him.

Perhaps Inspector Valdez has put Hemmings under surveillance, I doubt he'd be interested in my movements.

Through his mirror and before he pulled into the driveway leading to the gated community he noticed the BMW had disappeared.

Through the open car window in the hot, windless day, he pressed the digits 23 on the entry pad. The gates opened. Gomez parked in the visitor's area.

Conrad waited on the short flight of steps to the ground floor apartment, quite a fetching sight in his bright yellow shorts, a matching 'T' shirt, and looking mightily relaxed as he greeted Gomez. He led him through the lounge onto a magnificent terrace with far reaching views of the Mediterranean.

'All right for some.' Manuel too ensured his flippancy fell in with Conrad's mood. 'You must enjoy living in such luxury.' He admired the opulence of the place, its carefully selected furniture – a blend of antique and modern that didn't argue – and pictures that had to be worth a small fortune.

'I need something to keep me from losing my sanity,' Conrad said. 'I'm in no doubt Varley has set up 24/7 surveillance, making it difficult for me to leave my prison.'

'Yes, you are right. I noticed an unmarked car tailing me, and I'm sure reporting my movements to Inspector Valdez. I can assure you there is no need to worry, my business here is legitimate and totally above board.'

'I know: Look after number one eh?' He tried not to sound serious. 'Manuel, listen. I'm sorry not to have seen you since the shooting accident.' Conrad sounded as if he really meant it. 'I didn't wish to compromise the situation by appearing concerned. And I am truly pleased to see you have made a remarkable recovery.'

'And do allow me to say that I understand you followed the correct procedure in keeping your distance and not communicating with me.' Manuel clapped his hands. 'Now to business. A number of issues to discuss.'

'Well,' Conrad was unable to suppress a chuckle, 'I pray one of them covers my release from captivity!'

'Be patient, my friend, everything will fall into place, soon you'll be free of your shackles.' That sounded positive.

'Briefly changing the subject,' said Manuel, 'I haven't had an opportunity to tell you how I managed to get rid of Petrov, leader of the rival gang Malysharkya.'

Without invitation Gomez settled in a wing back chair and accepted what he guessed would be a glass of finest red wine from Conrad, who then joined him.

'The only way I could obtain a conviction and send their leader to Alhaurín was achieved by influencing the evidence given by witnesses. Needless to say, bribes played an important part.' He raised his glass. 'To whatever the future holds..'

'Offers much for thought,' replied Conrad and raised his own glass. Que sera, sera.'

Gomez went on: 'As chief prosecutor, Valdez never bothered to check the authenticity behind their statements. Petrov and his cronies were getting in the way of our successful operation and needed to be exterminated.'

'I see,' said Conrad, 'that's why members of the gang who jumped bail tried to kill you in revenge for the sentences you doled out to their friends.'

'Exactly,' said Manuel. 'The assassination attempt on my life was orchestrated by

Francois Estelle, the Frenchman aboard the Hercules who took photos of you and Dr Grant on the boat deck. You should realise Estelle was one of Petrov's gang, acting as undercover agent. Somehow he discovered your trip to Morocco was connected with a large quantity of hashish being loaded in Tangier.'

'Clever sod,' Conrad said. 'The sole purpose of involving a party of clients, and Maria of course, was to act as decoys for our covert operation. Unlucky the bloody Froggie wanted a smoke. But he didn't get the cargo, did he?' Conrad really laughed and rubbed his hands gleefully.

'We were lucky,' Manuel said. 'If the Hercules had not diverted to Gibraltar, you would have found Petrov's team on the quayside waiting for you in Marbella. The carnage would have been catastrophic. We would have lost a haul worth fifty million dollars and probably some of our clients.'

Manuel's cell phone bleeped. 'Buenas tardes, Gomez aquí.'

'Ah Manuel, good evening, David Wilshire SFO. I hope you've recovered after the horrific attempt on your life.'

'I'm fine now, thanks David and looking forward to an extended vacation.' Manuel wondered if the head of SFO would be sufficiently astute to pause and reflect on the real meaning of "extended". He thought not.

'Manuel, I have received your e-mail with the photo attachments. It looks as if they were taken in a violent storm. The figures of Grant and her attacker are I feel, at best, vague. In this event such visual evidence would not stand up in any court of law. Might there be any decent shots showing their faces?'

'I'm afraid not, you have all the pictures taken by the Frenchman.'

'Then it's a complete waste of my time and resources asking Dr Grant to make a statement. CEISD will need to produce something more positive if we are to stand any chance of gaining a conviction.'

'Sorry old chap, must go. Give my regards to Varley.'

'What on earth was that all about?' Conrad asked bemused.

'Before you answer, what say we crack some champers? I'm afraid Franco's cellar is out of Krug.' Conrad laughed. 'It's why I offered you the red to keep you happy.'

'Möet will be fine.' Manuel nodded his approval.

Conrad exited and a few minutes later returned to find Gomez had moved to the terrace. He unloaded glasses and the Möet in its bucket of ice.

The POP of the cork was loud. Conrad poured. 'Salud,' they said in unison clinking glasses.

'You were going to say...' Conrad prompted.

'I haven't got time to elaborate,' Gomez insisted. 'Basically your French friend, François Estelle, handed his mobile containing the photos to Valdez. I persuaded the Inspector to release the phone and then proceeded to download the nine images into my laptop. I deleted the pictures identifying you and the doctor, sending the rest to the SFO.'

'Clever move Manuel.' Conrad felt even more secure.

'The call from Wiltshire confirmed my intentions to confuse the enemy. Although he sounded upset when he discovered the images could not be used to pinpoint you or the doctor. In other words, my friend, there is no incriminating evidence apart from the pendant. Your previous money laundering activities can be forgotten for good.'

'My God Manuel, you have saved me again. I don't know what would have happened if you'd died. Truly, I am more than grateful.' Conrad placed his glass aside and embraced him.

'What are friends for?' Manuel said. 'Now to real business, we haven't much time.

You already know I have sold your share in the Elvira development to Franco for one million Euros. My costs will be deducted later.' He arched an eyebrow.

'Our investment account shows a balance in excess of 50 million Euros. I have opened accounts in Brazil and Monaco and completed the transfers. We'll need a further 50 million Euros for the development in Brazil. Franco will provide the balance.' He leaned back wearing a cat-that-got-the-cream-look.

Conrad raised his glass. 'It's apparent our strategy has worked. You have done well Manuel. By the way, I never dared ask how you and

Franco managed to have such a close relationship when you were always at each other's throats, especially in the courts?'

'A clever plan, devised at Barcelona University when we were law students. We've managed to keep everyone guessing for many years. The deception has worked well in our favour.

'When you first appeared in my office Conrad, your connections with Franco presented me with the golden opportunity to make plans for the future. With your criminal mind and charisma, Franco and I knew we could use your talents. Now we should all capitalise on our good fortunes and move on.'

'What about poor Maria, how does she fit into the game plan?' Conrad asked.

'Poor Maria,' Manuel sighed. 'A shame she has to be discarded. Then, perhaps she could join us when the dust settles.'

'There's Franco, Ernesto Carlos and your lovely family?'

'Franco will be joining us later. As for Ernesto, his passport has been withdrawn and a court hearing is pending in the UK. Regarding my family, well, they'll probably attend my funeral, very shortly.' He laughed. Nor was he joking.

'Conrad, we have little time to lose before warrants are issued for your arrest. Be ready to leave at three a.m. tomorrow morning. No luggage except your automatic, you may need it. I'll see you at Gibraltar airport. I hope you are a good swimmer!'

'My God Manuel, I'm not certain I want to come. Surely we are not going to fly over the Amazon in a Piper Cub and then ditch in the sea, are we?'

CHAPTER 31

Varley was talking to Nacho Valdez on the phone.

'Philip, I hope you are sitting comfortably.'

'Why? Don't tell me Hemmings has slipped through your net.' He tried to joke.

The inspector disregarded the response. 'I've received a call from airport security at Gibraltar,' Nacho said. 'Three days ago, the pilot of a Cessna obtained approval for a flight plan to the coastal town of Ilheus in North East Brazil.' The pause hinted at something that Varley couldn't immediately guess. 'The plane never arrived, it crashed into the sea.'

'Why on earth should we be concerned about an aircraft going for a swim?'

'There is an article in the Express which, if you will allow, I will read to you.'

Varley sat back and listened.

From Valdez's reading Varley learned the plane had been in contact with air traffic controllers eight miles out to sea, and some nine minutes before a scheduled landing. The pilots had announced they were switching from instruments to visual observation. Ellen Harte, business manager for the charter company, Aero Star, had said, quote: "It was flying perfectly. The pilot was maintaining visual approach to the airport . . . it was the last we heard."

Eye witnesses accounts then varied to the extent that the plane was flying unusually low, with another describing it as "a bit out of control" and that it "swung out towards the sea and then back to the forest. And that not long afterwards it disappeared." The latter from a student Carlina Nesquita.

Rescue teams had searched 400km of sea and rainforest. Two days later the search was called off after small pieces of wreckage were washed up sixty miles north of Illheus. No bodies had been recovered.

Conspiracy theories ranged from the outlandish to the more feasible. Some suggested the two crew and its passengers bailed out before the crash.

'Interesting story,' said Philip Varley.' If you've finished do please get to the point, I have got a meeting with the Chief in ten minutes.'

Nacho, without further preamble, did just that. 'The authorities in Brazil contacted Gibraltar and requested names of passengers. Passport control knew about the two Brazilian pilots but no passengers were registered on the flight plan, although the charter company confirmed there were two passengers aboard.

'They concluded this was odd so checked CCTV cameras. Two passengers were seen running to the far end of the runway and boarding the aircraft at four a.m. in the morning. I have seen the footage. Guess what?'

'OK,' said Philip, the penny dropping with a clang, 'Hemmings and Pérez.'

'Nearly correct. Hold onto your hat. The second passenger wasn't Pérez. But our friend and police prosecutor, Manuel Gomez.'

'Impossible,' Philip uttered.

Thing was, in his specialised game of law enforcement, nothing was impossible.

CHAPTER 32

Peter Grant re-filled his glass with Crianza. He was returning to the balcony when his mobile vibrated.

'Evening Peter, Philip Varley.'

'Hi Philip. I was enjoying a sundowner on this beautiful evening; the sunset is a wonder over Torremelinos.'

'Oh to be there rather than have this conversation from London,' Philip said.

'Sounds ominous. Tell me you're not going to spoil my evening. I've enough to worry about lately.'

'Been some major developments,' Varley said, slightly concerned for Peter. 'Bull Ring Properties are in receivership owing in excess of £200 million. The fraud squad have started investigations on my advice.

'Hemmings and Gomez have fled to Brazil. Having said that, there is a sting in the tale. Two crew members plus our two friends, were aboard a Cessna that crashed into the sea off the coast of Northern Brazil. No survivors have been found. Crash investigators who recovered wreckage think the occupants of the plane bailed out before the crash.'

'Gomez you say? I thought he was on our side. What about deposits in client accounts *and* my money, are they still safe?' Peter had to find a seat, shattered by the news on Gomez.

'You may well ask,' said Philip. 'Hemmings has been involved in criminal activities with Gomez and Pérez since he set foot in Spain.'

'Jesus! Franco Pérez involved? Can it get much worse?'

'Yes it can.' Philip told him, 'Gomez and Hemmings have raided client deposit accounts over the years and siphoned off in excess of £100 million, either spent, or it's in Brazil *or* deposited in banks around Monaco. The £150 grand you're owed is obviously lost in the scam.

'What is relevant,' Philip said, 'you remember the trip to Morocco? CEISD have evidence that 50 million Euros worth of drugs was loaded in

Tangier on the Hercules and shipped into Gibraltar. Our trio of musketeers were also running a gang of dealers.

Plus Bill Young must be held accountable for Hemmings's reign of deceit and fraud. Letting Hemmings loose in Spain without checking his criminal record was negligent and deserves a long jail sentence.'

Ever get the feeling you've run a marathon and come a pitiful ninety ninth out of a hundred? No? It was how Peter Grant felt at that moments.

'Thank you Philip, I've heard enough. My relaxing, peaceful balcony scene has just been shattered!

'I had decided to take action against the perpetrators who have made my life hell, nearly bankrupting me, and turning my Spanish Dream into a nightmare. That said, there' nothing left in this wicked and corrupt world for me, or the thousands of British people who have lost everything; their life savings, homes, loved ones, their dignity and health. Lives shattered by a small, deadly mob of criminals, hell bent on continuing to destroy the fabric of society in a devious, ruthless reign of terror.

'What can we do Philip? Philip?'

The line breathed static.

CHAPTER 33

Peter looked out from the balcony, transfixed by the sight of twinkling lights illuminating Fuengirola. He swallowed his last drop of Crianza as the door bell rang.

Looking over the balcony he was pleasantly surprised to see golden hair hanging loosely on bare shoulders and hearing his name called.

'Peter. Julie Nash. Have you got a minute?'

'Julie? JULIE. All right.'

How wonderful to be disturbed by someone who understood his dilemma.

He unlocked the door and slid back security bolts to be met by a miniature whirlwind as she entwined her arms around him. The news he'd been given over the phone nosedived. He had never felt so excited for years, mind over-active as he tried to guess Julie's next move, the passionate kiss most welcome. Eventually she let go. Pity.

'There,' she whooshed, ' I've ached to do that from the moment you crossed my threshold in Bath. Anyway with Angela shacked up with her consultant friend, I thought you might be in need of some excitement from an admirer.' Her eyes twinkled as she hoisted a bottle of Moёt in the air.

Peter could taste her. 'Nothing like a bit of passion and comforting words to end my nightmare.'

'That isn't all. The Moet is worthy of more. Just wait until I reveal the latest chapter,

Julie, smiling like that other cat called *Cheshire*, dragged Peter upstairs. The noise of a champagne cork broke the silence. Bubbles and smiles.

'Cheers,' they each chimed, one a beat behind the other.

'So what's next?' Peter topped up her glass.

From her copious bag Julie took out a copy of the latest weekly Spanish version of SUR, unfolded it and started to translate.

"'The owner of a trawler fishing off the north coast of Brazil found parachutes and life jackets tangled in its nets. The captain remembered the incident when a Cessna aircraft crashed recently and his boat was involved in the search for wreckage and the four occupants.

"Aero Star, the Cessna's charter company confirmed parachutes and survival jackets were registered to the aircraft.'"

"'Incredible,' shouted Peter, draining his glass, the mood and the moment making him decidedly squiffy, especially after the earlier red wine.

'That's not all,' Julie said, happier than she'd been in ages. 'It gets even better, full of intrigue and mystery.' She read on:

"'Following a tip off from CEISD and the British M15, the Brazilian Federal Police have arrested a lawyer from Marbella, one Signor Pérez, who recently arrived in Rio de Janeiro. According to the authorities he is wanted for drug trafficking in Spain and serious fraud offences in Britain. CEISD and M15 provided evidence connecting Pérez with another lawyer in Marbella, Signor Gomez, and an Englishman, Conrad Hemmings, alleged property developer, amongst various other occupations. Signor Pérez denied any connection with the gentlemen.

"'Brazilian Federal Police have decided to re-open their investigations on the crashed Cessna. They are suspicious about the circumstances now believing that two passengers, Signors Gomez and Hemmings might have escaped from the crash.'"

'Listen carefully to the ending Peter.' Julie was beside herself.

'Just précis it, Julie,' he said his own excitement hardly containable. But was he bothered about newspaper accounts, or perhaps it was more basic, more satisfying?

She did summarise. It appeared that following a search of private hospitals in Rio the police found evidence of two patients matching Gomez and Hemmings's descriptions. Plastic surgery had been involved. Police accepted they had assumed new identities and passports.

Julie scanned down and read, "'Spanish and British governments are offering a reward of 250,000 Euros to anyone who can assist in information leading to the arrest of these men.'"

'So . . .' she sipped more champagne, 'what do we do now?'

'Just a minute,' said Peter. 'It's just tumbled to me why Varley hung up on me.'

'What do you mean?'

He explained about the call from Philip Varley. Him being in a hurry to tell him about Bull Ring Properties going down the pan. 'Plus shattering news that our so-called whiter than white prosecution lawyer, Manuel Gomez. is an active member of the Hemmings – Pérez syndicate.'

Peter remained serious as he further revealed, '. . .an excess of £100 million has been extracted from Bull Ring client accounts and deposited around the globe. The large slice we're owed by the company is down the proverbial drain I'm afraid. To top that, as you've just read, the criminals have fled to Brazil.

'As to what do I mean, Julie? Short answer, Varley didn't mention anything about Pérez being questioned by the police in Brazil or the probable discovery of Hemmings and Gomez having undergone facial changes.

'Get it? It's apparent Philip Varley doesn't want me sniffing around, "getting involved" as they say.'

Julie's smile broadened and still her eyes sparkled. Her laughter came up from her toes. 'Fancy a trip to South America?' She tottered towards Peter and threw her arms around him. Her champagne glass bounced on the carpet.

'We'll find Hemmings and Gomez, claim the reward . . . Sound like a good plan?'

Peter agreed with another kiss.

She pulled away. 'And guess what, we leave for Rio to-morrow.'

From that copious bag of hers she extracted the BA flight documents for Brazil and waved them at him.

Peter wouldn't have been surprised if she'd got the bally plane in there too.

'Come here, gorgeous,' he said.

THE END

Lightning Source UK Ltd.
Milton Keynes UK
UKOW031052021211

183080UK00002B/11/P